Flowers by Felicity by Janet Lee
What publicity florist Felicity C
the bouquet she made for her friend's wedding isn't quite
what she'd wished for. And she certainly doesn't want the
attentions of the photographer responsible for taking the picture of her flying flowers. . .even if she is very attracted to him.
Can David convince Felicity that he's truly sorry and that he
is part of God's plan for her life?

Petals of Promise by Diann Hunt
Konni Strong can't seem to live up to her last name. Five
years after the death of her husband, she still feels the pain
and holds to the vow of that dreadful day. But when handsome Rick Hamilton enters her life and tries to sneak into
her heart, can she learn to let go of the past and trust God
with her future?

Rose in Bloom by Sandra Petit
Owning and operating Rosie's Catering is a 24–7 job for Rose
Bentley. She loves her career, but she is beginning to worry
that in her zest to "make it" in the business world she is missing out on life. Catering her friend's wedding makes her yearn
to have a "special someone" of her own. When Lucas Montgomery falls into the prize wedding cake she created, she is
certain he is NOT Mr. Right. But does God have other plans?

Flowers for a Friend by Gail Sattler
When a piece of the bouquet lands on Geoff Manfrey's
head, he quickly gives the flowers to a little girl he knows.
To Geoff's horror, she innocently declares her love for him,
then begins to follow him. Things go from bad to worse
when her big sister Clarissa falls in love with him, too. Can
Clarissa show Geoff her love for him is real and that God
put them together for a reason?

The Bouquet

Four Pieces of a
Wedding Bouquet Ignite
Four Romances

JANET LEE BARTON
DIANN HUNT
SANDRA PETIT
GAIL SATTLER

BARBOUR
PUBLISHING

ISBN 1-59310-140-6

Cover image © Jo Tronc

Illustrations by Mari Goering

Published by Barbour Publishing, Inc., P.O. Box 719, Uhrichsville, Ohio 44683, www.barbourbooks.com

Our mission is to publish and distribute inspirational products offering exceptional value and biblical encouragement to the masses.

Member of the
Evangelical Christian
Publishers Association

Printed in the United States of America.
5 4 3 2 1

The Bouquet

Prologue

by Gail Sattler

Prologue

Abby's hand shook as she reached for the bouquet. Her bridal bouquet.

After months of preparation, she was no longer Abby Edmonds—at least not on paper. She was now Mrs. Stanleigh Chenkowski.

For the first time today, Abby was able to stand by herself and not listen to relatives recount highlights of their own wedding day thirty years ago or pose for pictures. For a few minutes, she had some time to see what was happening around her.

Currently, a large group of guests had their attention fixed on the beautiful groom's cake, made to look just like Stan's dog. Since the cake resembled Bowser so much, no one, including Stan, had the heart to cut it. Even Rose, who made the cake, couldn't be the first one to insert the knife.

Guests sat at the tables around the room, nibbling goodies, eating wedding cake, and sipping coffee and tea. Other people stood in small groups, just talking.

Away from the action, Abby surveyed the banquet room

of the Country Meadows Inn one last time. The red and white streamers, hearts, and bells were exquisite, the decorating perfect.

Her wedding day was almost over. Everything had progressed without a hitch.

The ceremony had been beautiful, and there hadn't been a dry eye in the house, except, strangely, for her own. Because she'd caught Stan sniffling when she hadn't been, Abby promised Stan she would remind him on every anniversary. Abby snickered to herself. She always kept her promises.

Following the ceremony, because the weather was a typical March day for Vermont, they'd taken the portrait pictures inside a studio, then come back to the inn for the reception.

The meal had been delicious. The speeches were performed without incident or too much embarrassment, although she couldn't say the same about the video her brother and his friends had made and shown their guests. Abby wasn't very pleased her courtship with Stan had been turned into a comedic documentary, but the video had provided a nice break from the rush and festivities.

For now, the wedding cake had been cut, and it was time to get ready to throw the bouquet to her still-single guests.

Abby picked up the small bouquet and ran her fingers over the soft petals of the fragrant roses in varying hues of red, pink, peach, and even a few in yellow. Felicity had outdone herself with the beautiful bouquet. Abby almost didn't want to give it away, but of course she had to. Besides, her brother David was a semi-professional photographer, and he had taken enough pictures that she would never forget its beauty.

"Abby?" a little voice piped up beside her.

Abby looked down. "Hi, Jenni. Are you enjoying yourself? I want to thank you for spreading the rose petals so nicely at the church today. You did a good job as flower girl." She smiled, thinking of how cute Jenni and Cody, the ring bearer, were together.

Jenni beamed from ear to ear. "Thanks!" she squealed. "Mrs. Edmonds told me to tell you that it's time to throw the bouquet."

Abby bit back her grin. "Tell her that I'm going to do it right now."

As Jenni giggled and skipped back to Abby's mother, Abby sighed. This was her last official function of the day, and then her wedding would be over.

She craned her neck to see Stan, all decked out in his white tuxedo, through the crowd. At the same moment, he turned around and looked back at her, smiling.

Abby's heart pounded. She loved Stan more than she did yesterday, and even more than this morning. Today they had been joined as husband and wife in a ceremony witnessed by their friends, their families, and God. And now it was time to leave their guests and begin their lives together as a married couple.

Abby raised one arm and waved at the room full of people. "Attention! Everybody! I'm going to throw the bouquet! Everyone who wants to see if they're going to be next to get married, come now!"

Most of her single guests hurried into a circle behind her. She could see Kathy, Brenda, Nanci, all her cousins, and a bunch of Stan's cousins, whose names she couldn't remember, shuffling into a circle. Even little Jenni, who was only six years old, was in the middle. All faces were expectant and hopeful as they waited.

However, some faces were missing. But before Abby had a chance to tell them to join in the fun, the women already gathered began calling out to her to hurry up.

Abby turned around and tightened her grip on the bouquet. "Okay, Lord," she mumbled, "I've had my day. You gave me Stan, and You made me the happiest woman on earth. But now it's someone else's turn. You know who needs this the most."

Abby sucked in a deep breath, closed her eyes, and flung the bouquet over her head.

The weight of the flowers had barely left her hands when she spun around to see who would catch it.

Before she stopped moving, a collective gasp echoed through the room.

All heads were turned up, way up, toward the ceiling. Abby also tilted her head to watch.

The bouquet was not arcing gracefully through the air; she'd accidentally thrown it too hard. Instead of floating into the circle of anxious single women, the bouquet zipped through the air, straight for the whirring ceiling fan in the middle of the room.

Abby covered her mouth with her hands. "No!" she shouted, but her voice came out muffled between her fingers.

With a dull thud, followed by a series of crisp snaps, her beautiful bouquet shattered.

Only shredded leaves floated to the women below. The larger pieces of the bouquet, their speed increased by the force and velocity of the spinning fan blades, shot past the ladies huddled in the middle of the room and hurled along on paths of their own.

Flowers by Felicity

by Janet Lee Barton

To my Lord and Savior for showing me the way.
To my family for your love and encouragement always.
To my granddaughters, Mariah, Paige, and Sarah:
When it's time—remember to look to the Lord
for the mate of His choosing.
I love you all!

Chapter 1

F elicity Carmichael's heart slammed against the inside of her chest as she witnessed pieces of the bridal bouquet she'd worked so hard on fly out over the room in all directions. She caught her breath as one of the clumps shot straight toward her. Instinctively, she closed her eyes and reached up to catch it just before it smashed her in the face.

Opening first one eye and then the other, she looked down at the small tuft of flowers she held and fleetingly wondered if catching only a portion of a bouquet meant anything. She shook her head and sighed. *It was nothing but a near miss. . .just like her two previous engagements.* No. She wasn't going to think about that now.

Clasping the flowers to her heart, she took a deep breath and willed her racing pulse to slow down. She looked down at the mangled little cluster of flowers, and her heart sank. All her work had been torn to bits in a matter of seconds. She closed her eyes once more to fight against the threat of tears. When she opened them, it was only to immediately blink against the bright light of a camera flash going off somewhere very close.

David, the bride's brother, had been taking pictures of his sister Abby's wedding reception all afternoon. From what Abby had told her about him, Felicity was pretty sure he'd be teasing his sister forever about her pitching style. . . especially after witnessing the aftermath of that pitch.

She watched him turn to catch his sister doubled over laughing at the expressions on the faces of the women who'd hoped to catch her bouquet. Felicity couldn't help but chuckle herself. If Abby wasn't upset, she certainly shouldn't be. After all, it wasn't her wedding day.

Looking around, Felicity shook her head but couldn't keep from chuckling as she watched David continue to take pictures of the wedding reception and the havoc the flying bouquet had caused. He moved around the room snapping pictures right and left. How he could hold the camera still with his shoulders shaking with laughter was beyond her. No telling what those photos were going to look like. But she found it hard to take her eyes off him. A handsome man with thick dark hair and blue-green eyes, he was even better looking when he smiled or laughed—his eyes crinkling at the corners and a dimple suddenly appearing out of nowhere.

Felicity was surprised at the way her pulse sped up when he turned and caught her staring. He began to walk toward her. She didn't realize she'd been holding her breath until his parents stopped him and she released the pent-up air in her lungs with a whoosh.

Feeling the heat rising on her cheeks, Felicity didn't know

whether to be relieved or disappointed when he turned and started in a different direction, but the way her pulse began to race, she decided it might be for the best if she found something to do besides watch David Edmonds. It didn't take long. . .there were bits and pieces of the bride's bouquet everywhere. Felicity gently put the tiny portion of bouquet she'd caught into her skirt pocket and began to pick up some of the scattered blooms off the floor.

David hadn't had time to think since he'd dodged the flying flower bundle that flew past his ear. For a scant second he'd wondered if he was seeing things and then realized what it was he *had* seen. The look of shock on his sister's face as she'd thrown her bouquet had him aiming his camera first at her and then at her attendants who'd been waiting to catch the bouquet. Their expressions were priceless. As Abby dissolved into laughter, he turned to the room.

He took a picture of Felicity Carmichael, Abby's friend and the florist who'd made the bouquet, holding one of the errant flower bundles close to her chest. There was a vulnerable look in her eyes that made him want to stop and talk to her, but laughter from across the room had him aiming his camera in a different direction just in time to catch his best friend, Geoff Manfrey, reaching for the clump of flowers stuck on top of his head.

David felt the mirth building in his chest. . .his chuckles inching toward huge guffaws. . .but he didn't dare let them out as he watched the responses of the people who'd caught or been hit by parts of the shredded bouquet. Somehow he didn't think most of them would appreciate it. It wasn't easy holding the camera steady while he tried not to laugh, but he didn't want to miss one good shot. Thankfully, Abby didn't seem too upset. . .at first. But when her expression changed to one of concern and she darted across the room, he followed.

It took him longer as he framed first one and then another shot. By the time he got there, a crowd had gathered around the cake table—or what was left of it—and the caterer, Rose something, and Stan's best man, Lucas Montgomery. David couldn't get close enough to really see what was happening, and he wondered if the bouquet had anything to do with it. He then dismissed that idea. They were flowers after all. How much damage could they do?

He turned and saw Felicity across the room and suddenly remembered that Abby had suggested that he interview her for the newspaper—that it would be a way of helping Felicity's business out since she had given Abby such a great price on the flowers. It was the least he could do for someone who'd helped make his sister's wedding so beautiful, and he started toward her to try to set up an interview. But he was stopped by his parents telling him that Abby and Stan would be leaving soon, and when he looked back, he didn't see Felicity. He made a mental note to try to talk to her later. He took a couple more pictures and decided he'd better head toward the door so that he could take the going-away pictures of his sister and her new husband.

He looked at his watch. If the newlyweds hurried, he'd be able to get these pictures developed and into the Sunday paper. He turned quickly, stumbled, and almost tripped over Felicity, who was bent down picking floral bits up off the floor.

"Oh! I'm so sorry," he said, extending a hand to help her up. "Are you all right?"

Her laughter was light and lilting, and as he looked into her eyes, he was surprised by the way his heart began to beat faster. He'd seen Felicity many times through the last few months—at church, although they didn't attend the same Sunday school class, and at times on the street as they passed each other coming or going from his sister's house just next door to hers. But he'd never been really up close like this. Her eyes were the most unusual shade of brown. . .almost gold. They sort of shimmered as she looked up at him, and something in his chest seemed to flip into his stomach. He was pretty sure it was his heart.

"I'm fine," she said, sounding a little out of breath.

"Good. I think we've already had one casualty today." Funny. He sounded the same way—as if he'd been out running.

"Oh?" Felicity looked around. "Who?"

"The wedding cake."

"The cake?" She looked confused.

"Yes. It seems to have crashed to the floor." David looked back toward the cake table, but the crowd had dispersed and Rose and Lucas were nowhere to be seen. He shrugged. "I'm not sure what happened."

"That's a shame," she said, shaking her head. "I was looking forward to a piece of that cake. Oh, well."

David chuckled. "You can have a piece of the groom's cake."

"Of Bowser? Oh. . .I'm not sure I can do that."

The groom's cake was adorable. . .shaped and decorated to look just like Stan's basset hound.

"From what's left of it by now, you probably wouldn't recognize him." David wasn't sure what to say next, but he wanted to keep talking to her. "I noticed that you caught one of the pieces of the bouquet. I guess this means there will be more than one bride coming out of this wedding."

Felicity shook her head. "I don't think it works that way."

"No?"

"No."

Her smile seemed a little wistful, and David wondered why he hadn't noticed how really pretty she was before. "I've been—"

"David!" Abby called. She and Stan were hovering by the front door of the inn. "Are you going to get pictures of us leaving?"

He looked down at Felicity. "I'm sorry. Duty calls."

"Abby wants those pictures." She grinned and motioned back to the newlyweds. "And it looks like Stan wants to leave. You'd better go."

David turned to look at his sister and her new husband. Stan was motioning to him to hurry. He chuckled and grinned at Felicity. "Looks like you're right. I guess I'd better go. . .if you're sure you're not hurt?"

"I'm fine."

"Okay, then. I'll talk to you later." He hurried away, a little put off by his sister's timing, now that he realized he'd like to get to know her neighbor a whole lot better.

A light snow had begun to fall when Felicity left the reception. The temperature had been steadily dropping all evening, and by the time she'd changed clothes and fixed herself a light supper, the snow was beginning to accumulate on the sidewalk outside. She cleaned up the kitchen and then went to take a warm bath.

Dressed in her warmest robe, she made herself a cup of hot chocolate and carried it into the living room. Felicity looked out the window and shivered before settling into her recliner. She took a sip of the warm liquid in her cup and picked up the remains of Abby's bouquet that were lying on the table beside her. She still couldn't believe that it'd been sliced into pieces.

Had her work been inferior? Felicity shook her head. She'd spent hours on that bouquet. The fragile blooms just couldn't stand up to the force of the fan. She twirled the small clump around in her fingers and thought about what David had said. Could he be right. . .that catching a portion of a bouquet would have the same results as catching a whole one? She shrugged and shook her head. Did it really matter? No. . .not for her.

David certainly was an attractive man. Especially up close. She'd seen him many times, but she'd never really talked to him. She wondered why that was when she and Abby were such good friends. Of course they'd gone to college together, and David was already out of college by then. Felicity had only been living in Loudon for about a year, having moved here when her parents decided to retire in

Florida. Besides, Abby knew how relationship shy she was after her two broken engagements and probably hadn't wanted her to think she was trying to set her up with her brother.

Abby knew Felicity well enough to know she'd run the other way, because her heart had been broken too many times. Months ago Felicity had come to the conclusion that the Lord intended for her to stay single, and that was the reason she'd put everything she had into opening her own flower shop. Flowers by Felicity was all she had time for now, and she needed to put all of her energies into making a go of it.

She'd only been open a few months, and while she had enough business to hire one other person to help, she was barely getting by. It seemed her hired help was clearing more take-home money than she was. Of course, right now she was putting everything she made back into the business. She was just lucky the shop had a small house attached to it so that she wasn't paying for both a business and a place to live.

Abby's wedding was the first one she'd supplied flowers for, and she hoped word of mouth would garner her more business. Everything had looked lovely. Abby's attendants' skirts were multicolored, and she'd wanted the flowers to be made up of roses of those very same colors. Finding just the right shades of red, yellow, pink, deep rose, and peach had been quite a challenge. But Felicity had contacted all her suppliers and managed to order in enough for Abby's bouquet, the attendants' smaller ones, and the table arrangements at the inn.

Abby had been thrilled with the final result. . .and the

price Felicity had given her. She wasn't making much of anything on this project, but she hoped it would pay off in more business.

She sighed, thinking back over the day. It had been a beautiful wedding. Abby and Stan seemed to have found that elusive true love that Felicity had given up on. She really was happy for them. . .if a little sad for herself. She still longed for a love of her own, but it wasn't to be, and she certainly didn't need to sit around moping about it. She flipped on the television and tried to find something to take her mind off weddings and happy endings. It didn't take long.

It was the news hour, and none of the stories was uplifting. The weather was going to get worse during the night, with record snow accumulations for this time of year predicted. Felicity shivered and hit the off button on the remote. She took a sip of hot chocolate and picked up the book on the table beside her chair.

It held all the answers she needed and the assurance that she was indeed loved. She flipped open her precious and well-worn Bible. She loved seeing what the Lord had in store for her when she turned to His Word and sought His guidance.

Chapter 2

D avid looked over the Living section of the paper and chuckled. Abby would probably throttle him when she got home and saw this spread, but one day she would hug his neck for getting these pictures. He'd worked hard to get them ready to go into tomorrow's edition.

He especially loved the one of Abby as she realized she'd thrown her bouquet into the fan. He did feel a little funny about the one he'd taken of Felicity clasping that little bunch of flowers to her heart when she was looking so vulnerable, but it was too late to take it out now. At least she wasn't wearing it on top of her head! David laughed just thinking about what Geoff's reaction would be when he saw his picture. His friend would have plenty to say, of that there was no doubt.

David had looked for Felicity after he took the pictures of Abby and Stan leaving the reception but couldn't find her anywhere. He'd call and try to set up an interview tomorrow. There was no need to write a note to remind himself—he wanted to see her again. His sister's suggestion of an article for the paper just gave him a convenient excuse to be able to do that. He folded the paper under his arm and turned off his computer before heading home for the night.

The next morning, Felicity looked out her window to a snow-covered world. It was beautiful, even though she dreaded having to drive on slick roads the few miles to church. Hurrying downstairs and through her shop, she shivered and pulled her robe close as she opened the front door and quickly retrieved her paper. The sun was up—hopefully most of the snow would be melted by the time she got ready to leave. It didn't tend to stay around too long this time of year.

She stomped the snow off her shoes before going back inside and hurrying into the kitchen to pour herself a cup of hot coffee. Sitting down at the breakfast nook, she held the warm cup in both hands and sniffed the aromatic liquid before taking her first sip. She scanned the headlines and saw a note in the upper right-hand corner of the paper: "Edmonds-Perry Wedding: Article and pictures in Living section."

She quickly flipped through the newspaper sections until she found the one she was looking for and pulled it out. There on the front page was a beautiful picture of Abby and Stan leaving the church for the reception at the inn, and another one as they left the inn while everyone blew bubbles on them. They did make a beautiful couple. And David really was a great photographer. It was nice he could occasionally still use his talent for the newspaper he ran.

Felicity turned to the inside middle of the section and

almost choked on the coffee she'd just swallowed. There in full, living color was a picture of her bouquet flying in all different directions. The caption under the photograph read, "Flowers by Felicity."

The fan that shredded her creation was nowhere in sight. Nowhere in the small accompanying article was there an explanation of *why* the bouquet had broken apart. But all over the two-page spread were pictures of the aftermath. One showed her holding her little clump close, looking. . .confused? Sad? She wasn't sure, but she wasn't thrilled that David had caught her with that expression on her face. In another photo, a man she recognized from church wore one of the bundles on top of his head while observers laughed. It *was* kind of funny. Felicity found herself chuckling in spite of herself—but only for a moment. As she looked back over the picture layout and saw absolutely no mention of the fan, she wondered just how many people were going to think she did shoddy work. Worry about the effect on her business fueled a building anger.

David could have managed to show the fan along with the flowers, couldn't he? Or at the very least, the article could have explained it all. Didn't he realize how much damage he might be doing to her business with these pictures?

Well, before the day was out, he'd know. She couldn't wait to give him a piece of her mind. Felicity was pretty sure he was in the other adult Sunday school class—she knew he wasn't in hers—but she always saw him at church. While she usually sat with Abby, he sat across the way with friends from his class. One thing she was certain about: she would make sure to find him. Oh, yes, she would.

Felicity hurried to get ready, wanting to allow herself plenty of time to get to church. She dressed warmly in a long brown suede skirt, soft butter-yellow sweater, and her favorite boots. The calendar might say spring was just around the corner, but it sure didn't seem that way as she pulled on her coat, opened the front door, and headed for her car.

She was glad she'd allowed a little extra time as she followed a snowplow down the road. By the time she'd parked her car and made her way up the front steps and into the building, there wasn't any time to look for David. She slipped into class and was a little relieved that no one had time to ask about the pictures in the paper.

As soon as class was over, however, several people came up to ask how the bouquet had fallen apart. Her fears that those who weren't at the wedding to see what had happened would get the wrong idea were realized. Thankfully, several people had been there, and they jumped in with the explanation of the fan before Felicity had a chance to. She was too busy trying to tamp down her anger at David. It was probably a very good thing they weren't in the same class.

Felicity sent up a silent prayer that the Lord would help her get past her frustration with the situation and her irritation with David. By the time she'd taken a seat for the worship service, Felicity was having second thoughts about talking to David at church. Once she sat down for the worship service and saw him across the room talking to old Mrs. Donaldson, she decided she'd be better off just going to the paper the next morning and confronting him there. This wasn't the place to make a scene. . .and maybe by tomorrow she could laugh about it all.

David saw Felicity across the room and smiled at her, but she didn't smile back. In fact, she looked almost angry from the way she was frowning, but then she looked away with the same expression on her face, and he wondered if she might be nearsighted.

Once the worship service started, though, the frown left her face, and David found himself glancing her way off and on during the rest of the service. There was something about her. . .she seemed kind of reserved, and he admitted to himself that he wanted to get to know her better. He hoped he'd be able to talk to her after the service.

It quickly became apparent that wasn't going to happen as he was stopped by first one and then another church member laughing and commenting on the pictures in the paper of Abby and Stan's wedding. By the time he got free, Felicity Carmichael was nowhere to be found.

He thought about asking his best friend, Geoff Manfrey, to have lunch with him, but he seemed in deep conversation with Clarissa Evans and her little sister, Jenni. Hmm. When they all walked off together, he wondered what the conversation was about. It looked like lunch with Geoff was out.

Normally content with his own company, David couldn't understand why he suddenly felt so alone. . .but he did. He could go grab a quick bite somewhere and then play a little golf. *Right. In the snow.* Maybe he'd pick up some fast food and go home and watch a little golf on television. That was something he did a lot in the winter, but it didn't sound so great to him now. He headed down the aisle and into the foyer.

"David! Son, where are you going in such a rush?"

David turned to see his mother hurrying up to him.

"Want to come over for Sunday dinner? Your dad and I feel a little at loose ends with all of Abby's wedding preparations over with."

"Oh, so now you have time for me?" he teased.

"David, you know we always have time for you. You stay so busy, it's usually the other way around," his mother admonished him gently.

"Well, I would certainly love to have dinner with you, Mom. I'm feeling a little at loose ends today myself."

His mother raised an eyebrow and chuckled. "Oh, so now *you* have time for us?"

His dark mood immediately lifted, and he laughed as he put an arm around his mother's shoulders and gave her a hug. "It appears I do."

Laughing together, they headed toward his dad, who was waiting by the door. Family. What would he do without them?

Felicity was glad to see Monday morning come. Usually, she loved weekends—especially Sundays. But not this one. She'd spent most of the afternoon trying not to think of David and the pictures he'd put in the paper, but she hadn't been very successful. The day was too quiet and gave her too much time to think about the handsome newspaperman.

For weeks now, she'd spent most Sundays with Abby,

helping her plan the wedding. Staying busy. But yesterday there was nothing going on—no wedding showers to go to, no last-minute plans to attend to—and the day had stretched out before her. . .long and a little lonely.

She'd straightened up her house and emptied the trash, adding the offending newspaper to it. She never wanted to see those pictures again. Nor did she want to see David, she told herself. She'd worried and wrestled with whether to go see him most of the night, but she felt the need to tell him he should be more careful about what he put in his newspaper—before he hurt someone else's business.

This morning, she was trying to talk herself out of it until her helper, Nellie Barclay, came in at ten.

"Oh, Felicity—I saw those pictures in the paper! How in the world did that bouquet break up like that? I watched you tape those stems and put it all together. There's no way it should have come apart like that."

Felicity felt a little better just knowing that at least one person knew how carefully she'd put that bouquet together. But if Nellie, who worked with her on a daily business, was wondering about it, half the town would be, too. As the morning wore on, she knew she'd never rest until she made her way to the *Loudon Daily News* office.

Leaving Nellie in charge, Felicity pulled on a jacket and headed outside. The sun was peeking out behind the clouds, and she hoped that by mid-afternoon most of the snow would be gone.

Her shop was in an older section of town, just off the main street, and it was only a few blocks from David's office.

Nervous butterflies fluttered in her stomach as she made her way into the newspaper building. She took the elevator up to the executive offices and walked up to the receptionist.

"Is Mr. Edmonds in? I'd like to see him if possible."

The receptionist looked her up and down. "I'm sorry, but he's in a meeting right now. His schedule is pretty tight today. Would you like to schedule a meeting for tomorrow or the next day?"

Felicity could feel her courage sinking. If she left now, she probably wouldn't come back. "No, I'd really like to see him today if that's possible."

"Then you can take a seat. When his meeting is over, I'll see if he has time to see you. What is your name?"

"Felicity Carmichael."

"Oh. The *flower* girl." She shook her head. "Too bad that bouquet didn't hold together."

Felicity clenched her teeth and watched as the receptionist wrote down her name and glanced at her watch.

"He should be through anytime now. I'll check with him then to see if he has time to see you." In a condescending tone, she added, "But I don't think he will."

The receptionist bared her teeth in the phoniest and most insincere smile Felicity had ever seen and motioned across the room. "You can sit down and wait over there."

Praying for the Lord to forgive her for wanting to call the woman at the desk *guard dog,* and to keep those very words from passing her lips, Felicity somehow managed to find the nameplate on the desk. "Thank you, Myra."

And thank You, Lord.

She turned, let out a deep breath of relief that she hadn't made a scene, and took a seat in one of the chairs facing the door to David's office. She wanted to make sure that she could see when his meeting was over. If nothing else, she'd just wait until he took a lunch break and catch him then.

One way or another, the *flower girl* was meeting up with the *picture boy*. Today.

Chapter 3

When the office door opened fifteen minutes later, Felicity had only a moment to wonder if she could leave before David saw her waiting. Her bravado was quickly disappearing. Besides, what was the point? The damage had been done. She'd just have to depend on word of mouth from those at the wedding to let people know pictures didn't always tell the truth.

But before she could leave, David spotted her. "Felicity! What a nice surprise. I was just going to have Myra look up your number for me." He walked toward her with a smile. "Are you here to see me?"

Felicity nodded. "If you have time."

"Of course I do. Myra should have buzzed me to let me know you were here. I hope you haven't been waiting long."

"You were in a meeting, Mr. Edmonds," Myra said. "I didn't think you'd want to be disturbed. I'm sorry."

"It's all right, Myra. Just be sure to buzz me the next time Ms. Carmichael comes to see me, please. Felicity, come on into my office and tell me what I can do for you."

The look his receptionist shot Felicity wasn't pleasant, but at least it was apparent that Myra's guard status was self-imposed. Felicity held her head a little higher as she followed David into his office.

David couldn't believe Felicity was actually there to see him. She'd been on his mind ever since the wedding, and he had planned to contact her later in the day. He waited for her to take the chair in front of his desk before he sat down. "It's great to see you. What brings you here today?"

He watched as Felicity sighed and looked over at him with those big golden eyes. She was lovely, but she seemed a little nervous. "What is it, Felicity? Is something wrong?"

She let out a huge sigh. "Do you realize the harm you've done?"

David's heart skittered in his chest. "What harm? What are you talking about?"

"You honestly don't know?"

David shook his head. He didn't. But whatever it was, it was obvious that Felicity wasn't happy about it. She sat there, chewing her bottom lip and wringing her hands. He couldn't for the life of him figure out what he might have done that could cause her such distress. Whatever it was, it must have been bad. He stood and came around his desk and took the extra seat beside her. Propping his forearms on his knees, he looked into her eyes. "Felicity, I'm sorry. I don't know what I did. Please tell me."

"Those pictures you put in the paper of the wedding. . . the bouquet flying apart and no mention of the fan?" She flipped her hand in the air as if to remind him of the flying flowers. "It looks as though my work on the bouquet was inferior. . .that it didn't hold together."

David sank back into the chair, letting the breath he'd been holding swoosh out of his lungs. "You're right. I didn't mention the fan. I guess I assumed everyone there knew what caused the bouquet to fall apart."

"Everyone there *did* know. It's all the other people in town who read the *Loudon Daily News* who I'm concerned about—unless the only people who read your paper are the ones who attended the wedding? You'd have what? About two hundred subscribers?"

"Ahh, no. We wouldn't be in business if that were the case."

Felicity smiled at him, but it never reached her eyes. "I didn't think so. And that's my point. Are those subscribers who weren't at the wedding going to want to order flowers from a florist who they think does shoddy work? No, of course they aren't."

She shook her head and rubbed her fingers across her forehead as if to ease a headache. David was feeling worse by the minute.

"I'm just starting out, David. This wasn't the kind of publicity I was hoping would come from doing Abby's flowers."

"I am so sorry, Felicity. I truly am." And he was. He gave himself a mental kick in the seat of the pants. "Obviously. . . I wasn't thinking. How can I make it up to you? I can put an explanation in tomorrow's morning paper. . .a correction of sorts."

"No. That will only look like I complained and forced you to. It won't help." Felicity stood up and pulled her purse strap over her shoulder. "I just wanted to caution you about the next time you decide to pull a fast one on Abby. I know brothers and sisters like to pull pranks on each other, but this time it touched more than just the two of you."

David felt like a rat, knowing he'd hurt her. She turned to go, but he stood and beat her to the door. "Felicity, I truly am sorry. I never meant to hurt you or your business. Let me take you to lunch so we can talk about how I can make it up to you?"

For a moment he thought she was going to say yes. Then she shook her head and smiled at him. "No, thank you. I've got to get back to work. Besides, you've apologized. There's really nothing else you can do."

There has to be something I can do! I can't just let her walk out of my life, hating me. But before he could come up with any answer, that's exactly what she did.

Felicity swept past Myra and hurried to the elevator before she changed her mind and told David she would go to lunch with him. He'd really been very sweet, and he'd seemed sincerely sorry. She'd been tempted to accept his invitation to lunch. . .but she just couldn't. She had a feeling she could be way too attracted to David Edmonds, and that was the last thing she needed. She couldn't take the chance of being hurt again.

Besides, she'd said what she'd come to say. He'd apologized. That was it. That was all there ever could be. She had a business to run, and she'd best get back to it. It was lunch-time, and Nellie was probably starving. Felicity hurried down the street, trying to put David out of her thoughts.

She found Nellie on the phone, taking an order for an arrangement for a baby shower scheduled for that weekend. Felicity smiled. She loved doing those.

She waited on a man who came in from the street and ordered a dozen red roses. Maybe she wouldn't starve. And surely, one day people would forget the bouquet that flung its flowers from one end of County Meadow Inn to the other.

David spent most of the next few hours trying to figure out how to make things up to Felicity. . .and how to get her to go to dinner with him. He was interested in her. . .more than a little. Why hadn't he realized that he might be hurting her business by putting that picture of the bouquet breaking into pieces in the paper? David sighed and shook his head. He'd been too intent on putting together a layout that he knew would get a rise out of his sister.

They did that, the two of them. If he wasn't getting the best of Abby, she was playing a trick on him. That's what siblings did, wasn't it? Only this time, it looked as though someone else was being hurt by his prank, and for that he truly was sorry.

What could he do? Maybe he'd send Felicity flowers. Yeah. Right. From her competitor. That was bound to make her want to have dinner with him.

Myra buzzed him to remind him of a meeting with his advertising manager scheduled for later that afternoon. He had half a mind to cancel the meeting. Sales were up. Ed did a good job and didn't need any supervision in his area. They didn't have to meet today. David needed to spend his time trying to come up with something that would help Felicity, and. . .*advertising*. David tapped his fingers on his desk. Maybe he had the answer. Would Felicity go for it? He grinned. How could she not?

At first he thought Felicity was gone for the day, but he knew Ms. Barclay from church, and when he told her he was there to see Felicity, Nellie just led him back to a workroom where Felicity was working on a huge arrangement.

She didn't see them standing in the doorway at first, and David watched as she wrapped the stem of a purple flower with florist tape and place it just so in a vase among other flowers of the same kind and some yellow ones he thought were daffodils. It was a beautiful arrangement. Felicity was very good at what she did. It was too bad anyone might have other ideas from his own thoughtlessness.

"Felicity, Mr. Edmonds is here to see you," Nellie announced before turning to go back to the front of the shop.

Felicity seemed surprised to see him. . .and not very happy about it, either. She raised an eyebrow as if to ask what he was doing there. "David? What can I do for you?"

"Well, I came to make amends—I hope."

"You've already apologized. You don't need to do anything more."

"Oh, but I do. I have an idea. Please. . .have dinner with me and let me tell you about it."

Felicity shook her head. "I can't. I have to finish—"

"Don't say no. We can go after you get through. You choose the time."

She hesitated for a moment and shook her head again. "David, this really isn't necessary."

How was he going to convince her to have dinner with him? "Felicity, Abby is going to be mad enough at me as it is. Please let me at least be able to tell her I tried to make it up to you."

It worked. Felicity smiled at him and chuckled. "All right. I've seen Abby when she's angry. I'll take pity on you, 'cause she *is* going to be mad at you. Pick me up at about seven."

David nodded. "I'll be here." *With bells on if I thought it would help.*

Felicity looked at herself in the mirror and wondered one more time if she'd lost her mind. She had absolutely no business going to dinner with David. None. But the simple fact was she wanted to. And she was curious to find out his idea for making things up to her.

She had no idea where he was taking her for dinner, but she dressed in what she hoped would work for just about any place he chose. After much deliberation, she'd chosen an aqua sweater and matching pants. It was cold again and looked like more snow might be on the way. She was beginning to wonder if spring was ever going to arrive in Vermont.

When the doorbell rang, she hurried to answer it, trying to ignore the rapid beat of her heart. This was not a date.

David was here to make amends. That was all. And she'd do well to remember that fact.

But the smile on his face and the way he looked at her when she opened the door did nothing to slow her pulse rate. He looked wonderful in brown slacks, a cream-colored sweater, and a leather jacket.

"Hi. I hope you're hungry. I made reservations at Salvagio's. Do you like Italian? If not, we can go somewhere else."

"No, I love Italian food. And Salvagio's is one of my favorite places to eat."

"Good. It's one of mine, too." He helped her on with her coat and waited for her to grab her purse before guiding her down the walk to his car.

Felicity felt special as he opened the door and helped her inside. She kept telling herself it was only a business dinner. . . at the most, simply dinner with her best friend's brother. But when he looked over at her and smiled before starting the car and putting it in gear, she knew she was in trouble. Because suddenly, it felt like a date with a handsome man.

Chapter 4

David kept telling himself this wasn't a date. No matter how attracted to Felicity Carmichael he was. She was only with him because he had a plan to make things up to her for hurting her business—and to keep Abby from being furious with him when she got home—and because she was nice.

When they got to the restaurant and found a line already in progress even on a Monday night, he was glad he'd called ahead and made reservations. Salvagio's was one of the most popular restaurants in Loudon, and he considered Nick Salvagio a good friend. But when Nick kissed Felicity on the cheek, it didn't settle well with David.

"Felicity, you look lovely tonight. And, David. . .it's great to see you, my friend. What a good night—two of my favorite people, here together." He grinned at David. "Are you celebrating anything special?"

David had a feeling Nick was trying to find out if the two of them were seriously seeing each other, and he wasn't of a mind to let him know for sure. "More like I'm here to make amends to Felicity for something."

That stirred Nick's curiosity; David could tell from the way he raised an eyebrow in his direction and grinned. "I see."

David only wished what Nick thought was going on between him and Felicity was right. . .that they were dating. As it was, if she didn't like the idea he'd come up with, David wondered if it might be the first and last time he took her to dinner. Looking down at her as they followed Nick through the dimly lit dining room, he knew that he wanted it to be the first of many evenings they would share. Enough that he sent up a silent prayer. *Lord, please let me convince Felicity that I'm sorry and that I truly want to see her business succeed.*

Once seated at the candlelit table, they gave their attention to the menu. David knew what he wanted, but he was curious to see what Felicity would order. When the waiter appeared, he asked her if she'd decided.

Felicity nodded. "I'd like the Fettuccine Salvagio, a house salad, and iced tea, please."

David grinned and nodded. "I'll have the same." Nick's specialty of sliced Italian sausages on top of a bed of fettuccini with a spiced-up Alfredo sauce had become his favorite dish.

He handed the menus to the waiter and looked over at Felicity. "Thank you for coming with me tonight. You know, I looked for you after I finished taking pictures of Abby and Stan leaving the reception. Abby had suggested that I interview you for the paper. I'd still like to do that, if you are willing."

She leaned her head to the side and smiled at him.

"David. It's all right. You don't need to do that."

"No. Really, I'd like to. And maybe we can slide in an explanation about the flowers and the fan?"

"This is your plan to help my business and make things up to me?"

David shook his head and took a sip of water before answering. "Not entirely. I think it could help your business if done right. But I was planning on doing that anyway, so it wouldn't really be making anything up to you. It would be a way to get your name out there, though. Some free publicity."

"I guess it would. . . ."

"I promise you can look over the copy before it goes to print." David grinned at her.

"Well, then. How can I refuse?"

The waiter brought their drinks and salads just then, and once the man left their table, Felicity put her napkin in her lap and asked David if he'd say a blessing. He bowed his head and gave thanks for the food they were about to eat, wondering when the last time was that he'd dated a woman who expected a prayer to be said before they ate. It felt good to be around Felicity. It made him feel like a better man somehow.

They took several bites of salad before David continued with their conversation. "The making things up to you part would be to offer you free advertising for the next year."

"Oh, David." Felicity looked startled. "That's quite an offer. And it's much too generous. I can't let you do it. Hopefully, in a year no one will remember those pictures in the paper."

"Please. I want to do it. It's my paper, so it's not like I'll be out any actual money."

"But you'll be losing money—I've checked the prices of running an ad in your paper."

David looked into her eyes and knew it would be money he could live without. "Felicity, you're a businesswoman. Can you really afford to turn down my offer?"

She looked up at him and then back at her salad. She took a sip of her tea. Her gaze met his once more. She chuckled and shook her head. "No. I can't."

"Good. It's settled then. We'll discuss layout ideas later this week." David extended his hand across the table and waited for Felicity to take it. When she did, he was struck by how small and warm her hand was as his fingers tightened around hers for a moment.

Felicity pulled her hand away when the waiter brought their meal to the table. "A small ad will be fine. . .more than enough, David."

"We'll see." Afraid she'd change her mind about the ad, he quickly changed the subject, "Now, how about getting to that interview? Tell me. . .when did you decide you wanted to become a florist?"

"Oh, I think when I was a child, I fell in love with flowers. . .my grandmother and mother always had flower gardens, and fresh arrangements were part of our daily life. I've always loved the different textures, colors, and fragrances of flowers. Loved working them into arrangements. I think they are one of the most beautiful parts of God's creation."

"And how did you get started in the business? Did you

need any kind of formal training?"

David thought he could listen to the sound of her laughter forever. "I started in the business when I was about sixteen. I went to the florist in my hometown and asked if they needed help. I've been working in florist shops ever since. But I majored in business in college and got an associate degree in Floral Design and Marketing. When I decided I wanted to open my own shop, I applied for a small business loan, and here I am."

Sitting across from me. As David spent the next hour learning all he could about her, he could think of nowhere else he'd rather be.

Sitting across the table from David and finishing up the cheesecake they'd ordered for dessert, Felicity couldn't remember when she'd talked so much about herself or her life.

"And why did you decide to open your own shop?" David asked.

"I couldn't think of anything else I'd rather do for a living." She wasn't about to tell him that when it became obvious after two broken engagements that she would be her sole provider, she realized she needed to decide what she was going to do with the rest of her life. And that if she was never going to be a wife and mother as she longed to be, she might as well make a living doing something she loved.

He smiled across the table at her. "Not everyone can lay claim to that."

"No, they can't." Felicity did feel blessed in her career

choice. . .especially if she could just manage to make a living at it.

"And you've been open for business for how long?"

"Just since the first of the year."

"Oh, you are just starting out, aren't you?"

Felicity leaned back in her chair. "I am. I'm just thankful that the shop has a house attached to it. Otherwise, I'm not sure I could make it. But I'm hoping that by the end of the year, I can see a profit."

David pushed his dessert plate to the side and rested his forearms on the table, leaning in and looking at her intently. "I can see why you were so upset with me. I truly am sorry, Felicity. Please forgive my thoughtlessness."

How could she possibly refuse to forgive him? He was sincere; she had no doubt of that. Besides, she already had forgiven him. "David, of course I do. I know you meant no harm."

"Thank you. I promise to do all I can to help you make that profit by the end of the year."

"That isn't your responsibility, David."

"Maybe not, but I do feel that I might have hurt your chances some. I intend to change that, though. I'll come by tomorrow afternoon. What time do you close up shop?"

"Usually around five o'clock. Sometimes I work longer, but the shop closes to business then."

"So I'll be there about quitting time. I'll have a copy of the article for you to approve, and hopefully we can talk about advertising."

"I'll be there."

David asked a few more questions about her business, but they finished their meal making small talk. . .finding out about the people they both knew, trying to figure out how they'd never really met with his sister living right next door to Felicity.

By the time David pulled his car up to her house, Felicity found herself wishing the evening didn't have to come to an end. She couldn't remember when she'd had such a good time. The meal was wonderful, which was no surprise; the food at Salvagio's was always superb. It was David's company that made the evening stand out. He seemed genuinely interested in her work. . .in her. Of course, he was trying to make her feel better. . .and he didn't want his sister to chew him out when she got home. Besides, he was a newspaperman. He knew how to interview.

Aware that she'd enjoyed herself way too much, she opened her car door almost before he came to a stop. "Thank you, again, David. It was a wonderful meal. No need to see me inside."

"But I—"

"No—really," Felicity was already out of the car. "I left a light on. Thanks again." She hurried up the walk, but in her haste, she got the heel of her boot caught in a crack in the cement. She turned and swayed, dropped her purse, and struggled to right herself before she fell on the hard walk.

David must have gotten out of the car anyway, because he seemed to appear out of nowhere and was by her side, steadying her. "Are you all right?"

Well, so much for the graceful exit. "I'm fine. Thank you."

49

He handed her the purse he'd picked up and held on to her elbow as he guided her to her front door. "I'm glad," David said, waiting as she rummaged through her purse, looking for her keys

"My keys aren't here."

"Did you drop them when you tripped?"

She dug some more. "I might have."

David was already back out on the walk looking for them. "Ahh! Here they are," he said, bending to pick them up from the lawn. He turned, sprinted back to the porch, and held the keys out to her.

Felicity took them from him and unlocked the door, trying not to let him see the embarrassed tears that were trying to form. What a klutz she must have looked! He really was sweet. "Thank you."

"You're welcome." As if he knew how she was feeling, he turned to go. "Thank you for a great evening!"

She waved at him before shutting her front door. *A memorable one, anyway.* One she certainly wasn't going to forget anytime soon.

<hr>

The next day, David found himself looking forward to stopping by Felicity's shop that afternoon. She'd been on his mind all day. He couldn't remember when he'd enjoyed an evening more. Felicity was wonderful company. He'd had to keep reminding himself that he wasn't on a date—he was there to interview her and to help undo some of the harm he might have done with the Sunday photo spread. But it didn't ring true. He wished it had been a date, and if he had anything to do about it, there would be another and another. But it wasn't going to be easy. While Felicity had been warm and open at the restaurant, by the time they got back to her house, she seemed to turn cool.

He did know he wasn't going to put all of his apples in one basket. He'd take the copy of the interview to her for her approval, but he was going to draw out a decision on the advertising for her shop. If everything were settled today, he wouldn't have a good reason to stop by her shop again. And he wanted every excuse he could get to see Felicity Carmichael.

Abby might not be happy with him about the wedding pictures he'd picked for the paper, but he wasn't too thrilled with her, either. His little sister had a lot of explaining to do when she got home. After all the times she'd tried to get him together with one or the other of her friends, he wanted to know just why she hadn't tried to set him up with Felicity— the one and only woman who'd captured his interest in months!

Chapter 5

Felicity looked at the clock for the fourth time in the last ten minutes. She'd had Nellie leave early so she could stop by the hospital to deliver a bouquet made up of tiny baby pink roses to the mother of a brand-new little girl. Felicity had been looking for David to show up ever since. She sighed and shook her head. She had no business looking forward to his visit. Hadn't she asked the Lord to show her what His will for her life was after her last broken engagement? And hadn't the opportunity to open her own shop come up just days later?

Besides, she couldn't afford to have her heart broken again. She just couldn't. First Ned and then Marcus. She'd thought she'd found the man of her dreams both times. And *both* times she'd been mistaken. Ned had decided marriage wasn't for him. Marcus had decided that one of her best friends was for him. Felicity had decided that men—none of them—could be trusted. . .with the exception of her dad and granddad. Evidently, the mold had been thrown away after them.

So why was she watching the clock and listening for the bell over her shop door to ring? Because she couldn't quit thinking about David Edmonds. He'd been so nice last night. . .showing real concern when she'd nearly fallen and going back to look for her keys.

At the restaurant, it'd almost felt like a date with the two of them getting to know each other a little better. She'd found out that he and Abby had been pulling pranks on each other all their lives. . .but he was a little nervous about this last one. He'd included a few less than flattering shots of his sister in the Living section layout, and he had a feeling Abby wouldn't rest until she found a way to pay him back. Felicity chuckled. Knowing Abby, David was probably right.

She finished the birthday bouquet she was making for a young woman turning eighteen. It was made up of a mix of cream and pink roses, and Felicity was pleased with the results as she put it in the cooler to be delivered the next morning. Next, she checked the order pad for the last few orders Nellie had taken to see what needed to be done before she called it a day.

There was an anniversary bouquet to be made for a man to pick up around four in the afternoon. He wanted it to be special for the forty years they'd been married. Then there were several orders to be sent to a funeral home. Felicity didn't recognize the name of the deceased, but it wouldn't matter. She always gave a lot of time and care to funeral arrangements, knowing how much they meant to those who were grieving the loss of a loved one.

She checked her stock and made a list of the flowers and

greenery that she needed to order from her suppliers early the next morning. As she was making a list, the bell over the door rang out, and a young man entered the shop.

Felicity put a hand to her chest and shook her head. "Oh, I'm sorry. We're closed. I just hadn't turned the sign around."

"Oh, please, Ma'am, I really need some flowers tonight." He looked about nineteen and was very worried. "I forgot my girlfriend's birthday, and I really need to make it up to her. I'll pay double."

Felicity smiled at him, thinking how lucky his girlfriend was. Would that either of her fiancés had cared that much about her birthday. "Let me see what I have."

She had her head in the flower cooler when the bell over the door jingled once more, and she wondered if maybe she should consider lengthening her hours of operation if she could have this kind of business later in the day. Her heart did a funny little somersault when she turned to see David standing there.

He looked at his watch. "I thought you closed at five?"

"Normally, I do," she answered, ducking back into the cooler. She hoped the coolness from inside it would excuse the give-away color she felt flood her cheeks.

She took a breath and brought out a half-dozen red roses and several sprigs of baby's breath. She held them out for the young man to inspect. "Think these will do?"

"They'll be just fine, Ma'am. Thank you."

"Do you want them in a vase or boxed?"

"Boxed will be fine." He reached for his wallet. "How much do I owe you?"

Felicity wrapped the flowers in green tissue paper and carefully laid them in a long box. She quoted him a price, and he grinned. "Are you sure? At this late notice?"

She nodded and took the cash he handed her. "I'm sure. Just let your friends know how reasonable my prices are, okay?"

"I'll do that; I certainly will. You have a good evening, and thank you."

"You're welcome," Felicity said, following him to the door. She flipped the closed sign to the outside before turning to face David.

He smiled at her. "That was nice of you. You could have asked twice as much for those roses."

"I know. But he seemed so worried when he came in, I kind of felt sorry for him. It's his girlfriend's birthday, and he'd forgotten."

"Oh. I see. Still, you gave him a great price."

She shrugged and grinned. "My prices *are* good. I try to make sure they are better than most of my competitors."

He handed her a piece of paper. "Maybe I should add that to this copy. I plan on putting it in the Living section of the Sunday paper. . .along with some great pictures of the flowers that you did. I did get some really good shots before the fan incident."

Felicity took the paper from him. "You don't have to do the Sunday paper, David."

"But I'm going to." He looked around the shop. "Are you ready to close? Want to go pick up a bite to eat? You can inspect the copy and give me the go ahead. . .or not?"

She knew she shouldn't. She should just look over the article and tell him yes or no and send him on his way. That's what she should do. Her heart skipped a beat as he inclined his head and smiled a slow smile.

"Come on. You have to eat sometime."

Oh, yes, she knew what she *should* do, and she knew what she wanted to do. The latter won out. "Okay. Only, it's my treat tonight. I put a pot of soup on earlier. We can eat at my place."

Thank You, Lord. Never in his wildest dreams had David expected to be having supper with Felicity, but here he was. . . sitting in her cheery kitchen, smelling fresh cornbread cooking, and drinking in the sight of her across the table from him.

She looked up from reading the article he'd written and smiled at him. "Thank you, David. It's very flattering and a wonderful plug for my shop."

"That's what we're aiming for—lots of business for you. Which reminds me, I've got several ideas for ads. Have you had time to think about what you'd like?"

"David, this article is enough. You don't need to. . ."

Oh, yes, he did. In just a few short days, he'd realized he wanted to get to know this woman much better. She was like a breath of fresh spring air. . .even with small patches of snow still on the ground. Besides, he truly wanted to help her business get on its feet. She'd been so nice to that young man. And she had given Abby a really great deal on the flowers for her wedding. "Felicity, that's already been settled. I'll get some ideas to you later in the week."

"All right, thank you, then. But there's no hurry. I know you have a business to run, too."

David sighed with relief when she gave in.

Felicity got up to check on the cornbread. It was golden brown when she took it out of the oven. She ladled up two large bowls of beef vegetable soup and set one in front of him. He couldn't remember the last time he'd had home-made soup. The very smell of it had his mouth watering in anticipation.

Felicity brought her own bowl and a basket of cornbread to the table. She refilled their tea glasses and sat down. "Would you say the blessing, please?"

David bowed his head. "Dear Father, we thank You for this day, for this food. And thank You for prompting Felicity to ask me to share this meal she prepared. Please forgive us our sins and help us to live each day to Your glory. In Jesus' name, amen."

They began to eat, and David felt a contentment he didn't quite understand, sitting at Felicity's table, eating her delicious soup and the cornbread that, spread with butter, melted in his mouth. But the meal seemed to satisfy more than just his stomach, and he knew it had more to do with whom he was sharing the meal with than with what he was eating.

"This is wonderful, Felicity. You are a great cook."

"Thank you. I like cooking almost as much as I like flower arranging."

"Well, if the flower shop bombs, you can always open a—oh, I'm sorry." David clamped his mouth shut and shook his head. Would he never learn to keep his foot *out* of his mouth? He shrugged and said, "Abby says I have no tact at all. I think I just proved her right."

"It's all right, David." Felicity laughed. "That isn't a bad idea, actually. I think I like florists' hours better, though. Speaking of Abby. . .she and Stan are due home at the end of the week, aren't they?"

"Yes. Stan couldn't take any more time off from work, and they wanted to have a little time to settle in before Monday. I still can't believe my baby sister is a married woman now."

"It will seem a little strange to find Stan answering the phone or the door. Abby and I have been used to running back and forth through the hedge. Maybe I'll start calling first."

"I'm sure you'll be welcome there anytime. Stan's a pretty easygoing guy. I think they are going to be very happy together."

"So do I. He's really nice, and I'm very happy for Abby."

Felicity refilled his bowl, and the next half hour passed much faster than David wanted it to as they talked about Abby and Stan, their families, and anything else that came to mind. He would have liked to stay longer, but he had a feeling he might wear out his welcome, and that was the last thing he wanted to do.

"Let me help you with the dishes," he said as Felicity took their empty bowls to the sink.

"Oh, no. That's not necessary. Besides, the house may be old, but the kitchen is modern. I have a dishwasher."

David glanced down at the gleaming, stainless steel appliance built in beside the sink. "So you do. I'll be glad to help, though."

"Thanks, David. I can handle it." Felicity smiled at him as she came back to the table and gathered their glasses and the empty basket that had held the cornbread.

Obviously, it was time for him to go. . .whether he wanted to or not. He stood up. "I guess I'll be on my way, then. Thank you for the wonderful meal."

Felicity walked him to the door. "You're welcome. I'm glad you enjoyed it. And thank you for that nice article."

David gazed down at her as they stood in the doorway. He wanted to ask her out, but he had a feeling now wasn't the time. Patience was something the Lord was continually trying to teach him, and he acknowledged that this might be one of those moments when he should try to exercise that quality. He smiled down at her.

"It was easy to write. I'll try to get some ad ideas to you soon. If you come up with anything you'd like to do, just give me a call."

"All right. . ." Felicity paused.

David decided not to linger. He didn't want her to refuse the advertising space. . .not when it was the only good reason she might agree to see him again. He started down the steps. "I'll be in contact. Good night, Felicity."

Chapter 6

Felicity watched until David got in his car and pulled away from the curb before going back to the kitchen. She'd enjoyed the company immensely, but she told herself it was just because she felt a little at loose ends. All the preparations leading up to Abby's wedding had kept them both busy, and now she wasn't quite sure how to fill her time.

With Abby married and on her honeymoon, Felicity admitted to herself that she still wished for a love of her own, and she was trying very hard not to be envious. She was happy for Abby and Stan. . .truly she was.

She just wasn't totally happy for herself. And she didn't know why she was dwelling on it now. Her life plan had been decided with the last broken engagement. She had a living to make, a new business to see to, and that's *all* she had time for.

She certainly didn't have time to mope around wishing for what couldn't be. . .or thinking about how empty her kitchen felt since David left. Sensing the need to keep busy, instead of loading her dishwasher, she filled the sink with dishes, hot water, and dish soap.

But washing them by hand did nothing to help her mood. It only made her wonder what it would have been like to share the task with David. He was much too nice for her heart's sake. It beat faster just thinking of him, and she was certain that wasn't a good thing. Besides, he was her best friend's brother. She didn't need to be thinking about him romantically. She didn't need to be thinking of him at all!

Dear Lord, I'm sure David Edmonds isn't in Your plan for my future. We've already mapped it out, haven't we? So, please help me to put him out of my mind. I don't need the distraction right now. And I certainly don't need another heartache. In Jesus' name, amen.

She finished cleaning the kitchen and went back into the shop to finish making up her list for what to order the next day and to see if there were any messages on the answering machine. The light was blinking, and she was pleased to hear someone from the Loudon First National Bank asking her to call the next day with a quote for doing a weekly arrangement for the bank's lobby.

Maybe the pictures David had put in the paper hadn't done too much harm after all. Felicity put a note on her "to do" list to call them first thing the next morning and replaced thoughts of her handsome supper companion with ideas of the different kinds of arrangements she could offer the bank.

The next day, Felicity was pleased with the order the bank gave her, but a little disappointed in business in general. She wasn't sure if it had fallen off or if she'd just hit a slow spell, but she tried not to worry about it. She hoped that the newspaper article in the coming Sunday paper would help.

David called several times that week, but each time she was in the middle of a project and asked Nellie to take a message. He always said he'd just call back later. Much as she wanted to see him or talk to him again, she was fully aware that she was trying to avoid doing just that. The way her pulse raced each time Nellie told her he was on the phone, Felicity decided that it would just be easier on her if she could keep from seeing him any more than absolutely necessary.

Abby and Stan had returned on Saturday afternoon, and when Abby called with an invitation to come over for brunch after church on Sunday, Felicity was happy to accept.

The interview in Sunday's paper went over very well. Several people at church were complimentary about it, and Felicity knew she needed to thank David for the publicity. She looked around for him, but he was talking to several people across the room and she didn't want to disturb him, so she went on home to freshen up. She brushed her hair and applied fresh lipstick before going outside and hurrying through the hedge to her friend's back door.

She was glad Abby and Stan were back and looked forward to catching up and hearing all about their trip. But it was only when David came to the back door, accompanied by Bowser, that she acknowledged deep down she was hoping he would be here, too.

"Hi, Felicity. Abby didn't tell me you were coming over."

"Hi." *She didn't tell me about you, either.* Felicity hoped the color she felt stealing up her cheeks didn't give away how flustered she was at seeing him again. She bent to pat Bowser on the head and let him lick her hand, trying to give herself time to regain some of her composure.

Abby came up behind David and shoved him out of the way. Hugging Felicity, she asked, "Did he apologize for that awful spread in the paper last week? I've been on his case ever since I looked at it. I can't believe he put so many unflattering shots of me in there!"

Felicity couldn't help but chuckle at the way David rolled his eyes behind his sister's back. She shook her head at him and answered Abby, "Yes, he did. And he's trying to make up for it. Did you see the interview he did with me in today's paper?"

"No, I haven't had time to read it, but it's a good thing he's trying to make amends. Otherwise, he'd be—"

"Disowned," David said, grinning, with his hand over his heart. "But I've asked forgiveness, sister mine. If Felicity can forgive me, surely you can, too."

"I know you better than Felicity does," Abby answered.

David looked over at his new brother-in-law. "You can step in and take up for me anytime now, Stan."

Stan laughed and shook his head. "Not on your life, Buddy. We're still newlyweds."

"Aw, please forgive me, Abby. I really am sorry," David implored his sister.

She winked at Felicity. "Well, if you promise to make it

up to Felicity and if you behave yourself from now on—hard as I know that will be for you. . ."

David gave her a bear hug. "Thanks, Sis. I really didn't mean to cause problems for Felicity. And you looked beautiful—even with your mouth wide open and your eyes closed. But I promise not to ever put that kind of picture of you in the paper again."

Abby punched him on the shoulder. "You'd better not."

He kissed his sister on the cheek, gave an exaggerated sigh of relief, and grinned at Felicity.

The doorbell rang, and Abby hurried to answer it. Felicity was relieved to see more of Abby's family and friends joining them, thinking that there should be a certain amount of safety in numbers. . .because she needed to keep her heart safe from David.

But by the time the afternoon came to an end, she knew she was in real danger. She liked the interaction between David and his sister, between him and his parents. Liked more about him each time she saw him. She wanted to see more of him. But when she looked over and found him studying her from across the kitchen and giving her that slow, sweet smile of his, Felicity knew that was exactly what she couldn't do. Not if she wanted to save herself from more heartbreak.

By the end of the next week, and after calling in favors from everyone he could think of—asking them to put any flower orders they might need, or even a few they might not need, into Flowers by Felicity—David began to wonder if he'd hurt his own cause.

Felicity was up to her ears with work. He stopped by on Friday evening, hoping to get her to go to dinner so that they could discuss some of the ad copy his advertising department had come up with, only to find her and Nellie knee-deep in buckets of cut flowers.

"What's all this?"

"Peach amaryllis, white amaryllis, purple anemones, red anemones, yellow tulips, roses, broom, artichoke leaves, and—"

"No. I mean, what's up?"

She shrugged at him and grinned. "I don't know. Suddenly, I have more business than I've ever had. I think I have you to thank for that."

"That's the point of it all, right?" He smiled at her and looked around. Her worktable was covered with vases and bowls of different shapes and sizes, some kind of green foam stuff, and greenery. Buckets of flowers were all over the place.

"The Wildwood Country Club called late this afternoon. Some kind of reception is being held there tomorrow evening, and they wanted thirty table arrangements by four o'clock tomorrow afternoon. I needed to get started tonight because I've never had an order from them before and I want to be sure and have everything ready on time."

Remind me to kick myself later, Lord. I want to help her business, but I certainly don't want her so busy she doesn't have time for me. David almost snorted at his vain assumption that she might want to spend *any* time with him—the goal was to get her to that point. But he had to have time to do that. . .and if she was working nonstop, what chance did he have?

"I was going to see if you wanted to grab a bite to eat and

go over some ideas for your ads." He could easily see that wasn't going to happen. . .at least not tonight.

"As it stands now, the only way I'm going to eat for a while is if I have something sent in, but thank you anyway."

"Well, how about I go pick something up and bring it back here?"

"Oh, there's no need. I can call and order a pizza."

How was he going to get around that, David wondered, thinking as fast as he could. "I can go pick one up. It'd be a lot quicker."

"I—"

"Let me do this for you, Felicity. Please."

She hesitated for a moment, then she smiled at him. "Yes, all right. Thank you, David. Maybe by the time you get back, we'll have everything set up so that Nellie and I can finish up first thing in the morning. She wiped her hands on her work smock and grabbed the phone. "I'll call in an order to Mario's Pizza. Any kind you are partial to?"

David shook his head, knowing he'd eat any kind she ordered. He headed toward the door. "You pick. Just put it in my name and surprise me."

Chapter 7

Felicity gave the order for the pizza and hung up the phone, staring at the door David had just gone out of. How had he done that? She'd been determined *not* to see more of him, and now it appeared she'd be sharing a meal with him once more. Did she have no backbone at all?

"Are you all right, Felicity?" Nellie asked, bringing her out of her reverie.

"I'm fine. I'm just trying to gather my thoughts." *And protect my heart.* But Felicity had a feeling it was already too late for that. She was afraid she was quickly losing her heart to David Edmonds. She shook her head. She was just going to have to be more on guard.

Trying to get her mind off of him and back on business, she experimented with several different arrangements to find the one she liked best. She made one up of white roses, ornamental cabbage leaves, and rose leaves, and another of anemones of different colors.

She was just putting the finishing touches on one made up of the peach and white amaryllis, broom, and sprigs of cineraria, all the while telling herself that she was going to make sure she didn't fall in love with David. And that was all well and good. . .until he walked back in the door with the pizza and a huge smile on his face. Her heartbeat went into overdrive.

"How did you know I liked a lot of meat on my pizza? And thick crust?"

"Just a wild guess?" Felicity arched an eyebrow at him and grinned. "I think Abby mentioned it one time. And besides, that's the kind Nellie and I like, too."

"Can you take a break and eat while it's warm?"

"I think we're at a good stopping place."

"If you don't need me, I think I'll take off and go home," Nellie said. "But I can come in early, if you want me to."

"That'd be great. Can you come in about seven o'clock?"

"I'll see you then," Nellie said, gathering her purse and a sweater before heading out the door.

"Are you finished for tonight?" David asked.

"I've just got to decide which arrangement I think will work. They left it up to me, and I'm a little nervous about it." She brushed off her hands, took the pizza box from him, and headed toward the door leading into the kitchen. "I'll set the table. Come on back, David. But first, look at those arrangements, will you? And let me know which one you like best?"

David followed only minutes later. "Can I help?"

"No, thanks." She'd already put out the plates and was bringing glasses filled with iced tea to the table.

She liked the way David waited until she sat down

across from her before taking his seat, and she was pleased that he bowed his head and said a prayer before she had a chance to ask him to. He opened the box and motioned for her to help herself first.

She slid a slice filled with cheese, pepperoni, and sausage onto her plate. "Hmm, this smells delicious."

"Not nearly as good as your soup does," David said, taking a couple of pieces out of the box.

Felicity knew she shouldn't be so pleased at his compliment, but she was. Very. She changed the subject. "Which arrangement do you think I should go with?"

"I'm not sure you should take my advice, but I really liked the peach and white one."

"Oh, I am so glad. That's the one I like, too—and it will actually take me less time to put together!"

"Do you need any help tonight? I'm sure we could get Abby and Stan over here for a while."

"Oh, I'd hate to ask them. . ."

David grinned and headed for the phone hanging on the wall. "I don't mind at all."

In only a few minutes, the newlyweds were knocking at Abby's back door. Felicity couldn't remember work ever being quite so much fun as they spent the next few hours putting together the flower arrangements. David, Abby, and Stan proved to be quick studies, and it only took a time or two of showing them how to fill the white bowls about three-quarters full of water, trim the flower stems to the right size, and place them just so in the bowls, before they got it right.

But the laughter and companionship were wonderful and well worth the few mangled flowers on the floor. After they'd put the finished products in the cooler, ready to be delivered the next day, Felicity turned to the trio of friends. "I can't thank you all enough. It would have taken me hours tonight or working up until delivery time tomorrow to get them ready without your help."

"It was fun," Abby said with a yawn.

"It really was," Stan added as he put an arm around his wife's shoulder and turned her toward the door. "Call us anytime."

Felicity saw them out and turned to David. "Thank you again, David—for helping and for calling in Abby and Stan."

"No problem. But we never got around to discussing the ad for the paper."

"Oh, don't worry about that."

"Felicity, there's going to be an ad. I'd like your input."

She yawned and chuckled. "I'm sorry. I'm too tired to think anymore tonight."

David nodded and headed for the door. "I can see you are. I'll get back with you about it tomorrow or the next day. Thanks for letting me help out."

He stood in the doorway a moment, then reached out and gently touched her cheek. "You look exhausted. Try to get some rest, okay?"

She nodded and missed his touch when he dropped his hand and backed out the door. Felicity shut the door behind him and suddenly felt like crying. This man was so sweet. She was afraid she was really falling for him. . .and she couldn't let that happen. Couldn't open herself up to more hurt.

She pushed herself away from the door and went to call Nellie to tell her there was no need to come in early. But it didn't keep her from thinking about David. Oh, why couldn't she have met him before she'd put up a wall around her heart and promised herself never to take it down?

❦

Felicity was avoiding him again. David knew she was. Oh, he'd seen her for a minute at church on Sunday. But each time he'd called the last few days, he either got Nellie or listened to Felicity's voice on her answering machine. He didn't bother to leave a message with either. He was afraid it would become way too obvious that she didn't want to talk to him if she didn't return his calls. So he kept hope alive by telling Nellie he'd call back or hanging up before the tone sounded on the answering machine.

He was afraid he was falling in love with Felicity Carmichael in spite of the fact that she seemed determined not to see him. But he wasn't a quitter, and he wasn't about to give up now. There was something about the way soft color stole up her cheeks when he looked at her a moment too long. And the way the pulse at the base of her throat beat when he touched her cheek the other night. He had a feeling she cared about him, too, but how in the world was he going to find out when she wouldn't even talk to him on the phone?

By quitting time on Thursday, David did the only thing he could think of that would work. He picked up the phone and dialed. "Sis? I need your help."

"What with?" Abby asked.

"Felicity." That's all he needed to say. Abby immediately asked him over for supper, and David silently sent up a prayer, thanking the Lord above for family.

On his way over to his sister's, and thinking he had the perfect excuse for being in the neighborhood because he really needed an okay on the advertising copy he'd made up, he stopped by Felicity's shop. While he finally got her to look at the ad, she still tried to talk him out of it.

"David, I know I keep repeating myself, but you *really* don't need to do this. Business is picking up. . .most likely because of the article you did. In a few months, I could probably afford to put an ad in myself."

"Felicity, please quit trying to talk me out of it. I owe you this. Do you like it or not?" His tone was sharper than he meant it to be; he was just so frustrated at feeling like his relationship with her was going backward instead of forward.

Her tone turned cool. "It's fine."

"Aww, Felicity. I'm sorry. I didn't mean to—"

"No, I'm sorry. You are the one doing me a favor. I'm being ungracious." She handed the ad copy back to him. "It's wonderful, and I do thank you."

Her phone rang just then, and she hurriedly answered it. David couldn't help but think it was odd how she never answered when he called. He'd planned to ask her to dinner the next night, but he had a feeling she'd turn him down flat, and he wanted to avoid an open rejection for as long as possible.

So he took his leave by just waving at her and heading

over to his sister's. He sure hoped Abby had some ideas that would help, because with the ad approved, he was fast running out of reasons to stop by Felicity's shop. He needed his sister's advice more than ever.

When Abby came over the next afternoon, Felicity was glad to take a break. They went to her kitchen, and she made some iced tea for the two of them.

"So? How's married life?"

Abby blushed and smiled. "It's wonderful. Stan is so good to me."

"I'm glad. It's wonderful to see you so happy, Abby."

"Thanks. I wish. . ."

"What?"

Abby shook her head. "Nothing. Catch me up on you. How's business?"

"It's great. I really do have your brother to thank for that. Between his article and the ad he plans to put in the paper, I think I may have to hire another person."

"That's wonderful, Felicity. And it's only what you deserve. He owed you after that spread he put in of my wedding!"

Felicity's heart sank. Abby only confirmed what she'd been thinking. That David was just trying to make things up to her. She was sure that was the only reason he'd been showing her any attention at all.

"Well, he's more than made up for that. I've tried to tell him so. . .but maybe you need to tell him."

"You sound a little put out, Felicity. Has David done something else to upset you?"

"No! He's been wonderful, and I—"

"He thinks he's being a pest and getting on your nerves."

"He told you that?"

Abby was quiet for a moment. "I think he's interested in you. He's a little aggravated at me. . .that I never introduced you to him."

Could what Abby was telling her be true? And what did it matter if it was? He wouldn't be interested for long. . .no one ever was. And she couldn't afford to find out because she already cared too much.

"You knew I'd run in the opposite direction—"

"So, you're still relationship shy?" Abby took a sip of her tea and waited.

"I think I always will be." She couldn't afford to be anything else.

Abby shrugged. "No reason you and David can't just be friends. I'd sure like you to be."

Felicity felt a sudden relief she wasn't sure she understood. But she liked the idea of being friends with David. . .a lot better than thinking their business was over with and she'd never see him again. "A person can't have too many of those."

For the next several weeks, Abby and her new husband did their best to get David and Felicity together. Abby had told him about Felicity's broken engagements and warned him that he'd have to go slow if he wanted to get past her determination not to get involved with anyone again. But she thought they'd make a great couple, and she agreed to help his cause.

It was growing warmer, and they had cookouts and

cook-ins, sometimes with other friends, sometimes just the four of them. It took a few weeks, but finally, Felicity seemed to be warming up to him again. David was beginning to feel he was making progress. . .little by little.

Felicity had even sat with them in church for several Sundays. Well, more to the point, she hadn't objected when he sat beside her. Neither did she seem totally comfortable with it. But he was beginning to think she did care about him. He hoped so. Because he was ready to let her know how he felt about her.

One night, Stan and Abby invited them over for supper and then to a movie. The plan was for Stan and Abby to back out at the last minute, leaving David and Felicity to go alone. David just hoped she didn't refuse to go with him.

He was standing beside Stan at the grill outside, pretending not to be watching for her, when Felicity cut through the hedge, bringing a chocolate cake. It was still cool out, especially of an evening, and she had on a lightweight moss-green sweater and matching pants. She looked lovely.

"You guys be sure and don't burn those burgers tonight, okay?" she teased them, reaching down to scratch Bowser, who was lying right next to the grill, behind the ears. "Bowser likes them medium well, don't you, Boy?"

David and Stan chuckled. Last time they grilled out, they'd been talking about the upcoming baseball season and their inattention had resulted in charred steaks.

"I'll watch real close to make sure Stan pays attention this time," David said as she headed inside to help Abby.

Felicity giggled, and when she smiled at him, David knew

he was a goner. He loved her. Loved her sweetness and her spunkiness. Loved the way she was a loyal friend to his sister and the way she conducted her business. He loved that she loved the Lord with all her heart. He just plain loved her. And he wanted to tell her. It was time.

He worried all through the meal that Felicity would refuse to go to the movies when she found out Abby and Stan weren't going. He held his breath, waiting for her response, when Abby said, "You know, I'm really tired tonight. I hope I'm not coming down with anything. Would you two mind if Stan and I don't go to the movies tonight?"

"That's no problem. We can all go another night," Felicity said.

David's heart sank.

"No, this is the last weekend it's showing, and we'll feel bad if you miss it, too. You two go and let us know how it is," Abby insisted. "If it's good, we'll buy it when it comes out."

"It's okay with me, if it's okay with Felicity," David said. *Dear Lord, please let it be all right with her.* He waited for Felicity's response.

She shrugged. "Sure. Let me help you with dishes, and we'll be off."

Thank You, Lord. Tonight, please guide and direct me on how to let her know I care.

The movie was a romantic comedy with a happy ending that left them both in a good mood. When David suggested that they go to a nearby coffee shop for a cappuccino, he was pleasantly surprised when she agreed. At long last, he felt like they were on a *real* date.

Chapter 8

Felicity couldn't remember enjoying herself more. David was just fun to be around. Over the past few weeks, spending time with him and Abby and Stan, they'd had some really good times. She'd gotten to know him so well. He enjoyed the same movies, the same kind of foods, games, and humor that she did. They both had a soft spot for old people, and sitting beside him in church, she'd found out their favorite hymns were the same. She had more in common with him than with anyone else she'd ever known. It was no wonder she found it impossible to say no to going to a movie with him tonight.

But as she sat across from him, sipping a hot cappuccino, she knew tonight was different. This truly felt like a date, and she'd convinced herself that they were just great friends. But her heartbeat didn't lie, and it told her she was only kidding herself. She cared about this man. . .more than a little. She was falling in love with him.

She hated seeing the evening end because she knew it couldn't happen again. It was one thing to spend an evening in the company of others. . .another thing entirely to spend it with only David. She might begin to think a relationship was possible, and she couldn't afford to do that. She couldn't. Truth was, she'd been fooling herself for the last few months, and the only way to handle things now was to put an end to the time they spent together.

Still, when David drove her home, she didn't want the evening to come to a close. . .she wanted it to go on forever. When he walked her to her door, took her keys from her, and unlocked the door, she turned to thank him, and the look in his eyes was almost her undoing. If she didn't get a grip, she'd convince herself that he really cared.

David smiled down at her. "Thank you for going with me. It was. . .nice. . .just the two of us."

Felicity's heart beat against her ribs as his hand came up to cup the side of her face. "I. . .it was a good movie."

David's head dipped close, and his lips quickly touched the corner of her mouth. He raised his head. "Felicity, I'd like us to do this again. . .go out. . .just the two of us."

"I'm not sure that would be a good idea." Her voice sounded breathless even to her own ears.

"Why not?" His head dipped once more, and his lips touched hers gently, tenderly.

"Hmm. . ." She couldn't remember why not as she responded to his kiss.

When she pulled back, David leaned his forehead against hers. "Felicity, I'm falling in love with you."

That did it. Snapped her right back into her senses. She'd heard those words before. . .from two other men. She shouldn't have believed them then, and she couldn't believe David now.

She backed up toward the door. "No, David. You don't mean that. . .and I . . . No. You can't mean that. You only think you love me. I've been here before."

"I'm not like those other men. I never want to hurt you, Felicity."

She shook her head. "I can't do this again. I just can't. Good night, David." She opened the door, slipped into the safety of her home, and shut the door, leaving David outside. She wanted nothing more than to open the door and rush right back into his arms. But she couldn't do that. She had to stop spending time with him. She had to.

The thought of not seeing him again sent a piercing pain shooting through her heart, but she knew she had no choice. She had to put a stop to the time they spent together. It wasn't meant to be. She and the Lord had a plan for her life, and it didn't include having her heart broken once again.

⁂

David thought his heart truly would break in the timeless moments he stood there just looking at the door. What had he done wrong? He forced himself to turn and step off Felicity's porch and start down the walk. He looked over at Abby and Stan's. There were lights on downstairs. He needed advice, needed to talk to someone. Now. He headed toward his sister's, but watched as the light went out first in the kitchen, then in the living room. Stan and Abby were calling it an evening. Evidently, he wasn't going to get any advice tonight. His sigh sounded almost like a moan to his ears.

He bowed his head. *Lord, please help me here. I think Felicity cares for me as much as I care for her. I don't think that kiss lied. But if I'm wrong, please make it plainer to me than a door closed in my face.*

He shook his head, sighed deeply, and headed for his car. How could it possibly be any plainer?

Felicity was glad when Abby asked her to come over for lunch the next day. She needed to confide in her. . .even though she was David's sister. Abby knew her past, and she would understand why Felicity couldn't continue to join her and Stan and David. Why she couldn't see him anymore. She left Nellie in charge of the shop and hurried through the hedge that separated the two properties.

Abby had everything ready when Felicity arrived, and they sat down at the kitchen table. She'd made a salad with crusty rolls on the side. After saying a blessing, Abby poured tea into their glasses and asked about the movie.

"It was great. You and Stan will like it."

"Did you do anything afterward?"

"We had cappuccino at that new coffee house near the theater."

"And?"

"He brought me home." *And kissed me.*

"And what?"

I lost my heart once more. "He told me he was falling in love with me."

"Oh?" Abby took a sip of tea and paused for a moment. "And what did you say?"

"I told him he only thinks he is. . .and I ran inside. I shut the door right in his face." Felicity laid her head on the table and began to cry.

"Oh, Felicity, Honey, don't cry. He'll be all right." Abby patted her shoulder. "How do *you* feel about him?"

"I. . .he's. . .I. . . It doesn't matter." Felicity sniffed and raised her head. "It's not meant to be. Oh, Abby. . .I certainly don't want to hurt him, if what he said is true. . .but you know I can't go down that road again. I just. . .it's not God's plan for me, and I have to accept that."

Abby got up to get her a tissue and handed it to her. "Felicity, I don't think David is lying to you. He does care very much."

"I thought Ned and Marcus cared, too, Abby. But they changed their minds at the last minute. I just can't take that chance again. You *know* that."

"I know you think the path for your life has been decided and that marriage and a family are out because of those two jerks. But what if you are wrong this time, Felicity?"

"But I asked the Lord for guidance, and He opened up the way for me to start my own business, Abby."

Abby propped her elbow on the table and cradled her chin in her hand. "And you've always assumed that meant you weren't supposed to fall in love again?"

Felicity nodded and wiped her eyes. "That's what I think, yes."

"What if the business was the way to get you together with your true love?"

"Oh, Abby. That would be wishful thinking."

"Would it? You do care about him then."

Felicity nodded and wiped at fresh tears.

"Maybe you've been assuming too much. . .been wrong about what God has been trying to do for you," Abby said, handing her another tissue.

Felicity's heart skipped a beat and then another. Could that be possible? She shook her head. "Oh, Abby. If that was the case, I think the Lord would make it very plain to me."

Abby chuckled and patted her hand. "As plain as the nose on your face, huh?"

"It sure would help."

"Well, I think you may have misread God's will for you, Abby. Sometimes we get ahead of His will for us. We don't always wait for Him. Pray about it and see what happens. You know that verse in Proverbs three, verse five. . .to lean not on your own understanding?"

"Yes."

"Well, maybe you need to tell the Lord that you don't understand and ask Him to make it clear."

Hope stirred in Felicity's chest. She tamped it down. The Lord had made it clear to her already. . .hadn't He?

David told himself to get over it. Obviously, Felicity didn't care about him the way he cared about her. But he kept reliving the evening before—the kiss they'd shared—and he just couldn't believe she didn't have some feelings for him. They'd shared so much the past few weeks, grown more and more comfortable with each other, laughed with one another, and there was just something about the way she looked at him, smiled at him. He honestly felt she had feelings for him, too. But she didn't want to care, and he didn't know how to get past the hurts of her past.

He couldn't concentrate on anything, and by Sunday he was truly miserable. Felicity was late for church, and she took a seat at the back of the sanctuary instead of sitting in her usual spot on the pew beside Abby, Stan, and him. When the service was over, she didn't linger. Instead, she hurried out the door.

Abby touched him on the shoulder. "Want to join us? We're going out for lunch."

He didn't have anything else to do. . .and felt like he never would. "Sure."

David followed the couple to a favorite Mexican restaurant, and once they'd given their orders, he started quizzing his sister. "Is Felicity all right?"

"Oh, I'd say she's as well as you are." Abby grinned at him.

"What do you mean by that? I'm fine." David dipped a chip into salsa and stuck it in his mouth.

Abby looked at her husband and grinned. "Does he look all right to you, Hon?

Stan chuckled. "Seems a little lovesick to me."

David sighed. "You know about the other night? Did she tell you she shut the door in my face?"

"You probably moved too fast. You are too impatient, David. I told you it would take time." Abby dunked her tortilla chip into some guacamole dip.

"I know. You're right. I am. I should have—"

"She's scared, David. That's all it is. She's afraid to believe she could have a future with you. And she has this idea that it's not in God's plans for her to marry and have a family. I think she's as impatient as you in her own way. She may not have waited on the Lord to show her His plan for her life before she decided what it was."

"Well, how do I convince her that I'm sincere, that I do love her, and that I won't hurt her? I want to do God's will, too."

"I know you do. So you need to pray about it. And I don't know how you are going to convince her. It's not going to be easy. You're going to have to do something big. . .something that will persuade her you truly love her."

"Got any ideas?"

"No, but I know it has to be big enough to prove to her that what you feel is real and lasting. And most of all that it's in God's plan for *both* your lives. In the meantime, don't give up."

David had no intention of giving up. And he prayed. But it took several weeks before he finally came up with a plan. During that time he questioned if he should keep trying. Felicity continued to avoid him. If he showed up at Abby and Stan's while she was there, she quickly found an excuse to leave. Once he even saw her start out her door and head toward his sister's until she saw his car in the drive. Then she turned and retraced her steps back home.

Yet each time he did see her, there was something in her eyes that kept him on target. . .trying to come up with something big enough to prove to her that he was serious about her. Abby seemed convinced that Felicity really cared about him and that if he went about it right, he had a chance to win her over. He prayed she was right.

Now as he thought about the plan he'd come up with—the one he was sure the Lord had given him because he didn't think he would have come up with it on his own—he prayed he was doing the right thing. And it was something big like Abby said it would need to be. Very big.

After tomorrow, there was no way Felicity could doubt that he truly cared about her. The only question left was whether she felt the same about him. David bowed his head, knowing that he was either going to be the happiest man in the world the next day. . .or become the laughingstock of the whole town. *Dear Lord, I pray that I am part of Your plan for Felicity's life. That there is a place for me there. I love her. I won't hurt her. Please let this work. In Jesus' name, amen.*

Chapter 9

The last few weeks seemed to have dragged by to Felicity. She missed the fun evenings with Abby and Stan. . .and David. She really missed him more each day. Oh, she saw him when she was at Abby's and he suddenly showed up, or at church—even though she made sure she was late coming into the sanctuary from class so that most seats were taken, making it necessary for her to sit in the back. But nothing was the same, and she was sure it never would be again.

Thoughts of closing her business and moving away had crossed her mind. She wasn't sure she could handle seeing him come and go from next door for the rest of her life. There would come a day when he'd find someone else, marry, and have a family. Then she'd have to contend with watching children who could have been hers grow up right before her eyes. The thought almost made her physically sick. She didn't want David marrying anyone else. Didn't want to watch him have a life that didn't include her.

But if she sold her business and moved, how would she

be living in God's will for her. . .or at least what she thought was His will? *Could Abby be right? Could I have gotten it all wrong? Oh, dear Lord, if I'm wrong, please show me. If I decided what Your will for my life was on my own, please forgive me. Please give me understanding.*

Business was good and getting better, and it kept her busy during the day, but her nights were lonesome. She'd almost quit running over to Abby's for fear of running into David—although that's exactly what she wanted to do. She hadn't realized just how much a part of her life he'd become until now—and the emptiness she felt with him gone seemed to be growing daily. It hurt that she hadn't heard from him, that he hadn't come by or called, that he'd given up so easily.

Okay, maybe not so easily. He told me he loved me—put his heart on the line—and I slammed the door in his face. Felicity's heart twisted over the pain she was afraid she'd inflicted on him. Tears formed as she thought how that must have made him feel. She would have been crushed had he done that to her, yet she expected him to ask for more awful behavior? Felicity shook her head. Not likely.

She threw herself into her work, but it didn't take her mind off of David. . .or the kiss they'd shared. . .or the love she could no longer deny feeling for him. It was getting so hard to face seeing David yet not really being with him that Felicity was seriously contemplating changing churches. Yet she knew she wouldn't. She loved her church family, and she was due to start teaching the preschool class for the summer quarter.

As she woke on Sunday morning, both wanting and

dreading to see David, afraid she'd see him sitting beside another woman one day, she prayed for strength to get out of bed, get dressed, and focus her mind on the Lord rather than on the man she loved. She prayed that seeing David would get easier to bear and that she would get over the love that seemed to be growing by the minute. *Dear Lord, please help me to accept Your will in my life, and most especially, to know what it is. If it's only to run this business You've made possible for me to have, please help me to get past this, to get over David. But if I've been wrong all this time in thinking You intend for me to stay single, please make it clear to me, Lord. In Jesus' name, amen.*

She went through to the kitchen to put the coffee on and then outside to pick up her Sunday paper. Placing it on the table to be read with breakfast, she left it there and went to get dressed for Sunday school.

She found a sleeveless green dress with matching jacket. It was light and summery, and she hoped wearing it would lighten her mood. Hard to believe that it was only late spring. Abby's wedding seemed so long ago. In truth she knew that it was only the past few weeks that had dragged. The time after Abby's wedding—with David—had sped by until the night he told her he loved her. Oh, how she'd wanted to believe him. But she'd believed two other men and had been wrong. How could she trust her judgment anymore?

She couldn't. That's why she needed the Lord to show her if she was wrong. . .or if David was sincere.

She warmed a frozen waffle in the toaster oven and

poured herself a cup of coffee. Sitting down at the breakfast table, she took a bite of waffle, pulled the newspaper out of its protective plastic bag, and opened it to the front page. Her heart seemed to jump and stop all at the same time as she read the headline:

NEWSPAPER EDITOR PROPOSES TO LOCAL FLORIST
SEE LIVING SECTION FOR DETAILS

Felicity's heart began beating again and hammered in her chest as she tore through the paper, trying to locate the article. It was short and sweet:

> *Felicity Carmichael, I think I fell in love with you from the moment I nearly tripped over you at my sister's wedding. I know I was in love with you the night I told you so. And I love you more each day. I can only hope you feel the same way. It's with that hope that I ask you now—Felicity, will you marry me?*

Tears rushed to her eyes. David. Silly, adorable, precious David. She turned the paper all around. It looked like an ordinary Sunday paper with ad inserts and all. But he must have had these few pages made up just for her. . .for this proposal to her. *Oh, dear Lord, can I believe him? I want to so badly. Please help me to know.*

Her phone rang. She hurried to answer. "Hello?"

"Well? Are you going to tell him yes?" Abby asked.

"What?" How could Abby know?

"You have seen the paper, haven't you?"

Felicity's heartbeat pounded in her ears. "You saw it, too?"

Abby laughed. "By now, half the town has seen it. I told him he had to find some big way to let you know how he felt. That brother of mine! I think he succeeded."

Felicity tried to chuckle around a joyful sob. "I think he did, too."

She'd no more than hung up with Abby when the phone rang once more. This time it was Nellie. "Felicity, if you don't tell that wonderful man yes, I will!"

Nellie didn't even wait for an answer before hanging up. The phone rang at the same time her doorbell did. Felicity took the cordless phone with her to the door.

It was in all the papers. All over town. He did love her. He had to. Only a man deeply in love would lay his heart out for acceptance or rejection in full view of the entire town. *Thank You, Lord, for letting me know how he truly feels. Thank You.*

David was at the door. . .and his mother was on the phone. Felicity could only stand there grinning at him as his mother said, "My dear Felicity. I just had to tell you that my son must love you very much. This is just not like him. If you had any doubts before, I can tell you he is sincere. I hope you'll tell him yes."

At a loss for words, Felicity could only nod into the telephone.

"Who's on the phone?" David asked.

She held it out to him and finally found her voice. "Your mother."

David took the receiver from her. "Mom? Yes. I'd like to get her answer now. You'll be the second to know, I promise." With that, he punched the end button and pitched the phone to the couch. He turned back to Felicity and took her hands in his, pulling her close.

"Felicity, have you seen the paper?"

Her heart felt as if it might burst with the love she felt for this man. She nodded.

Still clasping her hands, David knelt on one knee. "I meant it. I love you. . .with all my heart. I know you've been hurt in the past, but I only want to make you happy for as long as I live. Will you please marry me and let me spend the rest of our lives proving it to you?"

Tears streaming down her face at the way the Lord had answered her prayers, Felicity tugged David's hands, and he got to his feet. He pulled her into his embrace, and she looked deep into his eyes. "Oh, David. I love you, too. And yes, oh, yes, I will marry you."

He lowered his head. Their lips met in a lingering kiss meant to mend the hurts of the past and seal the promise of their love for each other. . .for all time.

Epilogue

They said their vows two weeks later on a balmy summer evening in Abby's backyard garden. Felicity was dressed in a white satin A-line gown with beaded Venice lace and delicate cap sleeves gracing the top of the shoulders. Her only attendant was Abby, dressed in a peach Georgette flutter sleeve A-line with a chiffon ruched empire waist.

David had pressed for the date, saying he didn't want Felicity to have a chance to back out, but she knew there was no chance of that happening. She was more than happy to comply. She didn't want him to change his mind, either. Deep down, she felt they both knew that wasn't going to happen. The Lord had brought them together. . .in spite of their blundering along the way.

As David took her in his arms and they shared their first kiss as husband and wife, Felicity thanked the Lord above for leaving her no doubt about how this man felt about her. And she was pretty sure the Lord approved of their impatience this time. . .after all, it'd taken them long enough to figure out His plans.

When the time came to throw her bouquet, she was thankful there was no fan to tear it apart. It sailed through the air the way it was meant to. . .a beautiful bouquet of white roses, gardenias, and lily of the valley made by. . . Felicity, of course.

JANET LEE BARTON

Janet Lee Barton has lived all over the southern United States, but she and her husband plan to stay put in southern Mississippi where they feel blessed that at least one daughter and her family live nearby. Happily married to her very own hero, Janet is ever thankful that the Lord brought Dan into her life. She loves writing stories that show that the love between a man and a woman is at its best when the relationship is built with God at the center. She also writes for Barbour Publishing's **Heartsong Presents** line of romances and is very happy that the kind of romances the Lord has called her to write can be read and shared by women of all ages—from teenagers to grandmothers alike.

Petals of
Promise

by Diann Hunt

To my mother-in-law and father-in-law,
Alice and Byron Hunt.
Thank you for the blessing of your son,
my husband, Jim.
I love you.

Special thanks to my coauthors,
Janet Barton, Sandra Petit, and Gail Sattler.
It was great to work with you!

Chapter 1

Konni Strong reached toward the smiling baby girl perched in her mother's arms. "Hi, Zoe. Want to come to—"

"Watch it!" a deep voice called out beside her.

Before Konni could turn, a bundle of shredded roses plunked into her open palms.

She blinked. Her mouth went dry; her throat constricted. She stared at the flowers that mocked her like a bad dream. Her mind whirled. *Weddings. . .bouquets. . .vows. . .*

"I–I have to go outside," she said to Zoe's mother between shallow breaths. "I'm sorry." The petals dropped from her shaking fingers to the floor. Without so much as looking up, she bolted.

Straight into the arms of the man with the deep voice.

Konni thought she heard him grunt when her body slammed into his chest like an amateur skier against a sturdy tree. His arms grabbed her, holding her perfectly still. Mortified, she reluctantly looked up into his dark, compassionate eyes. As if a slight breeze had swept across the back of her neck, she shivered. "I–I. . ."

A grin spread across his face. Firm arms continued to hold her. She glanced from his hands to his face.

Amusement fanned the corners of his eyes with fine lines. "Oh, sorry," he said, but the smirk on his face indicated he wasn't sorry in the least. He released her.

Oh, how she wished she could crawl into a hole.

Her eighteen-year-old daughter, Emily, stood nearby and leaned over to whisper in Konni's ear, "Hmm, beautiful widow reaches for baby, catches a piece of the bridal bouquet, and runs into the arms of a handsome stranger. It definitely has potential." Emily curled Konni's fingers around the dropped bouquet pieces.

The stranger held Konni's gaze, and she almost gulped out loud. She ignored her daughter's comments completely.

"I nearly got hit in the face with those flowers," he said, nodding toward the petals in her hands.

"What happened, anyway?" she asked.

He laughed and pointed toward the commotion in the back of the room. "I think the bride threw her bouquet a little too hard. It hit the ceiling fan and broke into pieces." He turned back to Konni. "By the way, I'm Rick Hamilton, the new superintendent of schools for Hartley South School District."

Emily let out a soft whistle in her mother's ear.

Konni turned to her. "Emily, Dear," she said through clenched teeth, "would you please get me some more punch?" She batted her eyes sweetly but felt sure she got her meaning across.

Emily frowned. "All right, but I'll be back." Though said in a singsong fashion, Konni thought the words held an unveiled threat.

Konni turned back to Rick. "Excuse me." She sounded positively nasal. With a quick cough, she attempted to pull up a rich contralto. "I'm Konni Strong, aunt of the bride. That was my daughter, Emily," she said, pointing to the young woman as she made her way toward the punch line. "We attend this church."

He nodded. "Your niece told me." His eyes twinkled with secrets.

"Really?" she asked, wondering what else Abby had told him. "Since Stan is a principal, I assume you are here on his behalf?"

"Yep. Couldn't miss the groom's wedding." Lifting his punch cup, he took a drink. "I moved here this school year from the Midwest."

"So is your family with you?" She tried to sound nonchalant.

"No family. My mom and dad are both gone. I'm an only child." His eyes pinned hers before he added, with emphasis, "Never married."

"Oh, I'm sorry."

"Over my parents or the never married part?" he teased.

Suddenly her tongue felt like a beached whale. Before she could make it move, he continued. "Dad's been gone ten years, Mom four. The never married part was a choice I made long ago."

She scratched away the nerves tingling her neck.

He took a drink of punch. "I do have a dog, though, if that counts. Read's a black lab. He doesn't like weddings." His mouth split into a wide grin.

"Read?"

"The basis of all learning."

"Good name."

"Abby tells me you're not married?" He lifted his punch to his lips, but his eyes held hers as if he didn't want to miss her response.

"Well, no, actually, I'm not married. Now." She paused a moment and scratched the top of her hand that held the bouquet pieces. "Eric died five years ago."

"Oh, I'm sorry," he said as though he meant it.

"Thank you." When Konni looked down, she could see a rash developing on her right hand. Her body's response to stress. She sighed and glanced up at Rick. He was looking across the room. Quickly, she shoved her hand behind her. Oh, she hated these rashes. There wasn't a thing she could do about them except scratch and try to relax. She felt like a walking scratch 'n' sniff sticker.

She took another deep breath. *Calm down. Everything is fine.*

A few people beyond Rick smiled and looked their way. Well-meaning friends nodded and gave her the thumbs-up. She felt her face grow hot. Goodness, couldn't she even talk to a man without friends trying to hook her up? She sighed, knowing she'd soon be on their project list. Again. She rolled her eyes.

"Something wrong?"

"Oh, no, I was just. . .oh, well, uh. . ."

"Here you go, Mom." Emily offered the cup filled with punch.

Funny how things change, Konni thought. Suddenly, she was glad to see her daughter. Konni breathed an inward sigh of relief. "Mr. Hamilton, this is my daughter, Emily."

"Nice to meet you."

"Yeah, you, too."

"Mr. Hamilton is the superintendent—"

"Please, call me Rick."

Konni looked at him with surprise. She glanced at Emily, whose eyes positively sparkled. Oh, just wait till she got that girl home. "Emily, Rick is the new superintendent of schools."

"Great!" Emily said with definite approval in her voice and far too much enthusiasm.

Konni made a face at her.

"Would you like to sit down?" Rick asked. "Seems a little crowded right here." Before she could answer, he was already maneuvering her through the crowd. "Oh," he stooped down and lifted something from the floor, "I think you dropped this." He handed her another cluster of the petals she had dropped.

"Oh, uh, thanks." Suddenly, the last five minutes became a tangle of confusion. If only she could run, get away from the stares, the handsome stranger, the warmth of his hand against her back. But no matter how she felt, good manners prevailed. Pushing panic aside, she took a deep breath and continued toward the table.

101

She wished the people would leave her be. Oh, she knew they meant well, but couldn't she talk to a man without them charting her social calendar for the next six months? She shrugged mentally. Key word here, *man*. They thought she'd been far too long without one. What did they know anyway? She had done just fine for the past five years since Eric's death, and she would continue to do so.

Rick, Konni, and Emily slipped into chairs at the corner of a table, away from other people—though not away from the glances. What must Rick be thinking? He surely noticed how people studied them like biology students over a microscope.

Emily grinned as if she knew something the others did not. Konni threw her a go-somewhere-else-to-sit look. A friend came up to Emily and they chatted quietly.

"Do I have a punch mustache?"

Konni looked at Rick in surprise. "I'm sorry?"

"My mouth. Is there a red punch mustache above my mouth?"

She felt almost too embarrassed to look. "No, why?"

"Everyone seems to be staring at us, so I thought I must look funny." He studied her with a smile in his eyes. "It certainly can't be you. I mean, forgive me if I'm out of line, but, well, you look, um, all in place." He stammered for the words like an awkward boy with his first crush.

Konni thought he said the words in a most charming way. "Oh," she finally answered, "people with nothing better to do, I suppose."

He drank more punch, his eyes looking at her, never blinking.

She squirmed a little in her seat.

Putting the cup down, Rick settled back in his chair, his lean torso stretched into a relaxed position. "Since I started in the middle of the school year, I'm fairly new to the community. I don't really know many people outside the school setting."

Konni nodded. She looked at her hands. Why did she bite her nails? For once, she wished she had taken Emily's advice and polished them. She sighed. "So, do you go to church anywhere?"

"I've been attending the big community church on Main Street, but it's really too large for my taste. I prefer a small, intimate fellowship."

"That's how this church is, and I love it."

"Maybe I'll give it a try."

She almost choked. As if she didn't have enough to do to quiet the tongues from today's little chat. If he started going to her church, the endless get-togethers pairing the two of them would never cease. Her friends would not be happy till they got her to the marriage altar. She groaned inwardly.

"So, how long have you lived here?" he asked.

"Forever. All my life, actually."

Emily's friend walked away, and Emily turned to join the conversation.

"Do you have any kids, Mr. Hamilton?" Though Emily tried to mask the question with an air of nonchalance, she was obviously on a searching expedition. She looked at her mother and smiled sweetly before biting into a sandwich.

Konni squinted and tried to imagine Emily with duct tape over her mouth.

"No kids. Never married." His knowing eyes sparked with good humor.

Several people stood and pushed their chairs back up to the tables, then headed outside. Konni turned toward the noise of people shuffling out the door.

"Well, looks like the crowd is thinning out. The happy couple must be preparing to leave." Konni motioned toward the crush of people. She stood, grabbing her coat and purse. She couldn't leave soon enough. Emily and Rick followed suit.

A cold breeze whipped past them, causing Konni's hair to blow all over her face. Though cropped to neck length, she had lots of it. She pushed the black strands from her eyes.

Rick smiled.

That made her feel good inside. She rebuked herself. After all, she'd kept her vow to Eric for five years and didn't want to break it now.

"Here they come," rippled through the crowd. Everyone lined the sidewalk as the happy couple came through the doors and headed for the limo. Well-wishes, farewells, and bubbles filled the air.

Once the car pulled away, the guests scattered like falling leaves on a windy afternoon.

"Where did you park?"

She pointed toward her car.

He nodded and continued to walk with her. "Did you say you work outside the home?"

"No, I didn't say, but I do. I own an antique shop. Forgotten Treasures."

He nodded. "I've heard of that."

"It's a great little shop," Emily piped up. Konni had forgotten her daughter was still there.

"I'm sure it is. I like antiques myself. I might come in and check it out."

"Good." Why did she say "good"? She didn't want to encourage him. Not that he cared one way or the other. She stopped at her car door and turned to him. "Well, Mr. Hamilton—Rick—it's been a pleasure." She shifted the bouquet pieces into her left hand so she could extend her right hand.

"Konni, the pleasure has been all mine." He dwarfed her hand in his. "Hopefully, I'll see you again."

Before she could respond, he turned and walked toward his car. Her heart swirled with emotions she didn't want to deal with just now. She didn't like the effect this man had on her, and the farther away she stayed from him, the better.

She turned to get in the car, but not before glancing at her daughter who stood on the passenger's side waiting to get in. Emily looked at her. "At least give him a chance, Mom."

"Get in the car, Emily."

Emily climbed in, and Konni turned her head once more toward Rick, who was driving by just then. He caught her staring and raised his hand to wave. She waved in return, mad at herself for glancing back.

After all, she didn't want to give him the wrong impression.

Chapter 2

Rick stared at the paperwork spread across his oak desk. Seemed no end to his responsibilities. He didn't especially enjoy working on a Saturday, but he'd been swamped with paperwork since the wedding a couple weeks ago. He didn't mind too much. Work energized him. In fact, he looked forward to it each day. His chair squeaked as he scrunched into the soft leather and leaned back.

Yet things seemed different somehow. He couldn't understand it. He liked his job; it was going well. Why did he feel unsettled?

Konni Strong's image intruded his thoughts, surprising him. More and more, her face seemed to pop up like an energetic kindergartner. The short dark hair, delicate features, thick lashes that fringed eyes the color of rich, brown leather. Eyes that held a hint of sadness. A look that made him want to shelter her, hold her tight, and tell her everything would be right with her world. He shook himself. How could he make a promise like that? With his upbringing, what did he know about taking care of a woman? He didn't trust himself.

That's why all these years he had dabbled only in surface relationships. No tangles. No worries. Still, he couldn't deny his loneliness. He blew out a sigh. He decided he needed some good companionship. As they say, "All work, no play. . ." He thought a little longer. Konni didn't seem interested in a serious relationship. Maybe he'd attend her church in the morning and invite her out to dinner. No harm in that. He stretched long and hard in his seat. That's what he'd do.

With his decision made, he bent back over the papers and set to work.

The next morning, Konni got a call from Rick, asking about church service times. She gave him the information, hung up the phone, and stared at it a full moment. Since she hadn't talked to him in two weeks, she'd figured he had decided against coming to Hope Village. Well, she didn't have time to think about it now. She needed to get ready. Rummaging through her dresser drawer, she pulled out a packet of black pantyhose.

With her fingers wrapped around the ends of the package, she yanked off the tape. When she shook the nylons free, her jaw dropped. "I'd have to be Malibu Barbie to wear these things!" she said out loud. She blew out a gust of air and made a gesture of rolling up her sleeves.

With the tip of her tongue poking slightly through the right side of her mouth, she worked the socks between her fingers until she could gracefully slip her toes in. Gradually, she inched the material up her legs. Once she reached her knees, the delicate fabric fought back. "Come on, work with me here," she said between grunts and labored breathing.

She paused a moment to catch her breath. Like a rubber band, the hosiery snapped tight against her thighs, cutting off circulation. Her pulse throbbed through her leg veins with the steady rhythm of marching soldiers. She figured that couldn't be good, so she fell onto the bed and declared war.

Yanking, twisting, and basically squirming her way across the scattered bed covers, Konni worked with determination to pour her legs into the pantyhose, come what may. Perspiration beaded her forehead, but still she persisted. Harder and harder, she tugged like a woman on a mission. With victory just in sight, she gave a final thrust that catapulted her body across the family cat. Trixie's meow would have won an Oscar for special effects in a horror movie. Konni screamed. Her thumbnail ripped through the material as her legs tangled with the cat, the covers, and the control tops.

Things were not pretty.

Emily's footsteps pattered from the hallway to the bedroom door. "You okay?"

Konni gasped for air and stared in disbelief at the white pad of her thumb that poked through the ragged hole in the hose. She didn't know whether to cry or create a finger puppet. She made a face at her daughter. Emily covered her mouth to stifle a chuckle.

"I'm fine," Konni said in a huff, trying to stand, "but I'm not so sure about Trixie."

This time they both laughed.

When had she put on the extra pounds? Had she really

let herself go after Eric's death? She hadn't thought so, but now, her eyes opened to the truth.

Though it took some doing, Konni pulled herself free from the covers and the nylons. With renewed determination, she decided she would start a diet and exercise program.

After her morning doughnut.

"Do you think he'll come today?" Emily asked while examining her fingernails, as if only partially interested in Konni's response.

Konni played along. "Who, Dear?"

Emily looked up at her with a start. "Rick Hamilton, that's who."

Konni feigned surprise. "I'm sure I don't know what his plans are."

Emily stared at her.

"Okay, he just called. He'll be there this morning."

Emily was more excited than she let on. "That's nice," she finally commented before heading back to her room.

Though Emily had loved her father, she made it clear time and again she wanted Konni to move on with her life. No doubt before going off to college, Emily wanted her mother's happiness intact.

What Emily didn't understand was that Konni didn't need a man to be happy.

Konni sighed. She was a bit curious as to why Rick hadn't called or come to church before now. At the wedding, he had seemed anxious to get to know her. Maybe he had met someone else. Not that it mattered. She meant it on the day of Eric's funeral when she vowed to never remarry.

Though others had told her she needed to get on with her life, she didn't care. Eric Strong was the only man for her.

Past, present, and future.

⸺

Tired from the long week, and restless for reasons she couldn't explain, Konni punched her pillow into position for the umpteenth time. Rick's presence at church the previous Sunday had done little to calm her inner turmoil. Once she finally got comfortable, the phone rang. Grating her frazzled nerves, she almost fell off the bed. "Okay, so I'm a little edgy," she said to Trixie, as the feline walked by appearing as though she couldn't care less about Konni's problems. "Hello?"

Rick Hamilton's deep voice greeted her on the other end of the line. "Hi, Konni. Hope I didn't wake you."

She shot straight up in bed. Her heart leapt to her throat. "Uh, no." From where she sat, she could see herself in the dresser mirror. She worked her fingers through her hair to straighten it.

"Good. I'm not trying to stalk you or anything, but Emily gave me your number and said I should call you." He paused a second, then added, "We didn't really have a chance to talk last week at church."

"I know. I'm sorry about that. What with the Sunday school promotion and all, there was a lot going on."

"Not a problem. Those things happen." He cleared his throat. "I was wondering. . .well, I didn't know if you might want to go to dinner on Friday night. Nothing real fancy. Steak and potatoes restaurant. Are you game?"

Her mind screamed *no*, but her voice said, "Yeah, why not?" before her good sense could stop her. After all, shouldn't she offer Christian kindness and friendship? Though the feeling there was more to it than that gnawed at her.

"Great. I've been so bored around here. I mean, I have coworkers but no real friendships, you know?"

She smiled. "Yes, I understand."

"Thanks, Konni. I'll look forward to it."

"Me, too."

She gave him her address; they chatted a little longer and finally said their good-byes. Konni could hardly get through the conversation as she tried to think of a way to move and leave no forwarding address for her daughter. . . .

The next evening, Konni clicked off the TV and dabbed at her eyes.

"Why do you watch *Little House on the Prairie*? You know it always makes you cry," Emily said from her recliner before biting into an apple.

"I know." Konni grabbed a tissue and blew her nose.

"So, what's going on?"

Konni sat on the couch with her feet propped on the coffee table. An empty popcorn bowl perched in her lap, she shoved the last kernel in her mouth and looked up. "Nothing. Why?" She brushed the crumbs from her pajama top.

"Well, it's just that you only eat like that when you're nervous."

"Eat like what?"

"Well, you know, kind of fast and furious. Last meal kind

of thing." Emily's words held no disrespect, just bald truth.

Konni resisted the urge to whack Emily up the side of the head with the bowl. Visions of fighting with her pantyhose surfaced. She gave an inner wince. "I'm fine."

"Come on, Mom. Something is going on. I know you. Can't you tell me what it is?"

Konni scratched her neck. Uh-oh, the rash was back. She felt like a dog with fleas. Emily saw her scratching and threw her an I-caught-you look. Why did Konni feel like the kid here instead of the mom? She hated this role reversal thing. Wasn't it too early for that? She took a deep breath. "All right, I don't want you to make a big deal out of this—"

"Are you sick?" Emily's worried eyes searched her mother's.

"Oh, no, Honey, nothing like that."

Emily visibly relaxed. Poor kid. Last thing she needed was to deal with another blow like that in her young life.

Konni licked her lips. "It's really nothing. I'm just, well. . ." If only Emily would quit looking like she was hanging on her every word. Konni swallowed. "Well, I don't know why I'm stammering like a child. I'm just going to dinner with Rick Hamilton on Friday night, that's all."

"What?" Emily let out a scream and jumped off her chair. She ran to the couch. "Mom, that's fantastic!" Emily hugged her fiercely.

"Now, you see. That's why I didn't want to tell you."

"Why?" Emily pulled back, surprised.

"Because it's not a big deal, and I don't want you to make it into something it's not."

"Mom, it's a huge deal! You are going on a date! I'm so proud of you." Another hug.

"No, it's not a date. We're friends, period."

Emily nodded, giving her mother a patronizing smile.

"You stop that this minute, Emily Marie."

"Okay, okay, so it's not a date." Emily parroted what Konni wanted to hear. "Where you going?"

"Roy's Steakhouse."

Emily nodded. "Nice. Nice."

Konni stuffed a pillow in Emily's lap. "Glad you approve."

"What are you wearing?"

Konni thought a moment. She started to chew on her thumbnail. "I don't know."

"Mom, stop chewing your nails." Emily was off and running. "Oh, Mom, you could put your sign up at the store that you're closing early and get your nails done."

Konni raised her chin. "Absolutely not." She felt down-right offended at the suggestion. After all, she wasn't changing her routine for anyone, certainly not a man with whom she had no intention whatsoever of getting involved.

Emily raised her hand. "Okay, okay, just a suggestion." She tapped the eraser end of a pencil against her forehead. After a moment, her eyes lit up. "I know! You look great in that red pantsuit."

"Oh, Em, you know how I hate that thing."

"You hate it because men stop and take notice. Aunt Cheryl knew what she was doing when she bought it for your birthday. You look awesome in that suit, Mom."

"You and my sister are conspiring against me."

"Your red shoes with the gold buttons look great with it."

Konni chewed off her next nail. "I don't know. Might be too fancy."

Emily brushed the comment aside. "No, no, it's casual classy. Perfect to wear there. I've got some polish that will look good on your nails." Before Konni could comment, Emily ran to her room and came back with a bottle of cherry nail polish.

"I'll look like a tomato in all that red."

"You'll look gorgeous. I'll just put this on and you can see if you like it." Emily placed a board on her lap and pulled her mom's hand to her. Quickly, before Konni could chew off any more nails, Emily opened the polish and began to apply it to Konni's fingernails.

"Oh, Emily." Konni hated all the primping, but she knew her daughter enjoyed every minute of it.

Once Emily finished the job, Konni had to admit her nails did look nice. Besides, they matched the rash on her hands.

"Now, if they chip at all, just touch them up with this," Emily said as she replaced the cap and screwed it tightly closed.

Konni blew out a long sigh.

"Mom, everything will be fine. You'll see."

Konni nodded. "He's just a friend. You remember that." She waggled a red fingernail under Emily's nose.

"I'll remember," Emily said, doing the Scout's honor sign.

"You still going to Alexis's house Friday night?"

Emily smiled. "Yeah. Why, are you trying to get rid of me?"

Konni gasped. "Absolutely not!"

"Okay, okay, I'm just teasing." Emily turned a serious expression to her mom. "I'm really glad you're doing this, Mom."

Upon seeing her daughter's hopeful face, Konni didn't know how to respond. Emily reached over, dropped a kiss on Konni's forehead, and headed for the door. "See you in the morning."

"Okay, Honey."

Emily walked into the hall.

"Em?"

She turned. "Yeah?"

"Thanks."

A huge grin spread across Emily's face. "No problem." With that, she went to bed.

Konni watched her daughter and smiled in spite of herself. She knew Emily felt proud to help her in this way. Still, Konni wanted everyone to know right from the start, she and Rick were friends. Only friends. Period.

She walked over to the closet and pulled out her red pantsuit. Maybe she would wear it Friday night.

Chapter 3

Rick clicked on the wide-screen TV and raked his fingers through his hair. What had he gotten himself into? He wanted a friendly date. That's all. Yet after talking with Konni, he sensed this was a big step for her. Maybe a bigger step than he wanted her to take.

He turned on a reality show and walked into the kitchen. Plopping some ice cubes in a glass, he poured himself a soda. The fizz rose up over the rim of the glass and spilled onto the counter. Rick grabbed a dishcloth.

"I mean, it's not like we're getting married or anything," he said to Read. The lab's ears perked, his eyes fixed on his owner. Rick sipped the remaining suds from the top of his glass, cleaned the overflow from the counter, and looked back at his dog. "I haven't stayed single this long for nothing. I'm not about to get into that trap. Those people live in misery. That's not for me."

Read cocked his head as though listening with a compassionate ear. The action seemed to shake Rick to his senses. He laughed, bent down, and scratched behind Read's ear.

"Thanks for listening, ol' buddy. There will never be anyone but you for me." Rick stood, grabbed his glass again, and headed back into the living room. Read jumped up, wagged his tail, and trotted alongside.

Rick placed his glass on the coffee table. He leaned back and sank into the plump leather cushions of his sofa. With a glance at the reality show, he picked up the remote and clicked his way through the channels, pausing here and there along the way. His eyes glazed as images flickered across the screen.

Thoughts of his childhood surfaced again. He was nine. His mom clutched him close to her side, trying to leave the house while his alcoholic father blocked their way. No matter how hard he tried, Rick could not erase the memory of his dad's face at that moment, twisted in anger, breath reeking of whiskey. A twinge of fear from that scene haunted him still.

He blew out a sigh and clicked off the TV. Looking down, he stared into his open palms. Never did he want to break a woman's heart the way his dad had broken his mother's heart. Better to stay single and not risk it.

Read pushed his head under Rick's hands for attention. Rick smiled and rubbed the dog's neck. "You know, Read, it's not unusual for me to work late. Maybe I'll just let Konni know I need to stay at the office Friday night." Read's eyes met Rick's. "Well, there's truth in that." Rick felt defensive. "My desk is piled with papers needing my attention. I'll just stop by her antique shop tomorrow. That will be best for both of us," he said, ignoring the doubt that pricked his heart.

Konni flipped through the musty magazines a customer had dropped off. The periodicals appeared in pretty good shape despite their years. Recognizing some of the products and famous people of her youth, Konni sighed at the passing of time. Why couldn't things stay the same forever? She hated change, and she hated growing old. Why, just that morning she had plucked a gray hair. Okay, maybe two or three. . .hundred. Time to color. The thought made her mood dive south.

Stacking the magazines in a neat pile, Konni pulled out her inventory book, slipped on her reading glasses, and added the items to her growing list.

The bell on the front door jangled.

Konni took off her glasses and looked up. A slightly bent, frail wisp of a woman entered the store. Wrapped in a green tweed coat, neatly pressed and buttoned to the top, the old woman walked rather sprightly toward the counter. A sheer green scarf covered the white hair that fell in soft curls and dusted the nape of her neck. She carried a shiny black handbag with a small handle and gold clasp. Rubber-soled black shoes covered her feet, while sensible hosiery supported her aged legs. Once she reached the counter, a kind smile touched her mouth and a twinkle lit her eyes.

"Hi," she said in a shaky voice. "I'm Irene Kenner." She extended a gnarled hand.

"Konni Strong. How may I help you?" Konni's heart went soft at the sight of the woman.

Irene Kenner looked about the store. "You got a place to sit around here?"

Konni liked the woman's no-nonsense approach. "Oh, yes." Konni grabbed a chair and brought it to the mysterious stranger.

Mrs. Kenner eased herself into a seat plumped with padding, laid her purse across her lap, and looked up at Konni with a smile. "My mind tells me I'm twenty-five, but my body tells me the truth." A slight smirk tinged the corners of her mouth. "I do okay for an eighty-five-year-old, I reckon."

Konni nodded and waited for the woman to state her business.

Mrs. Kenner's eyes grew serious. "Married to a wonderful man for thirty-five years," she began. "Orville." She looked away from Konni, as if she'd stepped into the past.

Uh-oh. Something told Konni this could take awhile. Oh, well, the work would have to wait.

"I've wasted too many years. Too many," Mrs. Kenner said with a touch of sorrow. She seemed to linger in remembrance, then turned to Konni. "But no more." Bright enthusiasm flickered in pale, clouded eyes. She smacked the purse on her lap for emphasis.

"I want to sell a desk."

Konni smiled.

"Do you know I wrote love letters to my husband on that desk more than sixty-five years ago?" She waved her hand. "Of course you don't. We've only just met." She laughed at herself. "The desk was a good hundred years old then. My parents loved antiques." She shrugged again. "Got a neighbor girl who needs to go to college. She works two jobs, has all the financial aid she can get, and it's still not enough.

Parents barely make ends meet." She shook her head. "I mean to help her. I'm going to sell my desk." Her lips pursed into a thin line as though the matter was settled.

Amazed that someone could part with such a prize, Konni studied her. "The desk has been in your family for a long time. Are you sure that you want to sell it?"

The woman nodded emphatically. "What good does it do collecting dust at my house? Can't see a thing to write. For crying out loud, half the time, I can't even see the desk. I keep bumpin' into it." She groaned and rubbed her knee as if there was a fresh bruise underneath her dress. "Might as well do some good."

Konni stepped cautiously onto personal ground. "Might your family want it?"

"I have no family," she said matter-of-factly. Her hand steadied her purse.

Realizing the woman's mind was made up, Konni interrupted the brief silence. "Where might I see it?"

"I thought you'd never ask." With great care, Mrs. Kenner reached shaky fingers into her purse and pulled out a slip of paper. "Here's my address. I live just down the road. Within walking distance."

Konni looked at her in surprise. "You walked?"

"Course. How do you think I keep my figure?" An ornery grin escaped her.

Konni chuckled. "Would Saturday evening, say around seven o'clock, be all right?"

Mrs. Kenner nodded.

The doorbell jangled, causing them both to look up.

Rick Hamilton entered the store. Konni's heart flipped.

"Hi, Rick. Nice to see you," she said as he approached. Her eyes took in the heavy beige sweater that swept across his thick chest and broad shoulders. She ventured a glance at the well-scrubbed jeans that stretched down long legs and stopped short of brown leather shoes.

"Hi, Konni." He turned to Mrs. Kenner and tipped his head. "Ma'am."

"Rick, this is Irene Kenner. Mrs. Kenner, Rick Hamilton. Rick is superintendent of schools for Hartley South School District."

"Is that a fact?" She looked him over. "You'll do just fine. We need good men in such important positions." She studied him. "I can tell you're a good one," she said finally and snapped her head once with approval.

Rick looked at Konni, and they laughed. He turned to the old woman. "You can tell already?"

She attempted to rise. Rick reached over and assisted her to her feet. She poked a crooked finger under his nose. "Oh, don't let this body fool you. I may look like an old hound dog, but my mind is sharp. I can read people pretty well."

"Uh-oh, I'd better watch myself," he said with a laugh.

Mrs. Kenner smiled. Her slow, steady gaze drifted from Rick to Konni and back to Rick. "Well, I'll leave you young folks to your business. I'll see you Saturday, Konni Strong."

Konni nodded and smiled. She and Rick escorted Mrs. Kenner through the door into the crisp air. They watched her walk steadily into the quiet street lined with towering maples and quaint lampposts. High above, the whir of an airplane caught Konni's attention as it soared against the backdrop of a spring sky full of sailing clouds. Just once she would like to experience such freedom. To fly among the clouds, to allow her spirit to give way in complete abandon to protocols, convention, and. . .vows. She gasped almost audibly. Whatever made her think that?

"Nice woman," Rick said, jarring Konni to attention.

She nodded, though still stinging from the betrayal of her private thoughts. She mentally shook herself. "Do you know she's eighty-five?" Konni asked, her eyes once again on Mrs. Kenner.

"She gets around pretty well."

Konni turned to Rick. "So what brings you here?"

He swallowed hard and stared at her.

"Is something wrong?"

"Uh, no. I just wanted to look around your shop and, uh, remind you about dinner tomorrow night."

She laughed and opened the door into her shop. "You afraid I'll back out?"

Rick laughed, but something about his mannerisms made Konni wonder if there was more to his visit than he let on.

On Friday night, Konni's bedroom smelled of perfume and hair spray. Weary from the effort and stress of getting ready for a date, she finally allowed herself to edge in front of her full-length mirror. Her red neck matched her pantsuit. Emily came in and stood behind her mother.

"You look great, Mom."

"I look like Bob the Tomato. Round and red." She could

hear the panic in her voice. All she wanted to do was curl under a soft blanket and watch an old movie.

Emily laughed and shook her head. She walked over to her mother's dresser and picked through the jewelry. She held up a dainty golden necklace and turned to Konni. "Here, this will look great with your outfit."

Konni reluctantly walked over to Emily and looked at the necklace Eric had bought her on their fifth anniversary. "Not that one," she said in a whisper.

With knowing eyes, Emily looked at Konni. "I'm sorry." She squeezed her hand. "You don't really need one."

Just then the doorbell rang. They both jumped. Emily squealed and placed a kiss on her mother's cheek. Konni groaned and scratched her neck once more.

"Come on, Mom, you're going to have a great time. I promise." Emily grabbed Konni's hand.

Alarm shot through Konni. Her feet thudded to a halt. "I can't go like this. If people see me rush through the parking lot, they'll think I'm a flashing traffic signal. I'll cause a wreck. I'm much too conspicuous!" Konni turned to rush back to her bedroom; Emily grabbed her.

Holding her by both arms, Emily looked straight into Konni's eyes. "Mom, calm down. You look wonderful."

Konni thought she might lose her lunch, which, of course, would do nothing for her red pantsuit. She took a deep breath. She stood there a moment or two to calm herself. Goodness, what had gotten into her? *Dinner. Two friends going to dinner.*

The doorbell rang again. Emily and Konni both glanced toward the front door. "You gonna be okay, Mom?"

Konni closed her eyes, took another breath, and nodded.

"Okay, let's go." Emily helped Konni down the stairs to the front door; then Emily stepped aside and went into the living room.

Konni glanced once more at her daughter and received a thumbs-up. She opened the door.

Rick's approving eyes met hers. A large grin stretched across his face. "Hi."

He stood tall before her, dressed in khakis with a sharp crease, a button-down shirt, and a brown leather jacket. Konni stood mute like a figurine in a wax museum.

Rick's eyebrows raised; amusement danced in his eyes. "May I come in?"

Konni gulped. "Oh, yes." She let out a nervous laugh and stepped aside. She turned toward Emily and rolled her eyes. Emily covered a giggle.

"Just let me grab my bag and coat," Konni said.

Rick exchanged some chitchat with Emily while Konni stepped in the bathroom to check her rash once more. A glance in the mirror told her what she needed to know. Once at the restaurant, someone might possibly toss her into a salad bowl. Okay, a very large salad bowl. She sighed and walked back into the living room.

"You ready?" Rick asked

Konni nodded and looked toward Emily. "You and Alexis behave yourselves," she said in the expected parental tone.

Emily smiled. "We'll be good as gold. I promise."

Konni eyed her with suspicion. "Why does that make me nervous?"

Emily laughed. "I'll be back around ten o'clock tomorrow morning. Is that okay?"

Konni kissed her daughter on the forehead. "That's fine, Honey. You girls have a good time."

"You, too." Emily gave her a motherly look.

Konni felt like a sixteen-year-old going on her first date. She half expected Emily to dole out a curfew. Rick smiled and cast a wink at Emily, then ushered Konni out the door. She felt his hand on the small of her back. A gentle and protective touch. She liked it. Too much. She told herself to jerk away but argued it would be a rude thing to do.

It's okay. You're friends. You're only friends.

Rick opened the door and helped her in. While he walked back to the driver's side, she looked at her hands and admired her nail polish. Reluctantly, she admitted to herself she did feel quite feminine.

"Want some music?" he asked as he closed the door and started the engine.

"Sure."

He clicked on the knob and turned to an easy-listening station. A saxophone crooned a romantic melody that melted the stress from Konni's shoulders and soothed her down to her toes. It was just what she needed after her tension-filled day. She felt sure if she were a cat, she'd start to purr.

"You hungry?" Rick asked, breaking through her momentary trance.

She turned to him and smiled. "Yes."

"Good. I am, too."

Chapter 4

After dinner at Roy's Steakhouse, Rick and Konni went to the Chatting Grounds Coffeehouse. The clock inched toward closing time, but Rick didn't want the night to end. Seeing Konni at Forgotten Treasures had made him want to keep the date. He was glad he hadn't canceled it. He and Konni were having a good time.

Konni laughed at something someone had commented in passing; then she took the last sip of her latte. She placed the cup back on the table and glanced around. "Must be near closing," she said in a voice that hinted at disappointment.

"I know a diner, a fifties kind of place that stays open until one o'clock. That would give us a little more time. Are you game?" As soon as he spoke the words, he was afraid he had pushed her too far. One look in her eyes removed his fear.

"Why not?" A carefree grin lit her face—an expression that told him she truly was enjoying herself.

"Great."

They rose from the wooden chairs, threw their cups in

the trash, and left the coffee shop. In practically no time at all, they arrived at Della's Diner.

Rick shut off the engine and walked to the passenger's side of his navy SUV. He opened the door and let Konni out, noticing she had touched up her lipstick.

Once inside, she eased into the booth, and he slid across from her.

"Hey, Rick," a plump, gray-haired lady called from behind the counter of the near-empty room.

"Hi, Della. What's the owner doing working so late?"

She shrugged, edging her way over with menus. "The waitress called in sick. My backup left for vacation. That leaves me." She tossed a weak smile and pulled a pencil from behind her ear. Reaching into her pocket, she lifted a customer order pad. "What will it be?"

Rick held up his hand. "Sorry, Della, no food tonight. Just coffee will be fine." He looked at Konni to make sure that's all she wanted.

"Please. Decaf," she said.

"Better do the same for me, or I'll never get to sleep tonight," Rick added.

Della laughed. "You'll have trouble sleeping all right, but it won't be from the coffee," she murmured as she walked away.

Rick heard her and turned to Konni. She rummaged through her purse and didn't seem to notice the comment. He had to smile in spite of himself. Della, always the matchmaker.

Konni looked up at him. "What is it?"

"Hmm?"

"You're smiling."

"Oh, that." He ran his fingers absently across his chin and shrugged. "Just having a good time, I guess." He kept his eyes fixed on her.

Konni smiled back. "Rick, this has been a wonderful evening."

Uh-oh, here it comes. "It's been great, but. . ." He studied his fingers and gritted his teeth, waiting on what would follow. Silence. Surprised, he glanced up. She looked at him.

"Did I say something wrong?" she asked, concern on her face.

"Not at all. I just thought—"

Her dark eyes searched his face, causing his tongue to stick to the roof of his mouth like a glob of peanut butter.

"Well?" A smile played in her teasing eyes.

"Okay, I thought you were going to say something like, "It's been great, but, blah, blah, blah," you know, like maybe you didn't want to see me again." Oh, now he'd done it. A shadow flickered across her face. He had to slow down or he'd blow it. He reached his hands out and cupped hers in his own. "Look, I'm sorry. I don't mean to. . ."

She looked as though she wanted to rescue him from digging a deeper hole. "It's okay, Rick. I understand."

He blew out a sigh of relief and leaned back in his seat. Their eyes engaged, neither breathing a word.

Della approached with a pot of coffee, shaking them from their thoughts. She poured the steaming liquid into china cups she placed in front of them.

"Wow, fine china. I've not seen those before, Della. Are

we getting the red carpet treatment?"

The owner winked at Rick. "Just for you and your friend, Kiddo. Just for you." She patted his arm, then looked at Konni and smiled before walking away.

Konni chuckled. "I'd say you must come here quite often," she said, easing the hot liquid to her lips.

"Guilty as charged." He lifted his cup and took a drink. Putting it back in the saucer, he glanced at Konni. "What's a bachelor like me gonna do for dinner? Della keeps me from starving." He patted his midsection. "She does a great job, I might add."

"What, you don't cook?" Konni feigned shock.

"Can't even boil water," he said, trying his best to put on the sad look of a stray puppy.

Konni laughed. "Okay, that settles it. You'll have to let me fix dinner for you next Friday."

Rick's hand jerked and tipped his coffee. With his other hand, he stopped the spill. "Really?" he asked, cleaning coffee droplets from his cup and saucer.

She shrugged. "It's the least I can do for a starving friend."

He nodded his head with pleasure. "It's done then. Seven o'clock all right?"

She took another drink. He could detect a smile behind her cup. "Seven o'clock will be fine."

"To next Friday then," he said, lifting his cup to hers till they clinked.

The next morning, Konni put away the clean dishes from

the dishwasher, clanging pots and pans in the process.

"You okay, Mom?" Emily asked when she walked in the door.

Konni turned with a start. "Oh, hi, Em. I didn't hear you come in."

"You look a mess," Emily said, her eyes intent on Konni's face.

"Thanks a lot."

Emily grabbed her mother's hand and led her to the chair by the table. "What's wrong, Mom? Was the date a total bust? You look like you haven't slept all night."

"I haven't slept. Why, I didn't even get home until two o'clock this morning!" She could hear her voice rise; a panic attack threatened to strike. Her fingers scratched the rash on her neck.

Emily's eyes grew wide as grapes. "Mom, that's terrific!"

Konni's hands clamped the sides of her face. "It is not!" She rose from her chair and began to pace as Emily looked on. "It's not supposed to be like this. I'm not some silly teenager—" She stopped abruptly and glanced at Emily. "Sorry." She continued to pace, her arms raising and lowering for emphasis. "Look, I don't want to do this. I don't have the energy, nor the. . .the. . .well, I just can't do it, that's all."

Emily stood and faced her. "Why not? He's a great guy, and you obviously had a wonderful time. What are you worried about, Mom? What's stopping you?" She looked straight into Konni's eyes.

Konni stared at her, speechless.

"Mom. . ." Emily swallowed for a moment as if allowing

herself time to consider the words. "Dad is gone. Nothing we do will ever change that. We both need to face it and get on with our lives." Emily placed her hands on Konni's shoulders. "You know that's what Dad would want."

Whether from fatigue or the emotional turmoil of the last twenty-four hours, Konni didn't know, but try as she might, she couldn't stop the tears from falling.

"Oh, Mom." Emily pulled her into an enormous embrace. "It's gonna be okay."

There she went again, acting like the mom. It was just what Konni needed to bring her to her senses. She pulled away and wiped her face with a nearby paper towel. "You're right. We'll be fine." She raised her chin and shoulders. Her jaw tensed. They would be fine, but she didn't feel like talking to Emily about it just yet.

Emily seemed to sense it. "Anytime you want to talk, Mom, I'm here for you."

Now, Konni really felt like a failure. Her daughter had to take care of her instead of the other way around. Konni needed time to think, a place where she could not be bothered.

She knew just where to go.

⌁

Konni took measured steps under an overcast sky. The April winds blew a chill her way. She pulled her coat closer and glanced up. Gray clouds shadowed her footsteps like unexpected feelings shadowed her heart.

Frost kept the ground cold and hard. Winter. The season of her life since Eric's death. Gone were the soft, moldable ways of yesteryear. A hardened heart burdened her chest, making it difficult some days just to breathe. At least the ground would thaw soon, but Konni feared winter would never leave her.

Yet last night with Rick, a thin shred of warmth had seeped through her veins, frightening her. Not that she wanted to stay in a winter fog, but the vow reminded her that she had no choice.

A nervous squirrel darted across the path and scurried up a tree. If only she could do that. Run and hide, not have to deal with anything.

Her footsteps finally stopped in front of the familiar marker. "Eric Strong. Beloved husband and father. We will always love you."

As she read the words once again, they pricked her conscience. "Some love, huh, Eric?" Konni dropped to her knees beside the grave. Her knees throbbed from the impact, but she didn't care. Right now, nothing mattered. She pulled a tissue from her pocket as big plops of tears fell from her eyes and splashed onto her legs. "I shouldn't have gone out with him." She wiped her face, trying to keep up with the tears. "You took such good care of me, in life and in death. How could I possibly see someone else?"

She bit her lip. "Everyone tells me it's time to move on, Eric." Her eyes bore into the grave marker. "What do they know? Have they lost their best friend and lover? Do memories haunt them until their head hurts? Do they struggle to get out of bed in the morning? To put one foot in front of the other? To breathe?"

Blame shifted with the passing winds. "Why did you

leave me, Eric? Why? I needed you! I need you still!" She hit the ground hard with her fists until her hands started to bleed. She cried with abandon, like the wail of someone betrayed. Angry, swollen eyes glared at the heavens. "Why did you take him from me? It's not fair! I need him!" Things she knew she shouldn't say shot into the air like illegal fireworks.

Konni had rarely allowed herself to cry over Eric's death. Yet now, among the whispers of the wind, she held nothing back. Tears gushed like blood from an open wound. She cried until her strength was gone.

The wind seemed to echo her vow, taunting and mocking, as she made her way back to the car. Yet Eric's face brushed across her mind. A face that told her it was time to move on.

Without him.

By the time she settled behind the steering wheel, her breathing came easier, but she was no closer to answers for the future.

Out of nowhere, Isaiah 41:10, a verse she had memorized in her younger days, came to her: "Fear thou not; for I am with thee: be not dismayed; for I am thy God: I will strengthen thee; yea, I will help thee; yea, I will uphold thee with the right hand of my righteousness."

The words comforted her heart like good news from an old friend. Yet how could God be there for her when she had blamed Him for her pain? Konni put her key in the ignition and started the car. If only she could trust Him with her future.

"Fear thou not; for I am with thee. . ."

"But what if I lose someone else?"

"Be not dismayed; for I am thy God."

"I can't bear any more pain—"

"I will strengthen thee; yea, I will help thee—"

Tears flowed down her cheeks once again as she pulled onto the country road. "But. . ." Her words paused in her throat. "I haven't cared about anything for so long—even You."

"I will uphold thee with the right hand of my righteousness."

Peace spread over her cold heart like sunshine over snow. In the quiet of the country roads, inside her vehicle, Konni sensed her life was changing.

Was she ready for it?

Chapter 5

The morning quickly melted into early evening before Konni traveled the road toward Mrs. Kenner's house. Glancing through her rearview mirror, she could see the sun setting in a blaze of pink. Her car slowed in front of Forgotten Treasures, the soft glow from the security light spilling through the window onto the sidewalk. Everything appeared in order.

From her car radio, the oldies station beat out a song popular in Konni's teen years, and she ventured a few blocks farther. The familiar tune made her feel young and carefree, a feeling she had long forgotten—until last night. *Not now. I don't want to think about Rick now.* She clicked off the radio.

Once she arrived at Mrs. Kenner's house, she pulled next to the curb, causing tires to scrunch on the pebbly gravel. She reached for her purse, opened the groaning door, and climbed out. Cold, damp air chilled her face the moment she stepped into it, reminding her of the night before.

A brick path lined her way toward the porch. Konni glanced up to see Mrs. Kenner wrapped in her coat, rocking gently on a weather-beaten swing. Konni warmed with the sight of the old woman's wind-ruffled hair and the smile on her face.

Mrs. Kenner's hand clutched Konni's in a hearty greeting. The kind woman looked most eager for company. "You got a minute?"

"Sure."

Mrs. Kenner patted the seat beside her. Konni sat down.

The woman studied Konni for a moment. "You doing all right, Child?"

The woman has the heart of a grandmother. What a shame she has no children. "I'm fine."

"I'm not so sure," she said, pointing to Konni's eyes.

Konni dropped her gaze.

Mrs. Kenner paused a long moment. "Well. They say tea is good for the soul." She thumped her hands on her lap. "Let's have some." Without further ado, she stood and walked into the house.

Konni followed Mrs. Kenner like a child following her teacher. A small but tidy room lined the way toward the kitchen. Konni took a deep breath, pulling in a calming fragrance. On the table, she saw an antique crock overstuffed with a fresh bouquet. In the corner sat a ragged box littered with silk flowers.

Mrs. Kenner followed her gaze. "Oh, that." She filled the teakettle with water, placed it on the stove, then turned to Konni. "I used to set out silk flowers." She pulled some cups from her shelf. "They collected dust. Just like me," she said with a laugh. "Honestly, it occurred to me my life was like that. Stale as an old biscuit." She shrugged, placing the cups in saucers. "I might be eighty-five, but I'm still kickin'. I figure as long as I'm kickin', there's life to be lived. I keep fresh flowers to remind me every day is new and exciting. Meant to be savored like a good bowl of grits. So on Saturday mornings, I go to the florist and gather my bouquets for the week."

Konni smiled and thought about the wisdom of her words.

"Guess you can tell I'm from the South, huh?" A grin tipped the corners of her mouth.

Konni laughed. "I admit I had my suspicions."

"Me and Orville came here back in 1965. Our kinfolk were all from Tennessee." She turned abruptly to Konni. "Course, they're all dead now," she said matter-of-factly.

The woman hesitated, her eyes fixed on Konni. "You must be anxious to see the desk." Konni nodded and followed Mrs. Kenner into a side room that appeared to be a study. Bookshelves lined one wall; a rocking chair and desk were the only other pieces of furniture.

Konni gasped when she saw the antique desk, recognizing at once its value. Her fingers ran along the fine wood, well maintained over the years.

"You like it," Mrs. Kenner said more as a statement than a question.

Konni nodded. "How ever can you part with it?"

The old woman shrugged. "To give a girl a future."

They discussed its value and made arrangements to get it to the store. With business settled, they grabbed their tea and sat on the soft cushions of a well-kept antique sofa.

Konni shared bits of her life with Eric while Mrs. Kenner listened with interest. "I've talked far too long," Konni said, with a glance toward her watch. Lifting her cup and saucer, she stood, reached over, and took Mrs. Kenner's empty cup and saucer, then headed for the kitchen. Placing the dishes in the dishwasher, she turned to go. The bright flowers caught her attention. Mrs. Kenner's words played over in her mind. "I keep fresh flowers to remind me life is meant to be savored." Something stirred inside Konni. Was her life stale? One glance at her outdated pants and top answered her. She knew when she had stopped caring.

"Oh, Dear, you didn't need to do that."

Konni turned to Mrs. Kenner with a start. "No problem. Thank you for the tea. I'll be back next week for the desk." Without thinking Konni reached over and gave the woman a hug. The action surprised her. She didn't normally hug people she hardly knew, but there was something about this woman. . . .

Rick pulled into the church parking area. A rush of adrenaline pulsed through him once he spotted Konni's car. Grabbing his Bible, he stuffed his keys in his pocket and headed out the door. A few people greeted him upon his entrance into the church, and someone passed him a bulletin. He made small talk as he looked around for Konni.

"Good morning, Rick," Konni's voice called from behind.

He turned to her. "Hello." The sight of her caused his heart to jump off track like a runaway locomotive. For a moment, neither of them said anything as they stood close together. Rick fingered the cuff of his shirt, feeling the jitters of a kid on the first day of school. He cleared his throat. "You want to sit together?"

"Well. . ." She considered his question for a long moment.

Rick wondered at her hesitation. Hadn't she enjoyed herself on Friday night? He thought things had changed a little between them.

Her eyes flickered downward.

"Konni?"

She seemed to have pushed away her fear for the moment and looked back to him with apology. "Sure." A guarded smile lit her face.

Rick led the way into the sanctuary. He pondered the complexities of the woman walking beside him. Complex, yes, but somehow he felt she was worth the challenge.

The service couldn't be over soon enough to suit Konni. She still didn't know how she felt about things. Her vow to Eric hung over her heart like a heavy cloud.

She and Rick made their way from the sanctuary, amid greetings and friendly chatter. Rick turned to her. "Want to go to lunch?"

His question surprised her. She stumbled over her tongue, trying to find an appropriate response. "I. . .uh. . . well, I—"

"I'll take that as a yes." He laughed and touched her elbow, leading her away from curious friends. They stepped through the church doors into the sunshine. A concerned expression shadowed his face. "I'm sorry. I shouldn't have asked you within the hearing of others. I didn't mean to put you on the spot." He lifted her chin, causing her eyes to meet his.

The tenderness in his voice made her feel as though a breeze had caressed her. Her resolve melted away like the morning dew. "Thank you, Rick," she said with all sincerity. "I'd love to go to lunch with you." She stubbornly pushed aside all guilt and confusion and allowed herself the luxury of a friend.

The surprise on his face was so abrupt that Konni struggled to hide a smirk.

He laughed. The sound of his laughter made her feel content, like enjoying coffee with an old friend.

Tuesday night, Rick stopped by Konni's house unexpectedly after dinner. Konni had just popped in a DVD, so she invited him to join her. She put some kettle corn in the microwave and poured soda into glasses stuffed with cubed ice.

Once the movie started, Konni sat on the couch, munching on their snack, and stole a glance at Rick. Her emotions tossed about like a bag of popping corn. Attraction sparked between them, she couldn't deny that. The more time they spent together, the more she liked him. Why, in the short time of their relationship, he had managed to make her rashes disappear.

Their relationship. Was this a relationship? She gulped and almost swallowed a corn kernel whole. A rather unladylike cough escaped her, causing Rick to jerk around.

"You okay?"

She nodded, grabbing her drink from the coffee table. His attention still on her, Konni felt herself flush. She swallowed the cold liquid, trying desperately to bring herself under control.

Once she put her drink down, Rick scooted closer to her and gently hit her back a couple of times. The coughing finally subsided.

"Thanks," she said when she found her voice. She turned to him. His hand still rested behind her. Their eyes locked, neither daring to blink.

A gentle nudge from his hand on her back pulled her closer to him. Konni's pulse rushed in her ears in thunderous throbs. As they inched forward, Rick's gaze fell upon her lips. She trembled in his arms, her lips eager to receive his touch. When he was but a whisper away, the sudden swoosh of the front door jarred them apart like two school kids getting caught in a smooch behind the bleachers.

Emily stepped inside the door and froze in place. Konni could almost visualize the image of their guilt-ridden faces. Rick broke through the awkward silence.

"Well," he said, with a hand slap on his knees, "I'd best get home."

"Don't you want to finish the movie?"

He shook his head, already making his way to the door. "Got a big day tomorrow."

Konni practically had to run to keep up with him. Emily stepped out of the way, still gaping at the scene but saying nothing. Konni threw her a make-yourself-scarce look. Emily quickly retreated to the kitchen.

Konni turned toward Rick, who was halfway into his car by now. When she arrived at his car door, he had already started the engine. He held up his hand to stop her from saying anything. "I don't know what got into me. I apologize."

Before she could utter a word, he rushed out of her driveway with a squeal of tires.

Chapter 6

When Rick finally settled into his bed, he folded his hands behind his head and stared at the spackled ceiling. He couldn't imagine what had come over him when he almost kissed Konni. That wasn't his style. He'd spent enough time talking to her to know she struggled with the idea of dating again. He exhaled. "She'll never want to see me again, that's for sure."

No matter how he worked it, he didn't know how to fix things. He'd blown it, pure and simple.

With a jerk, he yanked off the covers. He stood and pulled a lightweight robe over his bare chest and long boxers and made his way to the kitchen. Lifting the cold water jug from the fridge, he poured himself a glass and drank it down without stopping for a breath. He swiped his hand across his mouth, placed the glass in the sink, and looked down at Read.

Scrunching until he was eye level with the lab, Rick scratched Read behind the ears. "I really messed up tonight," Rick said, staring blankly into the black fur. The dog threw him a tell-me-all-about-it-but-don't-stop-scratching look. In spite of himself, Rick laughed and calmed down a bit. He continued to scratch; then with a final pat on Read's sleek coat, Rick stood and walked back to the bedroom. Once inside the room, he knelt down at his bedside and did what he realized he should have done the moment he met Konni Strong.

He prayed.

As always, Saturday found Konni working at Forgotten Treasures. She walked through the store and checked to make sure the inventory looked nice for browsing customers. Satisfied with the turn of a rocker here, the scoot of a trunk there, she made a few phone calls to follow up on possible purchases. Once finished with the calls, she settled into her chair with a glass of iced tea in front of her. She cleared various papers away like unwanted thoughts.

Flashes of Tuesday night with Rick confused her. First, she had determined to stay away from him; then just as she found herself wanting more of his company, he seemed to distance himself. Why?

He had called on Thursday night, saying he couldn't come for dinner on Friday. "Too much work." Still, she wondered if something else lurked behind his excuse.

Her hands reached for the logbook to glance over the length of stay for some of her antiques. The front door jangled.

When she glanced up, she saw Mrs. Kenner walking through the store. The old woman waved and inched her way toward the counter. Konni could see that her friend held a couple of books in her arms.

"I'm sorry, Mrs. Kenner, I didn't realize you were carrying something." Konni rushed to the woman's side and took the books from her hands.

"Posh! I'm not an invalid, for crying out loud. You treat me like I'm an old woman!"

Konni looked at her in surprise. She held a giggle in her throat.

The woman tossed an ornery grin. "Okay, I may be past my prime, but like I said, I'm still kickin'." She winked. "And my name is Irene." She brushed the air with a wave of her hand. "You make me feel like my mother when you say 'Mrs.'"

Konni laughed and laid the books on the counter. When she looked at them, she realized they were journals. She wondered how Irene could part with something so personal.

"They're not for sale. They're for you to read."

Surprised, Konni looked up at her.

Taking a few more steps, Irene slipped into the chair Konni had brought out on Irene's last visit. "I thought you might like to know some of my story. Of course, it's not the entire story, but it is the most interesting part," she said with a wiggle of her eyebrows. "It shows some of my thirty-five year marriage to Orville." She searched Konni's face. "But of course, if you're too busy—"

"Oh, my, no," Konni said with her hand up. "I would love to read your journals—if you don't feel it's too personal."

Irene shrugged. "For others to read, perhaps, but somehow I feel like the Lord wants me to share them with you."

Konni stared at her, not knowing what to say. How could

145

she argue with what the Lord wanted? Reading someone's journals was like taking a glimpse into their soul. Konni could never reveal herself to someone like that.

"I also have some china I'd like you to look at."

"Whom are you selling it for?" Konni teased.

"A single woman from our church who works two jobs just to put food on the table."

"I don't know that china will bring you much in the way of money."

"Oh, but I believe this china will," Irene said with a mischievous grin. "It belonged to my great-great-grandparents. Now *that's* old."

They both laughed. Konni shook her head. "You're full of surprises."

Irene took a few moments to rise to her feet. "I'd better get home before I tucker out. By the way. . ." She stopped and with intense eyes stared at Konni. "How is Mr. Hamilton?"

Konni blinked. "Uh, he's fine," she stammered.

"He's a good one, I'm telling ya." With an expression that said she knew more than she let on, Irene Kenner turned toward the door. "Come by the house after work, and I'll show you the china," she called over her shoulder before she stepped into the spring air.

⸎

"So how does that make you feel—reading those journals, I mean?" Konni's sister asked while they followed the hostess who led them to a table.

They eased into their booth. "I don't know, Cheryl. As I read the love story between Irene and Orville, it's like reading

146

of my own life with Eric. Wonderful marriage, both strong in the Lord, he died fairly young. Fifties, I think."

Cheryl sipped from the glass of water the waitress had placed before her. "That's too weird."

"Yeah. I suppose she wanted me to read them since I lost my husband."

Cheryl shrugged, then after a moment leaned into the table. "You know, Konni, God could be in this."

"Fear thou not; for I am with thee. . . ."

Konni nodded but said nothing.

"So, tell me about this Rick guy. Emily says he's really cute." Cheryl's voice was lighthearted and encouraging, but Konni wasn't sure she wanted to talk about it.

"I admit I like him a lot, but things are still, well, a little strained between us. Besides, I'm not sure I want another relationship." She shrugged. "It's really a non-issue. He hasn't called for a while."

Before Cheryl could comment, the waitress showed up and took their orders. They handed her their menus and went back to their conversation. "Maybe he feels your apprehension," Cheryl offered.

"I don't know." Konni sighed. "Life was easier before he came along."

Cheryl reached out and grabbed Konni's hand. "It's time to live again, Konni. Eric would want that."

Konni thought of her time at Eric's grave, the sense of him releasing her from the vow. Still not sure she could talk about it, she looked away. Her eyes fell upon a scene that made her stomach plunge. Across the room in a cozy corner table sat Rick Hamilton and a woman with hair the color of corn silk. She wore a shapely dress that complimented all the right places and accentuated her endless legs. No wonder Rick was acting strange. He had other interests. *How could I have been so stupid?*

"Hey, you okay?"

Konni barely heard the words over the roar of her confusion. She couldn't blame him really. She glanced down at her own frumpy clothes. Maybe it was time to make some changes. Reluctantly, she turned toward her sister. "I'm fine." A trickle of determination stirred, then charged through her like a rushing river.

"Ma'am?" Konni called to her waitress.

The woman hurried to the table. "Yes?"

"I'm not as hungry as I thought. Could I cancel my previous order and just get a house salad, fat-free dressing, no croutons or cheese, please?"

The waitress made a quick note, then scurried off.

"What was that all about?" Cheryl asked with a slight smile.

Yes, she'd make some changes. Starting right now. Konni lifted her chin. "You know, I think I'm going to get my nails done."

Cheryl's eyes widened. "Now I know you're not okay. What's up?"

Konni forced herself to laugh. "Nothing's up. I just want to take care of myself. Is there anything wrong with that?"

Cheryl eyed her suspiciously. "Why, no. Nothing wrong at all."

Konni worked out all the frustrations of recent days exercising to her workout video. Maybe her vow was made in haste. Jump, two, three, kick! Maybe the others were right. Eric would want her to branch out. Twist, two, three, pant, four, five, six, gasp!

Why didn't Rick tell her he was dating someone else? Arm thrust, punch, two, three. Not that he owed her an explanation. After all, they didn't have "an understanding." Punch, four, five, six. Her pulse thumped harder than her feet on the aerobic stepper. Nobody owed her anything. She pushed her body harder. It's time she started a new life. From now on—jump, push, kick, wheeze—others would see the new Konni Strong.

She only hoped the determination wouldn't ebb with her fading energy.

Rick finished his five-mile run and pushed through the front door. As usual, Read stood ready to greet him. Bending over, Rick patted the hound on the head a few times and staggered to the kitchen, pulling the water jug from the fridge. He'd hoped to settle some things in his mind during his run, but instead he found himself more confused than ever.

He missed Konni, no doubt about it. But should he risk a relationship? His father had failed. What if Rick failed, too?

Then, as if he didn't have enough to think about, Assistant Superintendent Haley Green showed up with "business matters." Though hidden behind a barrage of paperwork, her true agenda was all too obvious.

Admittedly, she was a beautiful woman. Still, he had no interest in her. How could he when Konni Strong bombarded his thoughts day and night?

He wanted to forget the whole thing. Shove Konni from his life, from his heart.

From his heart?

Where did that come from? He couldn't possibly be in love. He didn't know her well enough. His mind argued that he knew her well enough to know something was different about her.

Okay, he could live with that. Now what? He still didn't want to get into a serious relationship. Couldn't she stop haunting his every thought? His head hurt from thinking.

Lifting his glass, he guzzled the cold water as fast as he could, hoping the chilled liquid would refresh him and maybe clear his mind at the same time. It cooled his body, but his thoughts still burned with Konni's image.

There was nothing he could do. Their relationship shifted the night he had tried to kiss her. End of story.

End of relationship.

He stopped drinking for a brief moment. He was forgetting one thing. Rick Hamilton was not a quitter. He had apologized about the near-kiss attempt. Maybe she wouldn't write him off completely.

What about church? He liked Hope Village. Why stop going there? And if he happened to bump into Konni in such a small church, well. . .

Excitement surged through him. He finished his ice water. By the time he lowered his glass, his mind was made up. He would win Konni Strong back.

He just didn't know how.

When Konni spotted Rick inside the church foyer, her heart skipped a beat. She struggled to pull her gaze away from him, but he caught her attention and waved. Anticipation sparked through her with every step that brought him closer.

"Good morning," he said, sounding a bit hesitant.

"Hi."

"You look great." The look in his eyes told her he meant it.

Konni could feel herself flush. "Thanks." Maybe the diet and exercise were helping. She curled a wisp of hair behind her ear, hoping he'd notice her manicured nails.

He looked at her and smiled. "Want to sit together?"

His voice smoothed her heart like cool water over pebbles. Without hesitation, she nodded.

Rick led the way, and Konni followed, wondering just where her life was headed.

Chapter 7

The smell of steak and baked breads filled the air as Konni and Rick waited for their meals.

"I'm glad you agreed to lunch," Rick said.

Konni shrugged. "You saved me from a cold sandwich. When Emily goes to her friend's house, I never feel like cooking just for me."

Rick eyed her carefully, hesitating a moment. "I wasn't sure you'd want to see me again."

"Why is that?" She studied him.

Feeling a bit restless, he fidgeted with an edge of the cloth napkin. "Um, well, I know you're still a little uncomfortable with dating."

"What makes you think that?"

He stopped fingering the cloth and looked at her with surprise. "Well, aren't you?"

She paused a moment. "Well, okay, maybe a little."

They both laughed.

"But it's getting easier," she added.

Her words gave him hope. "Good!" He wanted to probe

further into her heart. To ask her about her feelings for Eric. After all, he didn't want to play second fiddle to anyone. Not even her late husband. Yet the time didn't seem right.

"How are things with the school corporation?"

"Going well. Very busy, winding things down for the year."

She nodded and spread her napkin on her lap as the waitress placed their food before them. When the waitress left, Rick reached for Konni's hand. He noticed the surprise on her face but bowed his head before she could comment. He offered the Lord thanks for their meal, then pulled his hand away.

Konni reached for her fork and looked to him. "That was nice. Thank you."

Her comment surprised him. Why would she thank him for praying?

"I appreciate your walk with the Lord, Rick. It's made me examine my own heart. I mean, I used to have that close communion with the Lord, but that was before. . ." Her voice broke off.

He understood. "You still miss him, don't you?"

They sat in the quiet of the moment while Konni searched for the right words. "I miss the life we shared." She blankly stirred the corn on her plate. "What about you? Why have you never married?"

He noticed how she quickly changed the subject, apparently uncomfortable with talk about herself. "I suppose it scares me," he answered. "I never had a good example of what a husband should be. Dad was an alcoholic. When he drank, he abused my mother and me. I don't want to be like that."

Konni searched his face a moment. "You think because your dad wasn't a good husband that you won't be?"

He laid his fork down. "Seems logical, don't you think?"

A warm smile lit her face. "You're not your father, you know."

"So you think there's hope?" He cocked an eyebrow.

"There's always hope."

"Really?" He winced inwardly as he realized he'd spoken almost too eagerly.

"Really," she said with conviction.

Oh, he liked the sound of that. Made him feel anything was possible.

If only he could believe it.

Konni rolled her head from side to side as she waited for her E-mail to pop up. She didn't normally receive much mail—an occasional letter from out-of-town friends and sometimes work-related notes since she didn't have a computer at the store. She had to admit since Rick started e-mailing her, she could hardly wait to check for messages in the evening. It had almost become the highlight of her day. Seemed they could talk easier via computer than on the telephone.

The E-mail displayed across her screen, but she saw nothing from Rick. Before disappointment set in, an instant message popped up, asking if she'd accept a message from "Readerleader." Konni laughed. She could only imagine who that must be. Though not an expert with instant messaging, she had IM'd with her sister a couple of times before. Her fingers tingled with excitement.

"Excuse me, Dear Lady, do you always accept messages from strangers?"

Konni felt as giddy as when she discovered a rare antique. "Only ones with obvious names like 'Readerleader.' " She clicked the message back with a laugh.

"Okay, so I'm predictable. I thought you might be online about now. This instant message thing is a bit mysterious and all, don't you think? I feel somewhat like Romeo sneaking a secret message to Juliet."

Konni let out a giggle. "I admit it's a little easier to talk this way than face-to-face. Takes the pressure off, don't you agree?"

"Definitely. Now, since rejection might be a little less painful this way, what do you say we go to dinner Friday night?"

Uh-oh, am I ready for this? After all, he had never explained his relationship to the other woman Konni had seen him with in the restaurant. Konni wondered if she should confront him. She bit her thumbnail. They had no claims on one another. Maybe she should just let it go and see how it all turned out. Her hands hovered over the keyboard. She noticed a growing rash.

Another message from Rick popped up on the screen. "Okay, you're hesitating. Am I pushing too fast? Please tell me, Konni. I don't want to make you uncomfortable."

Even though his words played on the screen, she could almost hear his voice. For an instant, she wondered what it would feel like to be held in his arms. She gasped. What was going on with her? "I have to work."

"Oh, okay."

She could read his disappointment between the lines. "How about meeting for coffee Saturday afternoon?" There. They wouldn't have to be out late. A quick cup of coffee, then home.

"Great! I'll pick you up around, say, three-thirty?"

"How about we meet there?"

"Oh, right. So family members don't catch us. Have it your way, Dear Juliet. See you then. R (Romeo or Rick, whichever you prefer)."

Dare she trust her heart to him? The answer came as a surprise to her. Rick Hamilton had already stolen her heart.

"Don't hurt me, Romeo," she whispered into the softness of her room. Then she looked toward heaven and prayed, "Please, God, I can't go through losing someone I love again."

"Hey, Gal," Irene said as she slipped into the shop.

"Irene! So good to see you. I was afraid you wouldn't come," Konni said, grabbing a chair for her friend.

"Ah, but it's Saturday. I have to come see you on Saturday."

Konni laughed. "I'll make us some tea and be right back."

Irene nodded, settling into her familiar spot.

Konni returned with the tea and handed a cup to Irene. She sat in her chair across from Irene.

"Thank you for selling the desk and china," Irene offered.

"I was so pleased to get such a price for them both," Konni said and sipped from her cup.

"I suspect you didn't take your cut." Irene looked at Konni as a mother questioning her child.

Konni wasn't offended but rather smiled. "Why should you get all the blessing of helping a girl go to school and a mother feed her children?"

Irene laughed, deepening the wrinkles in her soft but aged face. She took another drink. "You've read my journals then?"

"Yes." They grew quiet. Konni looked into her cup. "You knew they would help me." She glanced up.

Kindness glowed from Irene's face. "I hoped they would."

"I've been a fool. You see, I made a vow—"

Irene quieted Konni with a wave of her hand. "You needn't tell me, Dear. God knows your heart. What's important is that you move on from here."

Konni swallowed hard. "I loved Eric so much, Irene."

The old woman leaned over and placed her hand on Konni's. "I know. But our memories of Orville and Eric will always be with us. They shared a part of our lives that belonged to them alone. No one can take that from us. But now is the time for new memories."

A tear slid down Konni's cheek and plopped on Irene's hand. "Oh, I'm sorry."

The older woman reached up and brushed Konni's face with her fingers. "God has a plan for you. Trust Him."

Konni grabbed the gnarled fingers that rubbed against her face. She squeezed Irene's hand lightly. "What would I do without you?"

"No need to worry. I'm like an ol' wart—hard to get rid of."

Konni wiped her face and laughed.

"The world is uncertain, Konni, but God's love for us never changes. Oh, I almost forgot! I brought something else." Irene reached into a large bag beside her chair and pulled out a worn leather Bible. The old woman's eyes twinkled like a kid with a secret as she handed the sacred pages to Konni.

"Irene, you always surprise me." Konni flipped through the pages and saw that the Bible had been in the family for six generations.

"Oh, my, Irene, I can't let you part with this."

She shook her head. "Our church has a missionary family in Papua New Guinea. They need financial support. They're sharing the Good News. I'll sell this Bible and give them the money."

Konni stared at her. "I want to be just like you when I grow up."

Irene looked at her aghast. "What? I haven't grown up myself yet!"

* * *

Rick walked Konni out to her car. A sliver of moon sailed overhead, granting a shaft of light below. Konni stood beside her car door, facing him.

"Thanks for meeting me tonight," Rick said.

"I'm sorry I had to reschedule it for this late. Trying to get Emily ready for college is quite a job," she said with a laugh.

"No problem. I'm just glad you could still make it. I really enjoy our times together, Konni." Emotion touched his eyes, causing something inside her to stir. He looked at her, never blinking, as if waiting on her to say something. Finally, he released a sigh. "Well, I'll see you tomorrow at church."

A look of defeat shadowed his eyes before he turned to go. "Rick?" She grabbed his hand. "Thank you. For everything."

The words seemed just the encouragement he needed. Rick stepped closer. She felt her pulse race to her throat. He glanced around the deserted parking lot, then looked down into her eyes. With a gentle touch, his fingers traced the outline of her face. His hand reached tenderly behind her neck, working, sifting through strands of hair, causing her skin to tingle with life. His eyes held a question to which hers answered yes. He moved to her waiting lips and eagerly caressed hers with his own.

A tender moment that she never wanted to end fell upon them. It seemed as if the whole world grew silent while under moonlight shadows, Rick Hamilton took Konni's breath away.

Chapter 8

"H i, Rick!" Konni's voice called from behind him in the church sanctuary.

He turned to her. "Good morning." Her face looked as happy as he felt. No doubt about it, their relationship had taken a turn for the better.

"Want to sit over there?" she asked, pointing to a pew halfway toward the front.

"Sure." He escorted her through the room, passing out greetings along the way. The praise band played quiet songs of worship as Konni and Rick settled into their seats.

Rick warred with himself over whether or not he should grab Konni's hand. They were, after all, in public, and he wasn't sure how she would respond. His heart pounded hard against his chest like a schoolboy in love. He told himself he was being silly. After all, he was forty-eight-years old. Just as he lifted his hand to reach for hers, she abruptly turned to him. Fortunately, she didn't see him almost jump out of his skin.

"Oh, dear, I forgot to tell Rhonda where I placed her

new quarterly. Will you excuse me a moment, Rick?"

He swallowed hard. His Adam's apple seemed to wedge itself between his collarbones like an elevator stuck on the basement floor. "Oh, sure."

Konni smiled and walked away. Rick figured it was just as well. They'd had a great time last night. In honest moments over coffee, they shared their fears and dreams of the future. They talked of a relationship and the risks involved. Still, they had agreed to take baby steps together and see where it led them.

One thing Rick knew for sure, he didn't want to do anything to blow his chances with her this time. As fragile as her heart was, he may not get another chance.

"Well, good morning, Rick. I was hoping you'd be here. May I sit down?"

Rick turned to the voice and looked up into the smiling face of Haley Green.

⸻

"Hey, Mom, you doing okay?" Emily's expression suggested a problem.

Konni almost laughed, then thought better of it when she saw the seriousness on her daughter's face. "I'm fine. Why? Do I look all flushed or something?" She winked, remembering she had told Emily about Rick's kiss last night.

"Mom, let's go sit down somewhere." Emily tugged on Konni's arm.

"Emily, what is the matter with you? The service is about to begin. I need to get back in and sit down with Rick. He'll wonder where I am."

"Wow!" interjected Emily's friend Nate. "Who is that gorgeous blond with your friend, Mrs. Strong? Is that his sister or something? I'd sure like to meet the likes of her." Emily turned to Nate and gouged him in the side. "Ouch! What did I do?"

Konni stared at both of them, then went to the sanctuary door and peered in. There beside Rick sat the woman she had seen him with in the restaurant. Konni swallowed hard. She turned back to Emily.

"Mom, you want to go?"

Konni took a deep breath and shook her head. "I can't run from my problems, Em."

Emily reached up and gave her mom a hug. "I'll be praying for you."

"I'll be fine, Honey. You go on to service."

Emily nodded. Konni watched as Emily walked up to a group of her friends and they made their way into the sanctuary. Emily tossed one more glance toward her mom. Konni waved just before the kids stepped out of sight.

How humiliating. The whole church would notice Rick sitting with that woman. "Poor Konni," they would say, offering her sorrowful glances and hugs. She inhaled long and deeply. Her chin lifted, shoulders straightened. She could do this. Stepping into the sanctuary, Konni slipped into an empty spot in the back row.

The service seemed to take forever. Konni didn't hear a word of the message. It took all her efforts to contain her racing emotions. She wanted to teach Emily to face her problems, so Konni forced herself to stay. But as soon as the benediction was over, Konni rushed through the crowd to get to her car.

"Konni!"

She could hear Rick's voice but kept moving.

"Konni!" He was closer now. She had no choice. She turned to him.

"Yes?"

"Where were you? You never came back."

She couldn't let him think for a moment she was jealous. "Oh, I got caught up with some business."

He looked at her as though he didn't believe her. "Want to go to lunch?"

She shook her head. "Not today, Rick." Adrenaline made her bold. "You know, I've really been thinking about last night, and I just don't think I'm ready for a relationship, Rick." Her breath was short and choppy, like she'd been running a marathon. "I'm sorry." With that, she turned on her heels, all but ran to her car, and climbed in.

Starting the engine, she pulled her car into gear and never once looked back.

❦

Rick's jaw dropped. With honest confusion, he watched Konni's car leave the lot. "What was that all about?"

"Hmm? Did you say something, Rick?" Haley stepped up behind him, placing her hand possessively on his arm. Concern filled her eyes.

His glance went from her hand, to her face, to Konni's fleeing car.

The answer became all too clear.

Thankful that Emily wouldn't be home for a while, Konni went into her bedroom and threw herself on the bed. She couldn't believe she had fallen so hard for Rick and was now dealing with yet another loss.

She leaned back against her pillows. What had happened today? One minute, she sat happily with Rick; the next minute, someone had taken her place. Just that fast. Did she know him so little? Was he playing two women at the same time? He did, after all, call himself "Romeo." Maybe there was more to it than she realized.

She shook her head. It made no sense. Rick didn't seem that type of guy. Oh, she didn't know what to think anymore. Her heart uttered a prayer for guidance and strength. Only this time, a new verse came to mind, 2 Corinthians 5:17 (KJV): "Therefore if any man be in Christ, he is a new creature: old things are passed away; behold, all things are become new."

It seemed an odd verse to come to her mind at that moment. "What are you trying to tell me, Lord?" The words played over and over.

Hadn't she allowed the Lord to touch her life afresh? Hadn't she put her past behind her—or at least attempted to? Okay, she was still working on that one.

She had taken a huge leap, allowing Rick passage into her heart. Now pain exploded in her chest with one blow. In the midst of her turmoil, a thought struck her. She hadn't given Rick a chance to explain. But he didn't owe her an explanation, did he? She stared at the ceiling. Still, if he had wanted to offer one, she hadn't given him the chance.

Whether she wanted to admit it or not, she had run away. Just like she'd been running for the past five years. Running from anything that remotely resembled conflict, rejection, or loss.

Misery sank to the pit of her stomach. Just then, the phone on her nightstand rang, startling her.

She let it ring. The caller could leave a message. If it was Emily, Konni would know and could answer.

"Yeah, Konni, this is Rick. Hey, I just wanted to say, well, I'm not sure what happened this morning, but if it has to do with the woman you saw me with at church, I can explain. Will you give me the chance?"

Oh, she wanted to reach over and grab the phone and tell him how she truly felt, but the image of the woman beside him at church kept Konni perfectly still, like a mummy in grave clothes. She waited, then decided to give him a chance. She reached for the phone, but instead of Rick's voice, the dial tone buzzed in her ear.

She rolled over on her bed. She'd allow herself a little time to sulk, then she'd pull up her boot straps and get back into the game of life. Rick's excuses could not lessen the pain of her embarrassment at being replaced on Sunday. She balled herself into the pillow. Somehow, she'd get through this.

She had to.

***

"Are you okay?" Haley asked when Rick returned to their booth.

"I'm fine. I just needed to make a phone call." He sat down in his seat, and Haley made an obvious shift to his side. Though uncomfortable, he was glad he brought her to lunch to deal with this matter before it got out of control.

"I'm just glad you're back." Her hand reached over to stroke his arm.

He shrank away. "Look, Haley, you're a beautiful woman—"

"Don't. Please don't." She stopped him. After a moment's hesitation, she started gathering her things from the booth. "I knew you cared for her; I just thought I could turn your head my way," she said, edging toward the other end of the seat. "Guess I hadn't figured on you being in love."

Rick stared at her, not knowing what to say. He didn't want to hurt her.

"I know we still have to work together, but once I know where I stand, it's not a problem. So we'll keep things strictly professional from here on out, okay?"

"Look, Haley, I'm sorry."

"Yeah, that's what all the good ones say." She threw him a meager smile and left him to eat lunch alone.

Rick sat in his recliner and stared at the phone in his hand, the dial tone blaring at him like a sassy teenager. How many messages had he left on Konni's answering machine over the past two weeks? Couldn't she at least return one phone call? What about the E-mails? She made it obvious she wanted nothing more to do with him.

He hadn't returned to Hope Village. Though it had become his own church home, he didn't want Konni to quit going because of him. He prayed for guidance. The situation seemed hopeless. He told himself he should let her go. Yet she was the one who had told him there was always hope. There had to be something else he could do.

The coffee shop. Saturday was the day she usually showed up there. At least he could make one last effort. If she still brushed him off, well, then he knew what to do.

His heart would say good-bye to Konni Strong.

Chapter 9

Rick rushed over to Chatting Grounds Coffeehouse, all the while praying for God's direction, whether that meant a future with or without Konni. He had to know where this was going.

He stepped out of his car and pushed through the entrance of the shop. Looking around, he didn't see Konni. Disappointed but not yet defeated, he went to the counter and ordered a latte.

Once he received his drink, he sat down behind a wooden table and tried to relax. Sipping the hot beverage, he mulled the situation over in his mind like a child's hands worked through Play-Doh. Before he could come up with an answer, the door swished open and in walked Konni. His stomach churned.

He gave her a moment to order her drink, and while she waited for it, he walked up behind her.

"Konni, please don't run."

She turned to him with a start. "Rick! Hi." Her face flushed.

"Konni, please, can we talk? Just this one time, and I'll never bother you again." He kept his voice soft and low, for her ears only.

She bit her lip and looked toward the lady who fixed her drink. "Where are you sitting?"

He finally took a breath and pointed toward his table. She nodded. He went back to the table, and once her drink was ready, she joined him.

"Look, I'm not sure what happened between us, but if it has anything to do with Haley, it's all a misunderstanding."

"Haley?"

He nodded. "She's the woman you saw me with at church. She's works with me as an assistant superintendent. We're coworkers. Nothing more."

"You don't owe me an explanation, Rick."

He grabbed her hand. She looked up at him. "Yes, I do. I want to pursue this thing between us, find out where it takes us."

She pulled her hand away. "I've found out something about myself in the past few weeks, Rick. I care a lot about you. I really do. But I don't want a serious relationship. With anyone. Ever."

"You can't mean that, Konni. You have your whole life ahead of you."

"Why does everyone keep saying that? Life is full of pain. I don't like pain, Rick." She paused. "I guess I just want to play it safe."

"Occasional dinner and coffee dates, that's it?"

She looked at him with defeat. "I'm afraid so. I'm sure

you don't want that, so we'll leave it here."

His eyes pinned hers. "Actually, I'll take that. For now."

Konni shifted in her seat and took a drink.

"I'm not ready to give up on us, Konni Strong. Not yet." Rick threw her a look that said he meant every word.

⁓⁓⁓

The summer sun warmed Konni's back as she carried the last load of Emily's belongings into the college dorm.

"You sure you have to start now? Why can't you wait till the fall like most kids?" Konni asked.

"Mom, I told you, they only offer these classes in the summer. Might as well get them over with."

Konni nodded reluctantly.

"You sure you'll be all right?" Emily eyed her carefully.

"Here we go again, you playing the mom role."

They both laughed. Konni's eyes scanned the messy room. "The question is will you be all right?"

Emily laughed. "I'll be fine."

Konni pulled her daughter into a long embrace and kissed her on the cheek. "Call anytime, okay? Study hard; come home when you can. Go easy on the guys."

"Yeah, right. You know guys are off-limits for me. I can't risk losing my scholarship."

"Just don't forget to enjoy yourself once in a while, Em."

"You're a good one to talk," Emily said with a laugh. "Give Rick a chance, will ya, Mom? He's a nice guy, and I think he really cares about you."

"I'm doing okay, really. You don't have to have a man to be happy, you know." Konni poked her finger in Emily's side.

Emily giggled, then stared her mother square in the face. "Are you happy?"

The light bantering stopped. Konni shrugged. "Let's just say I'm working on it." Konni smiled. "Keep in touch, okay? I love you."

"Love you, too, Mom."

Konni walked out the door, feeling lonelier than she'd ever felt in her life.

Rick and Konni had met for coffee and dinner a couple of times, but staying true to her word, Konni kept her distance. They were definitely back at the "friend" level.

He knew she grieved over Emily's absence. Konni lived her days locked in a world of memories, and he had no clue how to break her free. Things had been going so well until the interruption with Haley. Konni had been too vulnerable at the time. Too fragile. Now he didn't know if she would ever trust him—or anyone else—again.

The TV murmured in the distance while he wondered where this left him. After all, he couldn't wait forever. Could he? The phone rang, jarring him to his senses. "Hello?"

"Yes, I'm looking for a Dr. Rick Hamilton, superintendent of Hartley South School District in Loudon, Vermont," the male voice said.

"This is Rick Hamilton."

"Yes, Dr. Hamilton, this is Dr. Wedgewood calling from Macon County, Florida. We are currently in search of a superintendent for our school corporation here in Macon County. Your name has been referred to us, and we wanted to talk to you about a possible job change. Would you be interested?"

Rick's mind raced with what to do. He didn't normally switch positions so frequently. After all, he hadn't been in Loudon for a full year yet. He wouldn't leave Konni for the world if he thought there was any hope, yet if she wanted nothing more than friendship, he didn't know if he could stick around.

"Dr. Hamilton?"

"Yes, I'm still here."

"Well, I can tell we have taken you by surprise. How about we give you a week to think about it? If you decide you're interested, call us. We'll talk. Would that work for you?"

"That would be fine. I appreciate your consideration," Rick said. He spent the next few minutes getting the necessary contact information. When he finally hung the phone up, his hands were trembling. After spending time in prayer, Rick finally decided what he would do.

Without telling Konni of his job offer, he would declare his love to her. If she accepted it, he would stay. If she refused him, he would leave. His future was in her hands.

He prayed Konni Strong would make the right decision.

***

"So, you doing okay?" Rick asked Konni over coffee.

She cradled the cup in her hands and looked up. "Yeah."

"Look, Konni, I called you here because it's a private place where we can talk. I can't put this off any longer."

She looked at him, apprehension in her eyes.

He held up his hand. "Just hear me out. Then you can come to whatever conclusion you want."

Konni nodded and kept silent.

"When I came here, I didn't know anyone. Attending Stan and Abby's wedding changed all that. They brought you into my life. We became great friends and then something more—or at least I thought it was more.

"I never thought I'd get serious about anyone. People thought of me as a confirmed bachelor, and, well, that's what I was—and I liked it that way. I told you the reasons why. Fear of failure, I guess.

"But you—you changed all that. I was willing to risk failure rather than risk losing you. Still, misunderstandings happened and brought us to where we are today.

"We can't change the past, Konni, but we can change the future."

Rick took a deep breath. "I know you probably don't want to hear this, but I have to say it anyway. I love you. I've loved you from the moment you plowed into my chest at the wedding; it just took me awhile to realize it."

Konni's head felt hot. Rick spoke the words she had longed to hear, and now she didn't know if she could accept them. Love held too much pain. If she didn't get involved, if she just lived her life in a safe haven, she wouldn't get hurt. Ever. Though she loved him in a whole new way from Eric, she didn't think she could give her heart away again.

Rick grabbed her hand. "Being a confirmed bachelor, I never thought I'd say this. I'm ready to take a risk, Konni. I want to share my life with you. I'm asking you to be my wife."

Konni sat speechless in a hazy fog of confusion.

"I'm not asking for your answer right now. I know you said you didn't want a serious relationship, but please, think about it. Pray about it. I'll call you in a couple of days. We can talk it over then."

The kindness in his voice, the loving words felt like a gentle touch to her parched senses. Outwardly, she merely nodded. How could she lose him? But then how could she open her heart to yet another wound?

Rick threw their empty cups into the canister. He grabbed her hand and walked her to her car. Once they got there, he pulled her hand up to his lips. A look of desperation shadowed his face. He closed his eyes and for one long moment pressed his lips hard against the back of her hand. He looked at her. "No matter what our future holds, I will always love you, Konni."

Without a word, she turned and slipped into her car. All the while, her heart cried out in the darkness, *Father, please, show me what to do.*

"Oh, Irene, I just don't know which way to turn," Konni said, after explaining and discussing her problem with her friend.

Irene quietly walked over to a carved wooden jewelry box. She opened the lid and slipped out a beautiful gold chain with a small watch encircled with diamonds. She walked back and placed it in the palm of Konni's hand.

"Oh, my, Irene, this is beautiful."

"My wedding gift. Orville gave that to me more than

sixty-five years ago." She shook her head. "Hard to believe it's been so long." She looked at the watch with remembrance. " 'Irene,' he said, 'we need to enjoy every moment together. Life don't hold no guarantees.' " Irene laughed. "His English wasn't the best." She turned serious once again. "Bless his heart, he was right."

Tears formed in Konni's eyes.

"I want you to have this."

"What?" Konni asked incredulously.

Irene folded Konni's fingers over the necklace. "It's my reminder to you. Enjoy your moments, Konni. True love doesn't always come when we're ready for it. Life doesn't hold any guarantees. You could marry Rick, and yes, he could die."

Her voice fell to a whisper; she looked Konni full in the face, still holding her hand. "Or you could let him go and *you* will die."

Konni understood. She nodded and pulled Irene into a strong hug. "I love you."

"And I love you, Dear." Irene pulled away.

They talked a little longer; then Konni excused herself, knowing she had much to think about. From her car, she waved to Irene and pulled onto the road. Her thoughts raced. Could she trust her heart again? What of the pain? She couldn't bear any more. Yet if she lost Rick now, she'd have pain just the same. Working the matter over in her mind, she drove into the country—how far, she didn't know. All the while, her cluttered thoughts tossed about like ragged books cleared from an attic.

By the time her car had turned back toward town and reached Rick's house, she'd decided Irene was right. Peace had settled over her, and her mind was made up.

Rick heard a car door in his driveway and couldn't imagine who would visit him at such a late hour. He brushed the chips from his T-shirt and denim shorts, making his way to the door. He twisted the knob and pulled the door open.

Konni stood in the entrance. "Do you have a minute, Rick?" Red, puffy eyes greeted him, but something in them said she had come to a decision.

Rick let out a shaky grin and stepped aside. "You want something to drink?" he asked, closing the door behind him.

"No, thanks." Konni sat on the couch. She smiled and patted the seat beside her.

That encouraged him. Surely she wouldn't be that chipper if she had bad news. Somewhat guarded, he sat down and looked at her.

She grabbed his hands, shooting sparks up his arms. "Rick, I've been wrong. I've been so afraid of getting hurt, it's like I put my heart in a box and tucked it in a secret hideaway that no one could reach. I won't tell you this is easy. I'm frightened. Very frightened. But I love you, and to quote the man I love, 'I'm willing to take this risk, because I can't take the risk of losing you.'"

Rick pulled Konni into his arms, his chest tight against her so that he could feel the beating of her heart. Never had he loved anyone so deeply. Feverishly, he kissed her hair, her eyes, her forehead, and finally her lips, as if the moment might slip away. Their laughs mingled with tears.

"I want to marry you, Konni Strong."

"And I want to be your wife, Rick Hamilton." She kissed him this time. Long and hard.

When they pulled away, Rick told Konni of his job offer and how he had let her make his decision for him.

"When I think of how I could have lost you forever. . ." Konni stopped. "Thankfully, the Lord used Irene to guide me and bring me to my senses." She showed Rick the watch and explained the story.

He wiggled his eyebrows. "Hmm, she did say I was a good one."

Konni laughed. "And she was right."

"So, when are we getting married?"

"Well, it takes awhile to get everything ready, but just a small wedding should do it—you've never done this before, so I want it to be nice for you."

"It will be great for me because you'll be there." He kissed her again. She snuggled into him on the sofa, her head against his shoulder.

"I know one thing for sure," she said.

"Hmm, what's that?" he asked, his fingers gently stroking her hair.

"I know just the petals I want to tuck into my bouquet."

"You still have those bouquet pieces?"

"Uh-huh. For some reason I couldn't part with them. But I never dreamed those petals would open a whole new world for me. For us."

"I like the sound of that," he whispered into her ear.

"Petals of promise. I promise to love you forever, Konni."

She turned her smiling face up to him once again. "Could you seal that promise with a kiss?"

Rick's eyes held hers. He lowered his lips, brushing them tenderly against her own, thus sealing his promise on her lips, and on her heart, to love her forever. . . .

DIANN HUNT

Diann Hunt resides in Indiana with her husband. They have two grown children, three grandchildren, and one on the way! Feeling God has called her to the ministry of writing, Diann shares stories of lives changed and strengthened by faith in a loving God. Visit Diann's web site at http://www.diannhunt.com.

Rose in Bloom

by Sandra Petit

God's timing is always perfect. And He wastes nothing.
Through every event, every activity, every person
who has touched my life, He has brought me to this point,
and I am truly grateful. Many have traveled along with me
through the journey, but a special few I'd like to acknowledge.
A big hug of appreciation to my husband, Todd,
and my children, Kati and Ben, for their love and support.
My parents, Leoncia and Austin Stevens, have encouraged
me wholeheartedly in whatever endeavor I have attempted.
Their faith in me has helped me to press on.
Lastly, a special thanks to my wonderful friend,
Gail Sattler, who was so generous in sharing
her most valuable asset—herself.

Chapter 1

The words Rose Bentley was about to speak froze in her throat as she caught sight of a movement out of the corner of her eye.

A small bundle of flowers, transformed into a missile when the bridal bouquet hit the ceiling fan, hurtled toward the prize wedding cake she'd made as her gift for Abby and Stan's nuptials.

Ignoring propriety, Rose sucked in a deep breath and leaped toward the flowers, praying she'd retained enough skill and agility from her softball days to save her culinary creation.

She stretched her arm to its limit, plucked the flowers from the air, and dropped neatly back to the ground in one smooth motion. She grinned as she stared at the blossoms in her hand. *Easy as snagging a pop fly.*

Her triumphant smile suddenly faded. The pink roses were beautiful, even though the fan had clipped some of the delicate petals, but these weren't ordinary flowers. Since they were part of the bride's bouquet, catching them traditionally meant she would be the next to marry.

That couldn't happen. Rose was still building her catering business, and at twenty-nine years old, she was finally starting to achieve some degree of success. Putting her business aside to marry wasn't on her agenda.

Rose wound her arm back to hurl the offending arrangement to the waiting single women gathered in the center of the large banquet hall at Country Meadows Inn—and hit a rock hard jaw.

Just as she began to turn, the jaw's owner grabbed her outstretched arm in an attempt to steady himself. Unsuccessful, he fell backward. Rose couldn't do anything except scream as he pulled her along with him.

Air whooshed out of her lungs, and the two of them crashed into the table, which collapsed beneath them. Plates, napkins, cake, and little bottles of Vermont maple syrup flew through the air. Then everything seemed to hit the ground at the same time with a resounding crash. Rose landed on her arm with a thud and felt a searing pain in her right shoulder as she lay still, holding the small piece of Abby's bouquet in her hand.

Best man Lucas Montgomery groaned, bringing her attention to his face. His wide blue eyes bored into hers. White frosting covered his strong, chiseled chin, and the tiny plastic bridegroom was lodged in his charcoal black hair, glued in place by a blob of the sticky white icing.

Abby's beautiful cake—the one Rose had spent days making—lay in ruins on the floor around them.

By the heat on her face, Rose knew her cheeks were

flaming. She tried to raise herself off Lucas, but sank back in pain.

"Ow!"

"What's wrong?" Lucas asked, his voice filled with concern. "Is it your arm?"

"Yes. No, the shoulder I think." She blinked back tears and gritted her teeth with the pain. She inhaled sharply as he turned her gently so her back was to his chest.

"I'll help you up."

He wrapped his arms around her to help her keep the injured arm immobile, then sat up, bringing her with him. She closed her eyes and fought the pain and nausea that rolled over her. She recognized the sensations, having dislocated her shoulder years ago playing softball. Her doctor had warned her it could happen again. The memories were not pleasant.

Lord, help me get through this.

Lucas helped her to her feet. Before she could say anything, footsteps echoed behind her. "Rosie! Are you okay?" Her bridal gown flowing around her, Abby came to an abrupt halt a few inches from Rose.

Laughter sounded from other parts of the room, but there were muffled conversations in the area surrounding the cake as some guests realized she'd been hurt. People began to gather around to see if they could help.

Rose opened her mouth to answer Abby, but the lump in her throat prevented her from speaking. She ached for someone to take care of her. It was at times like this that being independent wasn't such fun. The thought had no sooner left her than her widowed sister, Alexandra, raced up.

"Rosie. Are you all right?"

Lucas saved her the trouble of answering. "It looks like her shoulder is dislocated. I grabbed her as I was going down." He turned to face Rose. "This is my fault. I'm so sorry."

"It was an accident," Rose said quietly, though even she could hear the strain in her voice. She moved to step away from him, but his arm tightened around her.

"You need to see a doctor right away. I'll drive you."

"I can take her," Alexandra said.

"I–I can't just leave. . . ." Rose's voice trailed off. She closed her eyes against another wave of nausea as she leaned into Lucas.

"Yes, you can. Abby?" Lucas looked at Abby.

"You can't take the baby to the hospital," Rose said to Alexandra, before Abby could reply. "It's no place for Mia."

Stan appeared beside Abby. "Lucas, if you can take care of Rose, we'll take care of everything here. We already have a crew for cleanup, and I'm sure arrangements can be made to get Rose's van to her later."

Lucas nodded. "I'll take care of her."

Someone handed Abby a stack of napkins, and she began to wipe frosting from Rose's arm. "I'm so sorry. I feel like this was my fault. If I hadn't thrown the bouquet. . ." Her voice trailed off as tears filled her eyes.

Rose laid her hand on Abby's and moved it away. Abby couldn't know that even that slight jarring was painful. "It wasn't your fault. It wasn't anyone's fault."

Stan moved up beside Abby and put his arm around her. "It was an accident, Sweetheart."

Lucas looked at Rose. "We'd better get going."

Rose hesitated. "There are still some people who didn't get cake."

The three of them looked at her, and Rose felt her face heat once again. "I guess that's not really a problem since there isn't any more cake. I'm so sorry, Abby. I'll make you another cake."

"That might not be for a while," Lucas said.

Rose's eyes widened even as she grimaced. "I have to make a cake just like this for Wednesday night. It takes three days to make. I don't have any choice. It's too late for them to get someone else. And Abby needs wedding cake for her first anniversary. It's tradition. She has to freeze it."

Rose noticed Stan watching Abby. His brow was drawn with concern, his entire attention on his bride. Soon Abby would leave Country Meadows Inn as Mrs. Stanleigh Chenkowski. The thought caused moisture to pool in Rose's eyes, but it wasn't because of her physical pain.

Lord, what about me? I know I asked You to help me get my business started. And You did that. Thank You. But I admit I'm coveting the love I see in Stan's eyes, the way he looks at Abby as though she's the only one in the room. Help me to find someone who will look at me that way, Lord. Someone who will understand how important my business is to me. I feel so alone right now. I know that's foolish. You're with me, Lord. Please give me peace.

"We'll work out your baking schedule later. Right now,

you need to get to a hospital." Lucas's voice pulled Rose back to her current situation.

"Don't worry about the guests," Stan put in, his gaze shifting to Rose. "They can eat the Bowser cake."

Rose gave him a weak smile. She was proud of the groom's cake, which she had shaped to look like Stan's basset hound. The chocolate cake and frosting had turned out just right. Rose worried that no one would want to "eat" Bowser, but she guessed if it were the only cake left, they'd enjoy the tasty treat.

Rose glanced at Lucas. He had taken the worst of the fall, shielding her with his broad shoulders from being immersed in the creamy white icing. She cringed.

"It was my fault you fell in the first place."

"You do pack a wallop." He rubbed his jaw where her fist had connected, then winked. "Come on. Let's get this shoulder taken care of."

"All right." Rose turned to her sister. "I'll call you later."

Lucas placed Rose's coat over her shoulders since she couldn't move her arm to put it on. He gently wrapped his arm around her and guided her toward the door as they left the reception, the errant bouquet still in Rose's hand.

Lucas looked at Rose, asleep on the seat beside him, as he drove to her apartment. Rose's sister was going to meet them at the apartment and stay the night with her.

The trip to the hospital had been difficult. Rose was in a lot of pain, and more than once he detected a tear slipping down her face, each one a stab at his heart. The attending physician couldn't give her anything for the pain until X-rays were taken, which he'd ordered immediately. When the diagnosis was confirmed, Rose was finally given medication, and the doctor popped her shoulder back in, giving her some relief. He'd given instructions that she was to rest the arm for several weeks.

Rose said she'd dislocated her shoulder twice before in high school, and the doctor told them that was probably why it had been so easy to dislocate again. Still, Lucas felt responsible.

He drove into the parking lot, turned off the engine, and walked around to the other side of the car to open Rose's door. He touched her good shoulder lightly.

"Rose?" She glanced up at him, groggy from the pain pills.

He picked up the piece of the bouquet she'd caught at the reception. He assumed it meant a lot to her, so he wanted to make sure she didn't lose it. It was the least he could do. He crooked his arm around her waist and helped her up the stairs, surprised at how small she was. How could such a little thing pack such a punch? He chuckled at the memory of her fist hitting his face.

When he got to the door, he knocked softly. Rose's sister opened the door, holding her baby. A large cat was wrapped around her legs.

"How is she?"

"I'm fine," Rose grumbled. "And I'm right here."

"Like you'd tell me the truth. Lucas?"

"She's a little loopy from the medication," Lucas replied, "but otherwise, okay. She's to take it easy and not use that arm for a while." He guided Rose to the sofa, removed her coat, and eased her down. The cat crept up and plopped itself down beside Rose, who murmured to it. "She'll probably sleep through the night."

"Thanks for taking her to the hospital."

"If you need anything—anything—call me." Lucas pulled out a business card and placed it on the table next to the sofa. "My home and cell phone numbers are on there. I don't have a business number yet since those plans aren't finalized."

"I'm sure we'll be fine." She pulled a brightly colored afghan over Rose.

"I guess I'll get going. Rose, I'm really sorry about this."

Rose rolled her eyes. "I know. But you wouldn't have fallen if I hadn't hit you in the jaw."

He laughed. "Point taken. Your right hook almost knocked me out. Nevertheless, I feel responsible. If there's anything I can do, all you have to do is ask."

"Have you ever baked a wedding cake?"

His mouth dropped open. "No, but I am in the restaurant business. My brother is the cook. I can read, though, and I'm sure I could follow instructions."

"Like I told you, I have to bake an anniversary cake for the Warners for Wednesday night. It takes three days, so I don't have time to look for another worker. If you're really serious, I could use your help on Monday. I can probably find someone else for the rest of the week."

"You don't need to find anyone else. I'll be glad to help. Besides, I owe Abby that top layer. I need to replace it."

Her deep sigh tore at his heart. "I guess I don't really have any choice."

"Then I'll see you on Monday."

"Thanks." She reached into her purse and pulled out a business card. "Here's the address."

Lucas tucked the card into his pocket.

Rose gave him a small smile. "Don't feel so bad. It could have been worse."

He didn't know how, but he accepted her words to ease his conscience.

━━━❦━━━

Lucas steered the car toward home. He loved living in the suburbs of Loudon, Vermont. Though the two-story house reflected his prosperity, it was too large for a single man living alone. Now that his business success was all but assured, his greatest desire was to have a family to fill the big house. He prayed daily for God to grant his wish.

Sighing, he entered the house, threw his keys on the small table by the door, and hung his jacket on the nearby coatrack.

Since it was getting late, he headed upstairs to shower and prepare for bed. Pulling his loose change out of his pocket, he felt the card Rose had given him fall into his hand and glanced down at it.

Rosie's Catering
311 Arby Avenue

His eyes widened and a lump formed in his throat. He

and his brother, Nick, had just purchased 311 Arby Avenue for their new restaurant. It was apparently also the building Rose rented for her catering shop.

Lucas ran a hand over his face. This was not good. He knew his brother had scoured the city for the perfect building to use for the new venture that would bring them back home, close to their parents. Nick said the Arby property had all the facilities they needed in a perfect location. They had agreed to make the purchase when the owner assured them the present renter was not interested in buying. A suspicion crept into his mind, however, that if Rose was the tenant in question, she knew nothing about the sale.

A catering business brought the food to the customer, so location wasn't as big an issue as it was with a restaurant. He needed the location; she didn't.

If she didn't know the building had been sold out from under her, she would soon. He'd faxed the signed agreement to Jerrold Inkman that morning. He was now legally bound. Not only that, but he really wanted this building. It was perfect for his needs. However, he didn't want to hurt Rose. He'd already caused her enough problems. Besides that, she was a nice woman, and he wanted to get to know her better.

As trite as it seemed, the moment he'd seen her, he'd felt an attraction. He'd even gone so far as to ask Stan about her.

"Nice, but focused on her career," Stan had said.

His shoulders slumped. He'd finally met a woman who interested him, and very soon she was going to hate the sight of him. He didn't want that to happen. The image of Rose's deep brown eyes looking down at him as he lay among the cake would haunt his dreams tonight.

And he realized Stan was correct. Rose's business was her life 24-7. That being the case, he'd make it his life, too, at least until her shoulder healed—and she got to know him better. Of course, she might run him over with her van once she found out he was shoving Rosie's Catering into the street.

Lucas sighed. Maybe she wouldn't have to find out. Not right away. Not that he'd lie to her. He wouldn't do that. He simply wouldn't tell her everything, making him guilty only of omission. He could let her landlord be the bearer of the bad news. *After* she realized she couldn't live without Lucas Montgomery.

He headed for the shower, deep in thought. Before he went to sleep tonight, it would be a good idea to spend some time in prayer. A lot of time.

Chapter 2

Lucas stared at the recipe in his hands. It listed amounts and ingredients but didn't tell him when everything needed to be done or how. He glanced at Rose. She said she wasn't in pain, just uncomfortable. She refused to take any pills because they made her sleepy. There was nothing he could do about it. She was an adult. He couldn't force her to take medication she didn't want to take, so he gave up and moved on.

"What do I do first?" he asked.

Rose yawned. "Make some coffee, and let's have breakfast. It always takes me awhile to get going on a Monday morning."

Coffee. That was something he could do. He was glad he'd picked up breakfast on his way in. A few minutes later, he joined her at the table and said a brief blessing over the food. He watched closely to be sure Rose didn't have any trouble and refilled her cup when it was empty.

"What made you decide to become a caterer?" he asked, taking a bite of his bacon, egg, and cheese biscuit.

"Not what. Who. Abby. I was always interested in baking, but I didn't have the money for the course. She encouraged me to share my feelings with Mom and Dad. They financed my education at the Culinary Arts Institute. It took all their savings and then some."

"They must be very proud of you."

She bit her lip, and her voice caught as she spoke. "They were killed in a car accident the night I catered my first party—but yes, I think they were proud."

"I'm sorry. That must have been rough." He reached over and squeezed her hand.

"It was. I still miss them." She paused. "I don't usually talk about it except with Alex."

Lucas winced. Who was Alex? "I'm glad you can talk to me. I'd like for us to be friends." He gave her an encouraging smile, squeezed her hand again, and released it. She returned the smile with a sad one of her own. He couldn't pull his eyes away. Those deep brown eyes showed every emotion. Lucas's heart beat faster, but he resisted the urge to lift his hand and touch the light brown hair that framed her face. Instead, he stood. It was time to start baking.

* * *

Rose watched Lucas struggling to get the top off the tub of flour, frustrated that she couldn't help. "It should just come off," she grumbled. "I never have any trouble with it."

"I think it's glued on," Lucas muttered as he pulled hard.

Rose backed up, shielding her arm. Lucas jerked the top off; the tub hit the edge of the counter, then slid out of his hand. He reached to catch the tub and slipped. Both tub and

Lucas hit the floor. A cloud of white flour flew into the air and settled on top of Lucas. Rose giggled, and Lucas shifted his gaze to glare at her.

"You should have put your apron on," Rose quipped.

His scowl deepened. "Men don't wear aprons."

"Right."

Rose bit her lip and struggled to contain her laughter.

Lucas stood and dusted himself off. "Where's your broom and dustpan?"

Rose pointed to the closet in the corner. "I'd help if I could."

"Not a problem."

A wedding cake was not a beginner project. Doing it herself would take less time than explaining it to him, but she didn't have any choice. She had an obligation to make this cake for Wednesday. It took three days. There wasn't room for error.

Since Lucas was willing, she was going to have to accept his help, even if she wasn't sure she wanted to spend several days in his company.

The Warners had contracted her to bake an anniversary cake months ago. They would repeat their wedding vows and then host a reception where everyone could share in their joy. Fifty years together. It was remarkable. Rose wondered if she would ever find a man who would love her that much. When she married, she wanted it to be forever.

Her gaze moved to Lucas. He had dressed casually, in jeans and a yellow T-shirt. His face was clean-shaven, and when he'd helped her inside, the woodsy scent of his aftershave had tickled her nose.

His blue eyes had dark circles under them as though he hadn't slept well, and his black hair—now heavily dusted with flour—had that mussed look one might get from driving with the top down, though she knew he certainly wasn't doing that in Vermont in March. He looked like a man who desperately needed caffeine, which was why she'd suggested coffee. She knew he felt guilty about her injury even though she'd told him several times it wasn't his fault.

Lucas interrupted her thoughts. "All cleaned up. What do I need to do now?"

"Put on an apron," Rose said, laughing. "Then the ingredients need to be measured out. The measuring cups are in that cabinet to your right. Then you can get the pans ready."

Grumbling, Lucas reluctantly grabbed an apron, then gathered ingredients and sat at the table with Rose.

"Maybe I could help," Rose said.

Lucas looked up. "Your job is supervisor. Doc said you have to take it easy for a few days."

Rose sighed. "All right, but we can't mix it all at one time, so we'll make the four small cakes first. That's eight cups of batter."

Lucas finished measuring and set the ingredients aside. "Now you want me to get the pans ready?" At her nod, he looked at the pans and grinned wryly. "How does one make a pan ready? Do you want me to have a talk with it? Explain what's going to happen?"

Rose stared at him. Then her mouth turned up, and she started to laugh until tears streamed down her face. Lucas was smiling. Finally, she pursed her lips together and got herself under control. She suddenly realized she'd been so intent on making a success of her business, she hadn't laughed much lately. It felt good.

She took a deep breath. "Um. The pans. You need to spread a thin layer of cake release on the bottom and sides of each pan with a pastry brush. It helps the cake to slide out of the pan more easily. It's the yellow container there on the counter. I'll turn the oven on to preheat." She stood, half expecting Lucas to object, but he simply began to work.

While Lucas prepared the pans, Rose carefully carried the measured ingredients, one at a time, to the counter where her large mixing bowl sat.

"I didn't realize how much batter it would take."

Rose turned. Lucas was standing right behind her. Having him so close made her breath catch. She moved slightly to put some distance between them. "We're making six double-layer cakes, and one of those is sixteen-inches square. That's a lot of batter."

"Hmm. You can sit down now. I'll do this. Do I just put it all in there and turn it on?"

Rose blinked. "Well, yes, but slowly and carefully. You don't want batter to go flying all over the place. And you need to use the spatula along the sides." She sighed, frustrated. How could she explain it to him?

Lucas placed his finger under her chin and lifted it so her eyes met his. "Hey. I know this is hard for you, but there's no choice here. We'll do the best we can. I'm really trying. Okay?"

Rose bit her lip and nodded. He was trying. She could see that. It wasn't his fault he didn't know what he was doing. "You're doing a good job. I appreciate it." She watched him mix the batter.

"How much of this goes in each pan?" Lucas asked.

"Fill them halfway."

He nodded and proceeded to do just that. The first cakes were placed in the oven and the timer set.

"So that's that," Lucas said, a big smile on his face.

Rose laughed. "Not exactly. Now we need to prepare the cardboard pieces the cakes will sit on. The two large cakes are stacked."

"Cardboard pieces?"

"Uh-huh. We'll need waxed paper, scissors, and my cutter to make the center hole in the cardboard."

Lucas gathered the pieces, and Rose explained what to do.

"That doesn't sound complicated," Lucas said. "Why don't you rest while I do that? Want some more coffee? A Danish? A pain pill?"

Rose hesitated. "No pain pills, but I'll have some coffee."

Lucas brought her a cup of coffee, then began to work. As he worked, he talked, inserting humorous anecdotes about things that had happened at his restaurants. Rose found herself enjoying the time and laughing more than she had in a long time.

Lucas insisted on ordering lunch from the Chinese restaurant down the street. As they sat down to eat, Lucas reached across the table for her hand and bowed his head. Rose hoped he didn't notice the way her pulse had increased at his touch. As soon as he said "Amen," she pulled her hand away and began to eat. But she almost choked at the first words out of Lucas's mouth.

"So, Rose, who's Alex?" he asked.

Rose's brows drew together. Lucas sat staring at her, his elbow on the table, his chin propped up with his hand.

"Alex—Alexandra—is my sister. I thought you knew that. Didn't I tell you she was staying with me the night I dislocated my shoulder?"

"Your sister was there, yes, but you didn't say that Alex was your sister, and you were in no shape to introduce us."

"Sorry. Alex is my sister. She's twenty-five, four years younger than I am. She's a widow and owns her own carpentry business. You met her baby daughter, Mia." Rose grinned mischievously. "Is that what you wanted to know?"

Chapter 3

Lucas's eyes lost their focus for a second, and he smiled. Perhaps he would get the chance to know Rose better. If she could forgive him for not telling her about his latest purchase.

"I know you said your parents are gone, and now I know you have a sister. Are there any other Bentley siblings?"

"No. What about you?"

"Just Nick and me. We get together for lunch at my parents' house often, usually on Sundays after church when we can make it."

"That's nice. Sounds like you're all close."

"We are. My folks aren't pushy, but they do keep reminding us what's important. It's not all work all the time." He paused and pointed his fork at her. "Who reminds Rose when it's time to put down the mixer and have some fun?"

Rose choked on her drink, then raised her head to stare at him. "I have fun."

He lifted one brow. "What do you do for fun?" Lucas

fought a smile as he watched her struggle to come up with something.

"I–I–I go to church."

He couldn't stop his grin. "That's a good thing, of course, but I'd hardly consider it entertainment. What church do you attend?"

"Lakeview Bible."

"I've been there a couple of times. Large congregation." He didn't tell her that he'd tried Lakeview when he first returned to town and that he'd felt lost in the crowd there. While there wasn't anything wrong with attending a large church, Lucas felt more comfortable in a smaller congregation. When he'd found Hope Village, it had felt like coming home.

"Where do you go?"

He smiled. "Hope Village at the edge of town. It's like a family. Everyone knows everyone. Why don't you come to church with me on Sunday and see for yourself?"

"I don't know. Maybe."

Lucas nodded. He didn't want to push her, but he didn't know how much time he had. Surely it wouldn't be long before her landlord let her know her building had been sold, although hopefully it would be awhile before she found out to whom. When he'd entered the building that morning, he'd been surprised to find Rose only used the kitchen and office area. He hoped Inkman, the current owner, wasn't charging her for the entire building. He and Nick were going to open up the large front room for the restaurant and put in a refrigerated storage area in the attached warehouse.

If business was good enough, the warehouse could be converted into additional seating later.

Rose stood and began to clear the table, but Lucas gently moved her aside and took care of the cleanup.

He listened carefully as Rose showed him how to check the cakes and remove them from the oven. After a few minutes, he removed them from the pans and set them on cardboard to finish cooling.

Lucas noticed the garbage can was full and decided to empty it. He lifted the bag from the large container and stepped to the door. He was turning the knob to open the back door when Rose whirled around.

"What. . .oh, no! Don't open the—"

Lucas turned his head as he pushed the door open. "What did you say? I didn't hear—"

A massive weight bumped against him. Unable to regain his balance, he felt himself falling to the floor as two huge dogs raced over him. Too stunned to move, Lucas remained on the floor, flat on his back, still grasping the garbage bag in his right hand. Cold air entered the room from the alley.

Rose screamed, and a huge crash echoed in the room. Lucas released the bag, jumped to his feet, and rushed to her side. Assured that she was all right, he surveyed the room.

The cakes they'd just spent the morning baking were in pieces on the floor—at least the pieces that weren't inside the dogs were on the floor. Rose was trying to grab one of the dogs. Lucas had a vision of her falling and spraining an ankle to go with her dislocated shoulder—again because of him.

"Rose, wait!" He grabbed hold of the two dogs and dragged them back outside, shutting the door firmly behind them. Then he picked up the garbage bag that had started the mess and very carefully exited the door and set the bag in the bin behind the shop, making sure the cover was tightly closed.

Returning to the kitchen, he stood next to Rose as they appraised the damage.

"I'm sorry. I had no idea."

"It's not your fault," she muttered. "I should have told you about the dogs. I've never seen anything like it, but these dogs love cake. Whenever I'm baking, they sit and wait by the door."

Lucas studied the disaster. "Does this happen every time you take out the garbage? Have you spoken to their owners? Or the animal control office?"

She sighed. "No. They're really nice dogs. They just love cake. If I have to open the door, I'm really careful. If I time it right, they're distracted when Wang puts his garbage out and they're down the street."

Lucas ran a hand down his face. "I'll sweep it up. And I'll pay for what was wasted. Then I guess we have to start over."

"I guess so." Her voice was tight, but she didn't yell at him.

He didn't quite know what to say to get himself out of this, but before he could come up with anything, the *Mission Impossible* theme song sounded in the room. Grinning at Rose, he lifted the cell phone attached to his waistband and pulled it open, leaning on the broom. "Montgomery."

"Lucas. Where are you?"

Lucas ignored the question. "What's the problem, Nick?"

"The Arby building owner, Mr. Inkman, hasn't informed his tenant of the sale or prepared the building, but his wife's had an automobile accident. He needs more time to take care of her, so he'd like us to wait to take possession. What do you think?"

It only took Lucas a moment to see that this would give him more time with Rose before she discovered the sale. "That sounds okay, but I'll talk to him." Lucas opened his mouth to say more, but suddenly realized Rose could hear every word he was saying. "I'll get back to you soon."

He ended the call and closed the phone.

"Do you need to go?" Rose asked.

He shrugged. "There are always problems. It can wait."

"If you need to take care of something, I understand. Maybe Alex can come and help me. The cakes will have to cool overnight anyway."

"I'm not going to desert you."

She scowled at him. "It's not your problem. I usually bake alone. It's only because—"

"You work too hard."

"I work as hard as I need to. My reputation is important to me. Failing is not an option, even if I have to stay up all night. I'll figure it out."

Lucas heard the defensive tone in her voice and knew he'd stepped over the line. He had no right to tell her what to do. He remembered the late nights when he'd opened his first restaurant. Starting a business was hard work. Yet he couldn't help worrying about Rose and wanting to make sure she didn't drive herself too hard. He also realized this was her business, and she wanted it to succeed as much as he wanted his own to do so. "All right. Look, I'll mix up another batch of cakes, and while they're in the oven, I can take care of my problem and pick up some dinner for us. Does that sound okay to you?"

She sighed. "I suppose so. I'm sorry I snapped at you. Maybe it will go faster since we've done it once already. But we'd only done one batch, and there are six cakes to make, plus the replacement wedding layer."

"Abby's cake is no rush. She's not using it until her anniversary, right? I'll make it. I promise. We'll just take care of the rush job first."

He gathered all the supplies once again and set about making new cakes. As Rose had said, the second time went faster because he knew more about what he was doing. Once the cakes were in the oven, Rose went to lie down in the office, and Lucas hurried out the door to get their dinner and take care of Inkman, without Rose overhearing the conversation.

When he returned, Rose was sitting at the table. She looked up when he entered, relief evident in her face.

"Everything okay here?"

She nodded. "The cakes are almost done. I was worried you wouldn't get back in time."

"I said I would, and I keep my promises." It hadn't taken long to work things out with Inkman. The man was distraught and worried about his wife. Since Lucas was in no hurry to take possession, he'd okayed the delay and even agreed to give Inkman his money so his wife could receive the best treatment. Inkman promised to talk to his tenant as soon as things settled down for him. Since Lucas and Nick had agreed to give Rose time to find a new place to operate, he hoped that would ease the way to a relationship other than business with the woman who appeared to be capturing his heart.

Lucas removed the new cakes from the oven and mixed the next batch. It was very late when they finally finished all the baking, but Rose insisted all the cakes had to be finished before they could leave. They needed the next two days for other things. While he didn't understand how it could take three days to bake one cake, he had already caused Rose enough distress. If she wanted the cakes baked today, they'd be baked today. Her eyes were drooping, and he could see how tired she was.

When he'd taken the last cake out of the oven and cleaned up, he drove her home, promising to pick her up the following morning.

He left quickly because he was afraid after the dog disaster she might decide she'd rather have another helper.

He didn't want her to say something like, "Don't come back."

Chapter 4

Lucas hesitantly knocked on Rose's door at six o'clock the next morning. He knew how tired he was, and he was sure Rose was in no better shape. After yesterday's disaster, he couldn't imagine what his welcome would be. Rose had been upset with him, he knew, though she hadn't reacted as he'd expected.

Before he'd fallen asleep, he'd prayed for Rose and for God's will regarding their blossoming relationship.

"Morning." Rose stood with the door open, wearing a button-down blouse and long denim skirt. Dark circles lined her eyes, and she yawned. "You're right on time."

"You look exhausted."

She frowned. "I'm fine. We can go now."

She stepped out, and Lucas moved his hand to the small of her back to guide her. Rose, however, didn't seem to want any assistance. She stiffened and moved ahead of him. He knew it distressed her to accept his help in making the cake. He wondered if she even allowed God to help her. That would be something they'd need to discuss before he allowed their relationship to go further. He knew she attended church, but he also knew that not everyone warming a church pew was a true believer, and it was important to him that any woman he was seriously involved with put God first.

When they arrived at the shop, he made coffee and set out the doughnuts he'd picked up for breakfast. He bowed his head and said a blessing before biting into a powdered doughnut, being careful not to get the fine powder all over everything. He'd seen enough flour yesterday to last him quite a long time.

"Do you always come in so early?"

Rose smiled. "Sometimes earlier. Depends on what I need to do."

"I'm not trying to criticize. It just seems you work so hard, even with an injury."

"I work hard because I want my business to be a success. I'm sure you work just as hard at your business. Why aren't you working, by the way?"

He shrugged. "My other restaurants are out of town. I have a manager at each restaurant, and I keep in touch through phone and fax. My brother left for Boston this morning to handle some problems."

"Oh. I thought your brother was the chef."

"He is, but we share the responsibilities. It's Nick's turn." Lucas watched as Rose took a sip of her coffee. "I was thinking about the wedding," he tried again.

"The wedding where we decided to wear the cake instead of eat it?" Her lips curved upwards into a soft smile, and Lucas felt his heart kick into gear. *Slow down. She's just a friend. A beautiful friend. At least right now.*

He grinned. "That's the one."

"I remember." This time she chuckled.

"You caught those flowers like a pro."

"Alex and I were on the school softball team for years. I wasn't really that much of an athlete, but Alex loved it. That's where I hurt my shoulder before."

"We could use you on our church softball team. Your sister, too."

"Isn't it too cold for softball?"

"Actually, we start practicing in a few weeks, though it's a little cool, and our games begin locally in late April or May, depending on what other teams are available. Of course, your arm has to heal before you can play."

Rose grinned. "I've seen guys play football the next week after dislocating a shoulder."

Lucas gave her a scowl. "The doctor said weeks."

She laughed. "I know. I'll think about it and talk to Alex, too. Don't team members have to belong to your church?"

"We often invite friends to help us out since the church is so small. We play other churches in the area. Both sides have booths for donated foods, which we sell during the games. Each game's profit goes to a different charity or ministry effort. People come out to have some fun and support their favorite charities."

"Sounds like fun and a worthwhile project, too."

"It is. It's family entertainment, and it helps people who need it. My offer's still good to come to church with me on Sunday. You could meet some of the other members of the team even if you can't practice yet."

Rose looked down. "I don't know that I want to change churches."

"I didn't ask you to change. I just asked you to visit. Pastor Charles is a terrific speaker. I think you'll enjoy hearing him." Lucas angled his head slightly in the direction of the radio, tuned to a Christian station. "I also notice you like contemporary Christian music. We have a praise band and sing a lot of the contemporary songs."

"Sounds nice. I'll think about it."

"Great! I'll pick you up at nine for Sunday school."

"I didn't say I'd go."

He gave her a wide grin. "You didn't say you wouldn't."

⟡

Rose handed the cake leveler to Lucas. "You're going to level the cake so the layers will fit well together. Keep the legs of the leveler flat on the counter and cut into the cake at the same height, using an easy sliding motion." She demonstrated with her free hand. "Each cake needs to be leveled, so you'll have to adjust the height of the leveler with the different cakes. If you'll open the cans of apricots, I'll make the glaze while you're doing that."

"What's the glaze for?" Lucas opened the cans, then picked up the leveler and eyed the cake as he adjusted the height of the equipment.

"To keep the crumbs from messing up the icing."

"Will we have to let that cool overnight?"

"No. It will harden in fifteen minutes." She hesitated. "Then we start the fondant."

Lucas tilted his head to stare at her. The leveler wobbled, but he returned his attention before any damage was done. "The what?"

"Fondant. I used European fondant on the first cake." Rose bit her lip as she wondered if perhaps she should use an easier rolled fondant or simple icing. European fondant was difficult to make correctly. It took timing and skills she'd developed in her years as a pastry chef.

Besides that, her head was starting to ache. She lifted her hand to massage her temple.

"Problem?" Lucas raised an eyebrow as he looked at her.

"No." If she told him she had a headache, Lucas would insist she rest, and there wasn't time for that. She had to deliver this cake on time. Lucas was right. She did work hard, but it was necessary. For Alex and Mia. She owed them this.

Lucas finished leveling the cakes as Rose boiled the apricot preserves for the glaze. She approved his work, and then they each took a pastry brush and coated the cakes with the glaze. Though it was more difficult with her left hand, she could still handle the brush, and it made her feel useful.

Cakes set aside to dry, Rose considered her next words carefully.

"This is when I would normally make the fondant."

Lucas nodded.

"It's very precise. And it takes a long time."

Lucas grinned. "Are you trying to politely tell me you don't think I can do it?"

The heat of a blush crept up Rose's neck as she swallowed and nodded. "You don't understand."

Lucas stepped closer, and Rose sucked in a breath. He was invading her space, and though she wasn't afraid of him, she was uncomfortable. When he lifted her hand, however, she couldn't seem to pull away.

"I do understand, Rose. You've been doing this for a long time. I don't have a clue what I'm doing. But you do. And you can get me through it. You're going to be right here beside me." The way he said the words made her blink. It sounded intimate, though she knew he was just talking about her help in making the fondant. "It's going to work out. Have faith. Okay?" He gave her hand a squeeze, then let it drop. "Now what do we do first?"

Rose released the breath she'd been holding and stared at him. He was right. She needed to have more faith. God knew what this meant to her, and He would help them through it. Hadn't He gotten them through the disaster yesterday? Though they'd had to do everything twice, it was done.

With focused determination, she gathered the glucose, sugar, and water. European fondant had to be heated to exactly 240 degrees Fahrenheit and then allowed to cool to 110 degrees or it would become coarse and tough rather than smooth and pliable as it was supposed to be.

Lucas didn't attempt conversation or interrupt her. He just did what she told him to do. He concentrated totally on the job at hand. Since he was busy, Rose was able to watch him work. No man should look so good—his black hair, strong chin, and gorgeous blue eyes made her feel like a teenager with a hormone overload. She refused to give in to it. She was more than the sum of her hormones. And Lucas was more than the sum of his good looks. He was gentle and kind. He'd taken time from his own schedule to help her with this job, something he didn't have to do. It touched her heart.

After he poured the mixture onto the marble slab and sprinkled it with water, he started to work it with a steel scraper, folding it onto itself over and over again. Though the work was physical, it was brainless, and Lucas talked to her as he worked, bringing a smile to her face with his stories of his brother, Nick, and vacations they'd taken as children. He even coerced her into sharing memories of her parents, bringing both happy and sad tears.

When the fondant was finished, Lucas insisted she lie down to rest while he cleaned the kitchen. She was so tired that she agreed. He walked her to the office, and when she lay down, he touched her cheek gently before he left.

Rose closed her eyes. The warmth from Lucas's touch stayed with her long after he left the room. She dozed, and when she awoke, the lamp was on low and muted sounds were coming from the other room. She slid off the sofa and walked back to the kitchen.

Lucas had cleaned all the dishes and sat at the table, radio playing softly, hands folded on his stomach, chin on his chest, sound asleep. A smile tugged at her lips, knowing he was still there because he hadn't wanted to wake her. It had been a long time since anyone had taken such care of her.

Rose tiptoed to the chair and laid her hand lightly on his shoulder. "Lucas?"

His eyes opened and he smiled, reaching up to hold her hand that rested on his shoulder. "Hey. How are you feeling?"

"Rested. I think we should go home now, though. Thanks for cleaning up."

"Not a problem. I'll drive you home."

She nodded and followed him out, locking the door behind them.

Chapter 5

Lucas felt great relief when Rose pronounced the fondant usable. He'd already made the filling for the cakes, and Rose had explained how to apply a border around the edges and then fill in the center. When the second layer was placed on top, the filling spread perfectly.

He understood how much it frustrated her not to be able to help. He would have hated standing by and watching someone else do his work. Regardless of that, he was impressed with the way she had handled things. She'd accepted his help graciously, not even yelling when things went wrong.

Working side by side with Rose, Lucas found himself enjoying the camaraderie as they bantered back and forth. He loved listening to her easy laughter and watching her eyes crinkle when he said something that amused her. He found himself working harder to keep that smile in place. And he found himself wanting to talk to her about things he didn't normally discuss with others. It was becoming harder not to tell her about the building purchase. The guilt weighed him down.

When the filling was done, Rose carefully coached him in the application of the creamy fondant.

Lucas then prepared to make icing from the recipe Rose gave him. His brow furrowed as he concentrated on the instructions. Making icing couldn't be that hard, could it?

"Don't worry. You can't ruin it." The musical lilt of Rose's voice caressed him from across the room. "I've laid out all the ingredients so you can't use the wrong ones. We can adjust the amounts when you're done if it's not the right consistency."

Lucas turned to quirk an eyebrow at her. "Do I hear a note of sarcasm? You think I'm going to mess it up, don't you?"

Rose lowered her head, and he knew she was giggling as her shoulders shook in a quick rhythm. He loved being the cause of her merriment.

He understood that Rose had no intention of starting a relationship. Her business was still in its infancy. Independent as she was, he was sure she wanted to make it on her own. And he was sure she'd succeed, if having to change locations didn't discourage her from continuing to try. He sighed softly.

Lucas worked carefully, wanting to show that he respected her work and could share in it if necessary. She seemed pleased with the effort when they stopped for the day to let the whole thing dry overnight.

They stood together at the sink. Lucas washed his hands and then took Rose's hand in his to wash it for her. Her skin was soft, and he lifted his head to tell her so, but the words stuck in his throat. The look in her eyes was almost too much for him. His gaze lowered, and he had to fight against an urge to brush his lips over hers.

"We'd better go if we're going to do this again tomorrow," Rose said softly.

Lucas swallowed and nodded. He patted her hand dry, then locked up the building and drove her home.

"Where's your apron?" Rose asked.

Lucas frowned. "We're not doing any baking today. No need for the aprons."

"Lucas." She stared at him, her eyes narrowing.

Lucas shook his head but acquiesced, tying an apron around his waist. He didn't want to think about why he gave in so easily, but he couldn't help smiling as he helped Rose wrap her huge apron around her thin frame.

"Let's get to that icing," he said with a laugh.

Rose showed him how to place the templates on the sides and mark them and then trace the designs with royal icing. He put together the church and steeple, then added icing to his creation. Rose had miniature flower arrangements to put on the four small square cakes.

When they sat down to eat a quick lunch of spaghetti with garlic bread, Rose complimented him on his efforts.

"I have to admit you've surprised me. I appreciate your help more than I can say."

"It's certainly been different from my regular workweek. I've enjoyed it." He wanted to say that he'd enjoyed being with her, but he didn't think Rose was ready to hear that.

At the end of the day, Lucas retrieved a camera from his

car and took pictures of the finished cake. He stepped back to survey their work.

"Job well done, Miss Bentley."

"I wasn't sure we could do it."

"I admit to having some doubts myself. Especially when those dogs bowled me over."

"The look on your face was priceless." Her eyes sparkled with glee.

Lucas chuckled. "I'm sure it was." He lifted a hand to push a strand of wayward brown hair behind her ear. "You deserve a reward for doing this twice in as many weeks."

"Reward?" Her eyes widened as he took a step closer.

"Uh-huh." He lifted a hand and cupped the back of her head, then leaned over and touched his lips gently to hers, careful of her shoulder. It was a sweet kiss, not meant to frighten or pressure her. He was relieved when she didn't pull back but accepted the kiss and even seemed to enjoy it. He released her and smiled. "It's been fun."

"Your fun is my work." She met his eyes briefly and then looked away.

His smile faded. "That's right. I don't have to do it 24-7." At her look, he changed the subject. "When do you need to deliver this?"

She hesitated. "We could take it over to the church now and set it up."

Lucas nodded. He noticed she'd automatically included him in her plans and was inexplicably pleased. "Then that's what we'll do."

It wasn't as easy as it sounded, but finally they were able

to load, transport, and deliver the cake to the church.

"Who's going to cut and serve?" Lucas asked.

Rose frowned. "I had planned to since I usually attend Bible study on Wednesdays anyway." She paused. "I think I could still do that. It only takes one hand to slice."

"Then it has to be put on plates. You'll need help, and you've already had a long day. I'll stay and help you."

"You've had a long day, too, and this is not your responsibility. You've done enough. Besides, don't you attend Bible study at your church?"

Lucas shook his head. "Not tonight. I'll take you home so you can rest awhile, and I'll pick you up in time for the ceremony. No arguments."

"I can't believe you helped Rose make this cake." Mrs. Warner gave Lucas a bright smile. "When I heard about her accident on Saturday, I was really worried, but everything looks wonderful—and tastes wonderful, too." She turned to Rose. "What a blessing Mr. Montgomery was available to help."

Rose smiled. "Yes, Ma'am, it was."

Lucas held his hands out in front of him in protest. "I only followed Rose's instructions."

He thought back to the ceremony they'd enjoyed just an hour earlier. The older couple had stood and professed their vows to one another, to keep God at the center of their lives and love one another forever. Their love was a wonder to see. Fifty years. Would he ever find a love like that?

His gaze moved to Rose, who stood chatting with other church members as she ate a piece of cake at Mrs. Warner's insistence. He cared for Rose. Perhaps more than cared. He had to admit he was hoping for a deeper relationship, but love? It was too soon to entertain those kinds of thoughts. He wanted her success as much as she did. He just wished it didn't have to be in his building.

He suddenly realized Rose was watching him, her brows bunched together, the skin between them wrinkled. He moved to her side. "Hey." He had a strange urge to lean down and kiss her cheek, but he reined it in. "No bouquets today, huh?"

She laughed. "No. This cake is safe."

"Good. I'd hate to have to spend the next three days making another one of these. As it is, we still have to remake Abby's cake."

Rose tapped her chin, a habit he'd noticed she had when she was concentrating—or pretending to. "You mean you didn't enjoy working at the catering shop this week?"

Lucas rubbed the back of his neck. "Yes, I did, but I don't think I'm cut out to do it full-time."

"Don't you do any cooking at the restaurant?

"That's Nick's job, and he loves it."

He paused, looking over the mingling crowd. This certainly was a much larger church than his. "Have you thought more about visiting Hope Village?"

Rose looked up at him. He almost lifted his hand to touch her face. Tiny freckles lined her nose, and she wore little makeup. *Lord, if this isn't the woman You want for me, please slam the door shut now.*

"Yes, I have. I guess I wouldn't mind going one Sunday."

A little voice inside him yelled, "Hallelujah!" but Lucas schooled his face into a neutral expression. "How about this Sunday? I can pick you up at nine for Sunday school."

"This Sunday?"

"Sure. Unless you've already got plans."

"I planned on going to church, so I guess that's fine."

"Great. So what's on the agenda for tomorrow's baking—besides Abby's cake?"

"I don't have a wedding this Saturday, but I do have a birthday party. The little boy doesn't like cake, though, so I'm making a chocolate chip cookie cake and several other kinds of cookies. It's nothing really difficult."

"Can I sample the wares?"

She laughed. "I suppose a taste test would be wise."

"It's a tough job, but I'm willing to accept the challenge." Lucas winked at her and linked his hand with hers. "Maybe the job wouldn't be so bad if I got to taste all the baking."

He stayed close to her the rest of the evening. Because of her injury, several ladies in the church insisted on taking care of cleanup and the leftover cake. He and Rose left early.

As Lucas made his way home, he rejoiced that Rose had agreed to attend church with him on Sunday. He'd see that she met the softball team members, but more than that, he would make sure she felt right at home at Hope Village Church. He wanted her worshiping next to him for a long time to come.

Chapter 6

Sunday morning Rose dressed carefully in a dark blue skirt and white silk blouse. A little nervous about going to a new church, she wasn't sure how Lucas had convinced her. Lakeview had been her home church since her parents died. Even so, she doubted anyone would even notice she missed today's service. She was just one person out of many. She took a last brief look in the mirror, knowing Lucas would arrive at any moment to pick her up.

The doorbell chimed, and she walked sedately to open it.

"Good mor—" Lucas stopped, his brow wrinkled.

"What's wrong?"

"You're. . .um. . ." He fidgeted.

"What?"

"Um, well, you're. . .too dressed up."

Rose looked down at her outfit. "This is what I always wear to church." Then she noticed what he was wearing. Jeans and a sport shirt with a casual heavy jacket. "You wear jeans to church?"

"Yes. I told you it was casual." He hesitated. "Look, if

you're comfortable, it's fine. Let's go." He picked up the coat she'd thrown over the back of the sofa and held it out to her, but Rose hesitated.

"I'll change."

"You don't have to. I shouldn't have said anything. It doesn't matter what you wear."

Rose bit her lip. "I don't want to stand out. I have jeans." She hurried to her room and pulled out a pair of jeans. The skirt came off easily, but unbuttoning the silk blouse with one hand and replacing it with a cotton one took time. She worried that they would be late. Finally, she finished wiggling into her jeans. She grabbed socks and a pair of boots and headed back out to the living room.

"Would you help me with these?" she asked nervously.

"Sure. Sit on the couch, and I'll do it."

She sat and Lucas knelt, working her feet into the socks. She giggled when his fingers brushed the bottom of her foot, tickling her. He held each boot out, she worked her foot into it, then Lucas zipped it up.

Lucas's lips curved in a bright smile of approval. Rose returned his look with relief, though she wasn't sure why what he thought mattered to her.

When they drove up to the small church, Lucas pulled into a parking spot and walked around the car to open her door.

"Want me to carry that for you?" He pointed to her purse and Bible.

"You want to carry my purse?"

Lucas grinned. "I'm a man of the twenty-first century. If

you need me to, I'm willing."

Rose laughed. "Thanks, but I think I can handle the purse. You can carry my Bible if you want to." He accepted the Bible, and Rose slipped out of the car.

Lucas placed his hand at the small of her back as he led her to the front door. A couple stood just inside, distributing bulletins. Lucas accepted one and slipped it inside his Bible.

"Hi, Don. This is my friend Rose Bentley. She's going to visit with us today." Lucas turned to Rose. "This is Don Barnes, the catcher on our softball team, and his wife, Marcia."

Rose nodded. "Nice to meet you." At her church no one really talked to her. She just entered and sat down. If she continued to attend here, she'd have to get used to being noticed.

Lucas greeted friends as he led her upstairs to his Sunday school classroom. Rose noticed that he kept his hand at her back and made every attempt to shield her injured arm from jostling by the crowd.

The Sunday school lesson was on following God's will for your life. She was impressed with the questions that were asked and by how generous the group was in sharing incidents from their own lives, making them very vulnerable as their faults were displayed for all to see.

When the class was over, they entered the sanctuary and found a seat close to the front. After a few minutes, the praise band started playing, and soon the congregation was singing a rousing chorus of "I Want to Know You" as people slowly made their way to their seats. The music eased into a worshipful "Amazing Love."

Rose joined in, glad she was familiar with the songs. As the service continued, she was surprised to find she recognized almost every song as one she had on CD at her apartment.

Rose was glad she had changed her clothes. Everyone was dressed casually as Lucas had told her. The pastor even wore casual clothes, though not jeans. His message, however, was anything but casual. Behind the entertaining humor was a suggestion that perhaps too many people let someone else carry the church load.

Church attendance, while good, was not enough. There were needs that could only be met if the people were willing to make sacrifices. Had she made any sacrifices lately that weren't for her own good or the sake of her business? Rose was ashamed to admit to herself she'd been focused solely on her own goals. She'd let God occupy the outer reaches of her life instead of keeping Him in front of her where He should be. She determined to do better in that regard.

"Want to go get something to eat?" Lucas asked as the closing chords of the last song faded away.

"I don't know, Lucas. I appreciate you taking me to church this morning, but I don't want to give you the wrong idea."

Lucas reached over and took her hand. It was a habit she was getting used to, and she was tempted to withdraw it for that very reason.

"And what idea would that be, Rose?"

She lowered her lashes and spoke softly so passersby wouldn't overhear her. "You know what idea. I don't have the time to invest in a relationship right now. I do want that in my life, but the timing isn't right. We've already spent the week together—"

"That was work."

"Yes, but—"

"I know what you're saying, Rose. I won't try to push you into anything. We can be friends. But remember, work isn't everything. I work hard, but I take time out for other things as well. Besides, God's timing and yours might not coincide."

Since she'd been thinking the same thing recently, Rose didn't respond.

"We'll just grab a burger. Okay?"

"All right," she finally agreed. "Just lunch."

Suddenly, someone called Lucas's name, and they turned as one to see an older couple walking toward them.

"Mom, Dad!" Lucas turned to Rose. "Mom and Dad don't attend here, but they do come occasionally because they're friends with Pastor Charles's family. They prefer 'Amazing Grace' to 'Bring It On.'" He grinned.

A woman with graying brown hair walked up to them, hand in hand with an older version of Lucas. "Lucas, we wanted to invite you and your friend to lunch. It won't be anything fancy. I have baked beans in the Crock-Pot, but there's fresh apple pie for dessert."

Lucas smiled. "Mom, Dad, this is Rose Bentley. Rose, my mom, Evelyn, and my dad, Lucien. Mom's a great cook. What do you say?"

Rose stared at Lucas. They seemed like a nice couple, but she'd just told Lucas she didn't want to get involved, and here he wanted to take her home to have a meal with his parents. It seemed a little too cozy for her, but she couldn't see a way to politely refuse.

"That would be nice. Can Lucas and I bring anything?"

"I think we have everything we need, but thanks for the offer. We'll look forward to seeing you soon." Evelyn smiled and put her hand on her husband's arm as the two walked off together.

Lucas sensed Rose was annoyed with him. He knew she didn't want a relationship. At least she said she didn't. While he knew he was ready to settle down, he wasn't sure if Rose was the one God intended for him. It was still early in their relationship to determine that, but it didn't seem as though God had slammed the door on the relationship, either.

There were so many things he liked about her. All he had to do was convince Rose to give them a chance. He was determined to be available to help her as long as she couldn't work. After all, it was his fault she was injured.

The meal with his parents went without incident, and he knew Rose enjoyed the food from her comments as they ate. His mother entertained them with embarrassing tales of his youth. He laughed along with the others. When the last bite of pie had been eaten, Lucas thanked his parents for the meal and escorted Rose to the car.

"Would you mind if I stopped at home for a few minutes?

I need to pick up some papers I promised to take to Nick. You're welcome to come along." Bringing Rose to meet Nick was risky. While he really preferred they never meet face-to-face, he knew that was unrealistic. He tried not to dwell on what her reaction would be when she saw the two of them side by side. Worst of all, Lucas didn't want to find she had more in common with Nick.

"I suppose that would be all right."

A short time later, he left her in his living room while he went to his office for the papers. When he returned, Rose was seated at the card table in front of a partially completed jigsaw puzzle of the Starship Enterprise.

"You build puzzles," Rose said. He could hear the smile in her voice as she took in the completed puzzles he'd mounted and framed and used to adorn his walls.

Lucas smiled. "Yes. I admit it. I'm a jigsaw puzzle fanatic." He crossed to the large picture window in the room, gazing out at his front yard. Without turning around, he continued. "I started doing them to relax during a difficult time in my life. I guess in a way the puzzles are representative of that time. Every day seemed like one big puzzle to me. I figured if I couldn't solve the puzzle that was my life, at least I could solve these." He took a breath and went on, wanting Rose to understand. "I was fighting God, angry with Him for some of the things that had happened to me. I ran with a bad crowd. I walked away from the church." He shoved his hands in his pockets. "I got an education, though. Some part of me knew that was important. God was trying to get my attention, but my eyes and ears were closed."

He lowered his voice. "Then Nick gave me some advice I've never forgotten. It certainly wasn't the first time I'd heard it, but I guess it was God's timing. This time it made sense. He told me to give God control of everything in my life, not just select portions."

"Easy to say, though not so easy to do." Her voice came from close behind him, but he didn't turn around.

"Exactly. Thing was, I thought I was following God's plan. I thought I trusted Him to handle things. Turns out I was just trying to turn God my way. I finally admitted I hadn't a clue what to do. I opened my heart to God and let Him work in my life." He faced her then. "Nick always loved to cook, and he's very gregarious. We decided to open a restaurant together. Neither of us ever believed it would be a national project. Boston, Napa, Denver, New Orleans."

"Is there a Mrs. Nick?" Rose asked lightly.

"No. Not yet, anyway."

"So you let God lead you, and now you've got all these restaurants. Successful?"

"Yep."

"And a new one soon?"

Lucas hesitated. "Yes. Nick and I plan to be based here, close to our parents. So what about you? How did you get to where you are?"

"I told you my parents sent me to culinary arts school."

"Yes, but anyone can go to school. Not everyone will make a success of it. You seem to have done that."

She nodded. "I'm doing okay." Her deep sigh tore at his heart. "I guess I'm not very good at letting God lead me, either. The catering shop is my obsession. I want to pay back the money my parents used for my education. Alex and Mia can use that money. It's not fair that she has no inheritance because my folks used it on me."

"That's admirable, Rose, but I'm sure Alex doesn't expect you to do that."

"Of course she doesn't, but I do." She stood. "Are you ready to go?"

He nodded and followed her to the car. Soon they were on the road to Nick's place, where Rose would learn another secret in his life. He hoped it wouldn't turn her away from him.

Chapter 7

"This is where your brother lives?"

Lucas glanced at Rose, who was staring at the red wooden building that resembled a barn. He smiled. "Yes." He walked around the car and opened the door to help Rose out. "Nick's house in California looked just like it. Wait until you see the inside."

Rose gave a noncommittal nod as she followed him to the front door. Lucas felt his heart speed up.

The door opened wide, and Nick greeted them, his gaze landing on Rose. "Lucas! And you brought an angel."

Lucas heard Rose's gasp and cringed.

"Nick, this is Rose. I told you about her catering business. Rose, this is my brother, Nick. You may notice we look a bit alike."

"A bit?" Rose's brow disappeared beneath her bangs.

Lucas glanced at Nick, who stood in the doorway, an amused smirk on his face. "Okay, more than a bit. Why don't we go inside?"

Nick stepped back and motioned for them to enter. "A

fellow chef. We should have lots to talk about."

Lucas clenched his fists as Nick gave Rose the smile that kept women at his side. He didn't want Rose at Nick's side.

The aroma of simmering food grew stronger as Nick continued on into the ultramodern kitchen.

Lucas turned to Rose and tried to read her expression. It wasn't very difficult. She was miffed.

"You should have told me you had a twin," she muttered.

"Don't you like surprises?" Lucas forced himself to smile, even though it was almost painful.

"No, actually, I don't. I never have," Rose said between gritted teeth.

"We'll have to change that. Maybe a more gradual introduction would have been better." Lucas gave her another weak smile. "Guess I should have told you sooner. I'm sorry. Yes, Nick and I are twins, but we're quite different. When we were kids, it wasn't cool for guys to cook. I spent a lot of time with a bloody nose, fighting boys who made fun of Nick's hobby." He glanced briefly at Nick.

Nick grinned. "Yeah. Lucas had the 'older brother' thing down pat. He *is* a few minutes older than I am. I liked to cook, and I didn't care who knew it. But in self-defense, and to keep Lucas from those bloody noses, I joined the football team. Kept me in shape. I had lots of friends, despite the cooking—most of them female."

Lucas grimaced when Rose giggled. Already she was succumbing to Nick's charm, and Lucas felt himself fade into the background as he always did when Nick was around and there was a woman in the room. "As we got older, things turned around. Nobody cares now that Nick cooks. Women flock to him like bees to honey." *Including you.*

Nick spoke up. "I think that's enough of a trip down memory lane, Lucas. I made lamb stew. Stay and have some." He spoke to both of them but looked at Rose, pulling out a chair and motioning for her to sit. Before either of them could answer, Nick winked at Rose. "I hope my brother is treating you right." He grinned widely.

"Yes, he is." A fine blush crept over her face, giving her a sweet innocence.

"Haven't fallen into any more cakes?"

Rose laughed, and Lucas felt the heat creep up his own neck. Then Rose replied. "That was an accident—my fault, really."

Nick snorted. "Right. You're a sweetheart. So, how about a bowl of stew?"

Lucas, still standing, pulled the papers out of his pocket and laid them on the table. "We've already eaten. We just stopped by to bring you these."

Nick picked up the papers and tossed them on the countertop. He glanced at Lucas. "Thanks." He angled his head toward Rose. "Lucas is efficient, a good business manager. I'm a good cook." He leaned in a little closer, invading Rose's space.

Lucas wanted to throw him against a wall, but Rose didn't seem to mind.

"Do you like to eat out?" Nick asked her, lowering his voice and waggling his brows.

"Yes, I do."

Lucas watched his brother flirt with Rose.

Nick waved toward the stove. "Come on. Just a small bowl?" He covered his heart with his hands. "You'll break my heart if you don't let me feed you."

Rose laughed. "Okay. A small bowl."

Nick rose and fixed two steaming bowls of stew, which he set in front of them.

Lucas sniffed appreciatively, hoping to take Nick's attention away from Rose. "I love your lamb stew, Nick."

Nick mumbled, "Thanks," but didn't move his gaze from Rose.

Lucas also looked at Rose. "We can't stay long. I have to get Rose home."

"What's the rush?" Nick asked, leaning over to stir Rose's stew. "It's hot. Be careful."

Rose lowered her eyes. "Lucas is right. I really have to get back." Nick dipped the spoon in the bowl and lifted a bite to her lips. Rose opened her mouth, and he slid the spoon inside. Her eyes widened. "This is fabulous."

Lucas clenched his hands at his side, watching Rose respond to Nick's attentions.

Nick dropped the spoon, which Rose picked up as she continued to eat.

"That means a lot coming from another cook. I think the new restaurant should do well. It's in a prime location. Has Lucas shown you—"

"Nick, why don't you put those papers in your office?" Suddenly, the room became too hot for Lucas. He hadn't considered that Nick might bring up the restaurant. This wasn't the way he wanted Rose to learn about the building purchase.

Rose was quiet on the drive home. Though Nick was a mirror image of Lucas, he was very different in personality, much more outgoing and flirtatious, while Lucas was quieter—not shy certainly, but not as comfortable in a party crowd as Nick would be.

"What did you think of Nick?" Lucas asked.

She turned slightly to face him. "I think he's very nice and a very talented cook, but you should have told me you had a look-alike in town."

Lucas had the grace to blush. "You're right. I just didn't know how to approach it. I wanted to get to know you first."

"Why would that matter?" He was quiet for so long, Rose thought he wasn't going to answer.

"Nick can be, um, overwhelming. Once he decides to pursue a woman, he doesn't really allow time for anyone else."

She lifted her brows in surprise. "I don't think Nick intends to pursue me, but even if he did, I have no intention of starting a relationship with anyone, particularly not a restaurant owner."

Lucas turned his head slightly. "Does that include me?"

"It includes every male in the city. I'm too busy building my business to expend time and energy maintaining a relationship. I thought I'd made that clear."

He frowned, then apparently decided to change the subject. "So are you going to join our softball team?"

"Is Nick on the team?" she teased.

"Yeah. He's a great hitter." She saw his sidelong glance but ignored it.

"He wasn't at church this morning."

"No, he attends with Mom and Dad. It's hard when we're both in the same place. People get confused. We've learned to handle it for the most part."

"Was Nick part of the puzzle you were trying to put together before you came back to the Lord?"

Lucas pulled into Rose's driveway. He shifted into park and turned off the ignition, then faced her. "As you could see, we're mirror images. Since we look alike, some assume we have the same personality as well. We don't. I didn't always appreciate Nick's unique qualities."

"Like his love of cooking. But you came to accept it?"

"Accept? Yes, and more. I value him. We get along well most times."

Lucas escorted Rose to her apartment. When she opened the door, a soft meow greeted them. Rose reached down to pick up the tortoiseshell Maine Coon that wrapped himself around her leg.

"I don't think you've been formally introduced," she said, lifting her head to meet Lucas's eyes. "Meet Bleu, named after Le Cordon Bleu Institute."

Lucas laughed and reached out to pet the cat, which purred softly. She lifted Bleu, kissed the top of his head, and then set him down.

"Would you like something to drink? Soda? Coffee?"

Lucas shook his head. "I really should go. The church youth meet in the late afternoon for a Bible study, and I usually try to be there. You're welcome to come with me if you'd like."

"Maybe another time. I'll think about the softball team." When his brow lifted, she added, "Of course it would have to be after I get the okay from the doctor. When do you need to know?"

"Whenever you're ready. Changes are accepted without question unless you're a really bad player."

"Then they'd kick me out?

"Nah, but they'd grumble at me."

She laughed. "When do you practice?"

"Saturday afternoons, two o'clock."

"At the church?"

"Yes. There's a big field behind the building."

She opened the door for him. "If I decide to participate, I'll let you know."

"Great. The team will love me if that throwing arm is any indication of your talents."

Rose laughed and shut the door behind Lucas. She leaned against it, feeling more alive than she'd felt in a long time.

Chapter 8

B atter up!"

Rose leaped from the bench and ran to stand at home plate. She hefted the bat and took a few practice swings. This was only her second time playing with the team, and it was an important game. It had taken more than four weeks for her shoulder to heal, and she was still supposed to be careful. She doubted her doctor would consider softball a recommended sport, but she decided she couldn't live her life worrying about being injured. She enjoyed playing with the group and wanted to do a good job.

She knew that Lucas, on the other hand, constantly worried about her playing so soon after her injury.

Nick yelled his encouragement over the roar of the crowd, and Rose knew, without looking, that Lucas was sitting quietly praying for her safety. It gave her a nice feeling, but it also concerned her that they'd become so close in such a short time.

Once Nick had seen she was only interested in his friendship, he'd backed off. He still liked to shower attention on her to tease Lucas. After that first visit to Nick's place, she and Lucas had not discussed relationships. She'd made it clear she didn't want one, but she had a feeling Lucas had conveniently forgotten that fact. Sometimes her conscience pricked her as they spent so much time together.

She closed her eyes briefly. *Lord, I know this is only a game, but it's an important one. I know the other team is praying just as hard, so I'll ask that no one gets hurt and we all go home friends. If You could see Your way clear to give us a reason to celebrate when it's over, however, I'd be grateful.*

The first swing was a strike. Rose put her head down and closed her eyes again. *And if I could not look too stupid up here, I'd really appreciate that, too, Lord.*

The second swing was a strike. Rose took a breath. The pitcher, a man, smiled at her and winked. Rose smiled back.

When the ball came at her, she knew she had to swing. She barely hit it and the ball rolled out of bounds.

"Foul!"

She could hear a combination of voices behind her.

"You can do it, Rosie!" That was Alex.

"Hit it high!" Nick yelled.

Rose took a second to glance over her shoulder. Lucas was standing, his fingers linked in the fence. He gave her a smile and a thumbs-up, and she turned back to face the pitcher, determined to win this game. If she struck out, it was over. If she got a base hit, at least someone else would be the one to win or lose. She'd have done her part.

Concentrating, she watched the pitcher. The man turned around and faced his teammates. She knew he was giving them hand signals, but of course, she didn't know which ones. Their team had similar signals depending on what kind of ball the pitcher had decided to throw.

When he turned around, his face was serious. He wound his arm and threw.

Rose watched the ball come at her, ready to swing. Her bat struck the ball with a satisfying crack. It flew high. She dropped the bat and ran, knowing the crowd in the stands was screaming. She prayed it wouldn't be a fly ball so she wouldn't have to walk back to the plate in disgrace. She kept her eyes on the base, trying not to think of where the ball was. As she got close to first base, Don signaled her to go on. She took his word and headed out. At second, Marcia yelled, "Go, Girl!"

Her side ached, and she was gasping for air. This was not the sort of exercise a caterer got on a daily basis. She continued to run, but when she rounded third, she had to look. The ball was in the air, heading home. She put on a burst of speed and dropped to slide into home plate, just as she heard the ball slap into the catcher's mitt and saw the player stumble while trying to tag her.

As Rose lay on the ground waiting for the call, she saw Lucas running toward her. It seemed forever before she heard the umpire yell. "Safe!"

The crowd went wild. The game was over, and her team had won.

Lucas reached her side as she started to get up. He dropped to the ground and laid his hand on her shoulder to stop her from rising too quickly.

"Slow and easy, Rose." Someone handed him a cup of water, and he encouraged her to drink. His hand unconsciously rubbed her back, and she felt his gaze on her as he tried to decide if she was all right.

Then others were crowding around, inquiring about her. She struggled to get up, but Lucas held her still. "Take it easy, Honey."

"I'm okay," she murmured in his ear. "Just a little winded. Don't make a fuss."

Alex dropped down beside her, holding Mia. "Big Sis, I'm proud of you." She leaned down and gave her a hug. Rose glanced over her sister's shoulder and saw Nick coming in for his hug. Lucas backed off, watching.

"I'll fix you a celebration dinner," Nick told her. "Everybody come to my house."

"We'll meet you there, Nick. I have to change my clothes." Rose looked down at her jeans, covered with dirt.

Lucas spoke up. "That sounds like a good idea."

Alex settled Mia on her hip, gave a little wave, and left the field, followed closely by Nick.

Lucas turned to Rose and helped her up. "You okay? You didn't hurt your arm again, did you?"

"I'm fine. My arm's fine. It's been a long time since I hit a home run."

Lucas grinned at her. "Felt good, huh?"

She beamed. "It felt terrific!"

He led her to his car and drove to her apartment where Rose stopped downstairs to pick up her mail. Bleu greeted them at the front door.

"Hey, Bleu. Miss me?" He watched her pick up the cat but quickly moved to take Bleu from her. Fortunately, the cat didn't object.

"You need to change quickly. Everyone's waiting for us."

"Okay."

Lucas sprawled on the sofa in the living room while Rose changed to clean jeans. When she returned, she stood in front of him. He smiled and held his hands out.

She took them, but before she could pull him up, Lucas pulled her down to the sofa.

"I've thought about it, and I think they can wait a bit. That was a tiring game," Lucas said, grinning.

Rose laughed and shook her head. "Nick is fixing food. I'm going. You can stay here if you want to."

Lucas groaned. "Oh, all right. I'm coming." He stood, lifting her up as well, and suddenly realized they were standing toe to toe. Rose looked up into his face, and his eyes met hers. "I was proud of you today. You did good," he whispered.

She ducked her head shyly, and he lifted her chin with his finger. Without thinking about it, he lowered his head and touched his lips to hers in a gentle kiss. Her arms went around his neck, and he pulled her to him.

He felt her smile as he captured her lips once again. Then he backed up. "Guess we'd better go," he said, his voice husky.

She nodded and led the way to the front door where Bleu had knocked the mail to the floor. Rose picked up the letters, scanning them quickly.

"Oh, look, here's one from my landlord." Rose picked out one letter from the group.

Lucas plucked the letter from her hand, hoping she'd forgive his rudeness. "You can read it later, can't you? Nick's cooking, remember?" Though Rose's brows came together as she looked at him, she said nothing and followed him to the car.

Time's up. I have to tell her today.

Cars filled Nick's driveway and spilled out onto the street. Apparently he had invited the entire team to join them.

Lucas walked with Rose to the den, where she was soon surrounded. She was everybody's hero, and though she'd never admit it, he thought she was enjoying the attention. He headed to the kitchen and found Nick busily preparing tacos. When he returned to the den, Rose was no longer there.

"Where's Rose?" he asked Alex.

Alex looked up. "She went that way." She pointed her thumb in the direction of the hall.

Lucas waited awhile, but when Rose didn't return, he began to wonder if something was wrong. He decided he'd better check and see. He walked down the hall and was passing Nick's office when he saw her.

She was kneeling on the floor near Nick's desk, scattered papers around her, one particular paper in her hand. Lucas recognized the purchase agreement for the Arby Avenue building.

"Rose?" Her head lifted, and the agony in her face made his breath catch. "What are you doing in here?"

She stared at him. "Nick said I could use the phone."

Her face contorted, and he cringed to see her anger directed at him. "You bought my building. For your restaurant." She looked down at the paper. "It's dated over a month ago. How could you do this? And how could you not tell me?"

He extended his hands, palms outward. "I can explain."

She stood and backed away from him. "There is no explanation."

Lucas watched the emotions crossing her face—rage, disillusionment, and betrayal. It was the last that tore his heart in two.

"It's not the way you think. There were reasons I—"

"I thought I knew you. I guess I was wrong. Please tell Nick I'm sorry. I'll get Alex to take me home."

"Please let me explain. Don't go like this."

She shook her head. "I can't stay here." She shoved her way past him and grabbed Alex's arm. "I need to leave. Will you drive me?"

Alex looked from her to Lucas and stood slowly, juggling Mia on her hip. "Sure. You okay?"

"Yes. I just need to leave. Now."

She turned and walked away without another word, head held high, not looking back once.

Lucas squeezed his eyes shut.

What now, Lord? I've messed up royally. I should have told her long ago. Is this it? Is it over?

Chapter 9

Rose stared at the letter in her hand:

Dear Miss Bentley,

Please be advised that I have sold the building at 311 Arby Avenue, which you presently rent. The new owners will honor your lease, which expires at the end of next month. That should give you sufficient time to find a new location.

My apologies for any inconvenience the change in ownership causes. I wish you success in your business.

Sincerely,
Jerrold Inkman

He had sold the building. *Her* building. And Lucas had bought it. The entire time he'd worked with her in the shop, he had known. The past weeks he'd taken her out to eat after practice, attended service and Sunday school with her, coaxed her to attend midweek Bible study with him—all that time, he'd known he was going to be evicting her. She clenched her hand in anger, crumpling the paper.

God never promised everything would go smoothly in life, but He did promise to be there with her whatever happened. *Sure need You now, Lord.*

She sank onto the sofa as tears began to fall. Bleu slipped onto her lap, and she petted the chubby cat. God's timing was always perfect. He had brought her closer to Him knowing she would need His comfort. The irony that God had used Lucas, her betrayer, to do that was not lost on her. She'd grown under Lucas's ministry, and now she had to move forward—without him.

She closed her eyes. Lucas had kissed her, right here in her living room, all the while knowing what he'd done. If he could do that, he didn't care for her as she'd hoped he did. It was best that he was out of her life. Her heart would be a lot steadier with Lucas gone. She could concentrate on her business, which was what she should have been doing anyway. Wherever it was located.

She regretted she'd have to give up the friends she'd made at Hope Village. She'd also have to leave the softball team. That was all right. She would find a way to minister in her own church. God would still come first in her life, even if she didn't understand why He'd allowed this to happen.

On Sunday, Rose returned to Lakeview Church. She found she missed the upbeat music and powerful sermons Pastor Charles delivered at Hope Village, the in-depth Sunday school classes, and the camaraderie that was shared. Still, every church had its good and bad points. She'd been pleased with Lakeview before, and she would be again. *But you were just warming a pew here. There you were participating.* She squeezed her eyes tightly shut. That was true, but that could change. A large church needed even more people to minister to the congregation than a small church.

When she returned home, the light on her answering machine was blinking. She sighed, sat down, and reached a trembling hand to hit the play button.

"Rose." Her heart caught at the pain in Lucas's voice. "I know you're angry with me—and with good reason. I should have told you about the sale. I thought—well, it doesn't matter what I thought. I was wrong. I didn't know you when I signed the papers to buy the building. But I have to be honest and tell you I would have bought it anyway. I'd like to talk to you and explain." He paused. "I hate that you didn't come to church today. I hope it wasn't because of me. I think you could be happy at Hope Village. Please call me." There was a pause and then a click.

So that was that. What they'd been to one another didn't matter. He still would have kicked her into the streets. A little sob caught in her throat.

The explanation for his deception didn't matter. Trust was important to her, and she couldn't trust him. As much as it hurt, it was time to move forward.

It was a long time before she could sleep, and even then, it was a restless night. When she woke, she knew what she had to do.

Lucas stared at the words on the front window of his new restaurant: MONTGOMERY'S. Plain and simple. It should have been a proud moment, yet all he felt was a sense of loss.

It had been weeks since he'd seen Rose. He'd come to see her at the catering shop, only to discover she'd already moved out. He'd called her several times, but she didn't answer the phone or return his calls. He'd even tried calling Alex, but Rose's sister would have nothing to do with him. Several times, he'd almost gone to her apartment, but her message was clear—stay away.

He had known he would miss Rose, but it surprised him how deeply he felt the loss. At the strangest times, he would be reminded of her by a scent or a word. He ached to see her again. She hadn't returned to Hope Village, which caused him further pain. He wanted to do something, but he didn't know what.

Rose was obviously not open to hearing his side of the matter. He knew she was hurt. He desperately needed to explain things to her, but she wouldn't give him a chance. The problem consumed him until he couldn't concentrate on anything else.

His shoulders slumped as he sighed deeply. Though he had renewed old friendships since moving back to Loudon and had family surrounding him now, he still felt alone. The word held a different meaning to him now. *Alone* meant being without Rose.

Though he longed for her, he had no idea how to make amends. Did Rose even care? Had their time together meant nothing to her? It amazed him that he could feel this way after spending only a few weeks in her company. Surely he hadn't misread her so completely.

He knew he needed to ensure this was a lasting love and not an emotional infatuation. Yet he'd never wanted to make a commitment to one woman like he wanted to make one to Rose.

What did it matter if he had a successful restaurant but no one to share the joy of his success? If it were only his decision, he'd gladly have given up the building, even with all the money they'd spent on renovations, but Nick was also owner of the building and had scoured the city to find a location perfect for their needs. Lucas hadn't known Rose then. The deal had been made before she was a part of his life.

How could he make everyone he loved happy when they were at cross-purposes? He blinked. Did everyone he loved include Rose? The thought made his heart race.

As he stood there contemplating this new piece of information, Nick walked up.

"We'll be able to open soon."

Lucas looked over at his brother. "Just another week."

"Do you think Rose will come?"

"I don't think so, Nick. Rose isn't very happy with me."

"She's a nice gal. I'm sorry things didn't work out for you two."

Lucas sighed. "She won't even talk to me."

Nick put his hand on Lucas's shoulder. "If it's the building that's the problem, why don't we just share it?"

Nick's simple statement stopped Lucas dead in his tracks.

"Share?" Lucas pictured the room in his mind. "Do you think it's possible?" Without waiting for his brother's reply, Lucas strode quickly to the kitchen. He was vaguely aware of Nick behind him, close on his heels.

Lucas looked over the appliances and the counter space. "It would be a bit cozy with two cooks in here, Nick."

Nick shrugged. "I'm sure we could work it out. Most of her jobs require her to bake during the day. I work mostly at night. She could keep her business. We could even pass on some jobs to her. Our other restaurants have occasionally been contacted for catering jobs, but we haven't wanted to go in that direction. This could be another service for our customers. There's also a lot of room for expansion if we want to do that."

"Right. That would give her more business, yet keep her independent. I just don't know if she would see it that way." Again, he studied the large room. "I know we've already put a lot of money into this place with the renovations in the dining area, but maybe we could add some counter space and another oven and stove on the other end of the room. That way you wouldn't be in one another's way."

His thoughts moving at warp speed, Lucas saw the new room in his head. He remembered that Alex worked as a carpenter, and from what Rose had told him, she was good and could use the money. Being a single mother wasn't easy. Maybe she would take the job.

It was a good plan, but would it make a difference to Rose?

He sat down heavily. He didn't know if it was fair to ask her, but he had to try.

He had hurt her once. She might forgive him that, but if he hurt her again. . . He needed to be sure. Was he ready to make a commitment to her? A lifetime commitment?

His head in his hands, Lucas pushed everything else out of his mind and began to pray.

Chapter 10

His finger poised above the doorbell to Rose's apartment, Lucas shifted from one foot to the other. He'd made the decision not to call first, knowing she probably wouldn't talk to him, and if she did, she would refuse to accompany him. She might even leave the apartment if she knew he was coming. It would be harder for her to refuse if he was standing right in front of her.

He pressed a finger to the bright piece of plastic and heard the tones chime within. No sound came from inside, so he rang again. Relief poured through him when he heard the lock turning.

"Why are you here, Lucas?" Her clipped tones told him he was not a welcomed guest.

He forced a smile. "I have a surprise for you."

"A surprise? Why would you show up at my door, with no warning I might add, with a surprise? Especially since you know that I don't like surprises. You also have no business being here since any relationship we had previously is over." She moved her head to look around him, her eyes narrowed, her expression unyielding. "I don't see anything."

He grimaced. "Yes, you've made yourself perfectly clear. I didn't give you any warning because you won't take my calls." He sighed, rubbing the back of his neck to ease the aching muscles. "It wasn't possible to bring it here. I need to take you to it."

Hands on her hips, she stared at him. "I'm not going anywhere with you."

He reached for her hand and gave it a gentle squeeze. "Please, Rose. I know you have no reason to trust me, but I'm hoping you'll give me a second chance. You don't have any plans, do you? You're not catering a party tonight?"

"Nooo," she said slowly. He suspected she was tempted to lie, but to her credit, she didn't.

"So you can allow me a little of your time. I wouldn't do anything to hurt you."

"You've already hurt me."

Lucas winced and dropped her hand. "Touché. I'm sorrier about that than I've ever been about anything in my life." He shoved his hands in his pockets and forced himself to meet her eyes. "Come with me. Please. It's important."

Her head tilted and her expression softened. "Is something wrong? Is it Nick? Your parents?"

It touched him that she still cared, even if it was about his family and not himself, but he wasn't going to lie to her. "No. Nothing's wrong. In fact, I hope to make everything right."

He waited tense seconds while she thought about his request. Then she turned and went back inside. She left the door open, though she didn't invite him in. Seconds later, she returned carrying a sweater and her purse.

Stepping ahead of him, she walked slowly to his car. Lucas opened the passenger door so she could slide inside, being careful not to crowd her, and soon they were on the road.

"Where are we going?"

"You don't expect me to tell you that, right? It's a surprise."

"I think we've established I don't like surprises."

"You'll like this one." *I hope.*

A few minutes later, Lucas pulled onto a dirt road. He knew Rose would soon see his surprise. It was hard to miss.

"What?"

He knew the moment she saw it.

"A hot air balloon? That's the surprise?"

"Yep. You've never ridden in one, have you?" His heart was beating wildly as he waited for her answer. She'd spent all of her time on her schooling and then her business. He didn't imagine she'd taken time for a frivolous thing like a balloon ride.

"No. And I'm not going to today."

Lucas pulled the car to a stop. "Why not? I chartered it especially for you."

"You should have asked me first, and I'd have saved you the trouble—and the exorbitant fee I'm sure they charge. Those rides take a long time. I have work to do."

Lucas turned to face her, trying to keep his frustration from showing on his face. This was his last chance. His only chance. He was desperate to have uninterrupted time with her. "Work. That's all you think about. There's more to life than work. Are you afraid of having fun, Rose? Are you afraid you might just like it and have to think of somebody and something other than business?" He drew a hand through his thick hair. "Rose, take a chance. Take a giant leap of faith. You need to do this."

"How would you know what I need?" Rose shoved open her door and strode away from the car in the direction from which they'd come.

"Rose!" Lucas's voice echoed behind her as she stomped off.

If she'd been thinking properly, she wouldn't have agreed to come. She shouldn't be here. She had a life. It just happened that work was a big part of it. She was grateful to Lucas for reminding her she needed to put God at its center, but that didn't give him the right to tell her what to do with the rest of it.

Lucas caught up with her and placed himself in front of her so she had to stop. She crossed her arms and stood still, tapping her foot in obvious irritation. When she refused to look at him, he lifted her chin with his finger.

"I'm sorry," he said. His voice was soft and quiet. "You're right. I should have asked you before setting this up. If you want to go back, you don't have to walk. I'll take you. But, Rose, I'd appreciate it if you'd give me a chance."

Rose looked into his earnest face. How could she trust him after weeks of deceit? She'd never risked her heart as much as she would today if she allowed Lucas to see how much she'd missed him.

Taking a balloon ride with him in a small confined space

would risk so much. Though she wished it weren't true, she was afraid she'd already lost her heart to Lucas Montgomery.

The gift of a balloon ride was a generous one. He'd gone to a lot of trouble for her. During the annual July balloon festival they offered rides, but they were early in the morning and in the evening. He would have made special arrangements for this mid-morning ride.

"All right. I'll go, but, Lucas, don't do this again."

"Deal. No more surprise balloon rides." He took her hand and led her to the basket. Before they entered, however, he stopped. "You're not afraid of heights, are you?"

Rose studied the basket in front of her. "I never have been, but then I've never been in an open basket in the sky, either." She took a step forward with determination. "Let's go."

She allowed Lucas to help her into the sturdy basket where the pilot already waited. Lucas slipped inside, moving to stand close to her. There was nowhere to go, so she gritted her teeth and waited to see what would happen next.

As they slowly gained altitude, Lucas risked a glance at Rose. She wasn't smiling, but she wasn't frowning, either. *Please, Lord, don't let her get airsick.*

"Rose?"

She turned toward him, and he once again thanked the Lord for placing this woman in his path. Her strength and courage constantly astounded him. He couldn't believe he'd ever doubted his feelings for her. Now he could only hope she felt the same way and would give him a chance to make up for the hurt he'd caused her.

"Yes?"

"I have another surprise for you." Her scowl reminded him she didn't like surprises.

"Another surprise? The first one turned out so well."

Her sarcasm didn't escape his notice, but he ignored it. With his finger he turned her head so she could see the land beneath them. "Look. All God's creation laid out before us."

She looked, and he saw the beginnings of a smile light her face.

"I've missed you, Rose."

Her gaze on the scene below, she admitted, "I've missed you, too."

"I'm sorry I wasn't honest with you about the building purchase. I thought if we got to know each other first. . . and then I thought it wasn't my place to tell you. Anyway, I was wrong, and I'm sorry. Can you forgive me?"

"Forgive you? Yes. God has forgiven me many times. But trust you? That's more difficult."

"I'd give anything to win back that trust. I had to buy that building. I'd already signed the papers when we met. I couldn't *not* buy it." He reached to take her hand and was grateful when she didn't pull it away. "I talked to Nick, and he agreed that our businesses are not in competition. We can help one another. We can share the building."

"Share the building?" She frowned as she turned to face him.

"Yes. If you agree. I've had your name added to the deed. Your copy is in the car." Swallowing hard, he lifted his gaze to meet hers. "Even more important than that, Rose, I want

258

to share my life with you. I love you. I'm asking you to be my wife."

Her frown deepened. Lucas felt his heart lurch. "So you're saying if I agree to marry you, I become a partner with you and Nick?"

He shook his head slowly. "No. The building is one-third yours—if you want it—regardless of your answer."

"I can't afford to buy a third of a building—any building."

"I'm not worried about that. We can work out the finances."

"You would continue to work with me if I refused to marry you?"

His heart breaking, Lucas hesitated. "No. I don't think I could do that."

Her face paled, but she met his eyes. "I see."

Lucas shook his head. "I don't think you do, Rose. You'll own one-third of the building, regardless of our personal relationship. But I couldn't stay here and watch you fall in love with somebody else. I would respect your wishes, however, whatever they are."

They were quiet as the balloon passed over the area.

Having been informed by Lucas that he didn't need the tourist spiel, the pilot remained silent except when communicating with the ground crew in the chase vehicle, which kept them in sight. When he began to make landing preparations, Lucas pulled Rose to the side.

"I don't want to pressure you, Rose. Take some time to pray about what I've said. Nick will be in touch with you about the shop. If you're willing to work with him, you can move back to Arby Avenue as soon as you're ready. The restaurant is open for dinner at five. I think the business arrangement will be beneficial to everyone, but if you don't want to do it, you can opt out." He wanted to say more, but he bit his lip to stop the words.

When they landed, the chase crew drove them back to his car. Rose settled herself in the front seat, and Lucas retrieved the revised deed from his briefcase, handing it to her.

Watching her face as she read through it, he realized he needed to get her home—before he did something stupid like pull her into his arms and never let her go again.

Chapter 11

Rose sat quietly in the seat beside Lucas. He said he loved her. He'd asked her to marry him. He'd even given her part ownership of the building she wanted. He was giving her everything she could want. Yet that was the point. She didn't want it given to her. Her independence was important. Rose wanted to succeed or fail on her own. Could she accept Lucas's offer and still do that?

Her mind was awhirl with mixed emotions. On the one hand, she hated working out of her apartment. On the other, sharing the building would be an adjustment to all of them. If it didn't work out, she'd have to move again.

Since she hadn't had time to find a new building, Lucas's offer would certainly fix one problem. But if she was to share the building, then she should share the cost. At the least, she could pay him the same amount she was paying Mr. Inkman for rent.

Though the finances were important, they weren't the real issue. Could she get past her hurt feelings and her distrust? She knew she loved Lucas. There was no doubt in her mind about that. But was it enough?

Her gaze moved to him. His blue eyes remained focused on the road—the eyes that had attracted her from the first when she and Lucas had fallen into Abby's cake. Even in profile, she could see he was tense. He'd laid his heart out to her. Could she do any less?

When he drove up to her apartment, she hopped out of the car before he could walk around, hoping he'd remain in the vehicle and leave. Rather, he escorted her upstairs and stood waiting patiently while she opened the door. She turned to face him then, uncertain of what to say.

Before she had a chance to speak, he placed his finger on her lips.

"Don't answer me now," he said softly. "Think about it. I love you, but I only want you if you want to be with me. It has to be your decision. Freely made."

He leaned down and kissed her cheek gently. Then he reached for her hand and held it, looking at it solemnly. He must not have been able to find the words, because he simply squeezed it as he'd done many times before, then turned to leave.

"Lucas." His name was out of her mouth before she could stop it.

He turned, and the hopeful look on his face tore at her heart. "Yes?"

"I *will* think about it. I do love you, but I'm not sure it's enough."

He looked at her seriously, though his eyes lit up at her declaration. "Love overcomes, Rose. Jesus showed us that.

Call me when you're ready."

Then he was gone.

The restaurant was crowded. The grand opening of Montgomery's was a rousing success.

Nick was in his element at the stove, creating masterpieces for their opening night. Lucas wasn't worried about Nick. The menu was set. Nick would shine.

Lucas barely had time to think as he moved from place to place, checking details, greeting guests. Though he'd hired a hostess, this first night he wanted to be in view. A visible owner made people feel special.

The bell over the door would have to go. It was driving him crazy. Why had he never noticed it before? When it rang for the hundredth time that night, Lucas gritted his teeth and glanced up. His heart caught in his throat.

In a combination of moonlight from the window and soft fluorescent lighting from the fixture at the entrance stood Rose, an uncertain smile on her lips, as though unsure of her reception.

His heart pounded, but he forced himself to move slowly toward her as she stood in the line of customers waiting to be seated. He knew the moment she saw him. Her eyes lit up, and her smile grew brighter, though the hesitation was still there. Didn't she know he would have given anything to have her by his side tonight?

"Rose," he said softly. Just saying her name made his heart soar. He moved to her side and reached a hand out to her. She placed her hand in his. He drew her to him, and they moved to the side, out of the flow of traffic. "Are you here for dinner?"

He didn't want to assume anything. He'd promised her no pressure. Perhaps she just wanted to be supportive since she was listed as part owner.

She pursed her lips and fidgeted. "Yes, I suppose. Could we go somewhere and talk first? I know this is a bad time." She chuckled. "A terrible time, I guess. You must be so busy."

"I always have time for you, Rose." He said the words quietly with as much sincerity as he could muster.

He led her to the back to the office that had recently been hers. Motioning for her to sit, he eased himself down next to her, close but not touching, waiting for her to speak.

Her eyes were shiny when she lifted her face to look at him, and his heart went out to her. Was she going to refuse him?

She lifted her hand and caressed his face. Lucas closed his eyes and laid his own hand atop hers.

"I need to ask your forgiveness," she said softly. Her voice was quiet but strong. "I've been thinking of only myself and my needs."

He opened his eyes and looked at her. "You don't need my forgiveness, but you have it if you'll give me yours."

Tears made little trails along her cheeks.

"Don't cry, Sweetheart." He couldn't stand her tears. Even if it meant he would never see her again, he wouldn't have her hurt. *Lord, help me to bear it if she's going to leave me. Your will be done. Not mine.*

"I was angry with you, and then I was confused because

you were giving me everything I wanted and I didn't understand why." She hesitated. "Then I found this." She reached into her handbag and withdrew the dried-up portion of the bouquet she'd caught at Abby's wedding. "It reminded me of the prayer I prayed the day I caught it. I asked God to help me find someone who would look at me with the love I saw in Stan's eyes when he looked at Abby. Someone who would understand about my business."

Lucas stared at their joined hands, resting on the sofa between them. "And did He?"

"Yes. I saw that look in your eyes the day we took the balloon ride. And when you offered to share this building, I knew you cared about my business."

Lucas nodded and lifted his head to look in her eyes. "Rose, did you mean it when you said you loved me?"

He held his breath while he waited for her answer. Her hand tensed, and she turned it over and entwined her fingers with his.

"Yes. I love you with all my heart. You reminded me that a life without God at its center is not a life at all. Your commitment to the Lord warms my heart. I've seen my own faith bloom as I watched you worship. I want to build a life, and a family, with you."

Heart soaring, he took her face in his hands. "You are God's answer to my prayers, Sweetheart." Lucas lowered his head, his lips meeting hers, sharing all the love in his heart with his kiss.

SANDRA PETIT

Sandra Petit grew up in southern Louisiana and lives in the New Orleans area with her husband of more than twenty years and her two teenage, home-schooled children. She believes God's timing is always perfect and welcomes the opportunity He has given her to share her faith through tales of romance. She prays that each of her readers will experience the love and joy of having Jesus in their lives and invites you to visit her web site at http://www.sandrapetit.com.

Flowers for a Friend

by Gail Sattler

Chapter 1

I'll bet they make the playoffs, maybe even win the Stanley Cup."

Geoff Manfrey opened his mouth to express his doubts when something lightweight smacked him on top of his head, then stuck in his hair. He started to raise one hand to find out what hit him when a crash resounded from the back of the banquet room. He turned to see what happened at the same time that he touched what felt like a plant on top of his head. Gales of laughter filled the room.

The closest laughing person was his friend Jason, who was also a guest at Abby and Stan's wedding. Instead of watching the action at the source of the crash—the caterer and the best man falling into the wedding cake—Jason was pointing at Geoff, laughing so hard his face had turned red.

"Look at you! You caught the bride's bouquet! You're going to be the next to get married."

"Very funny," Geoff mumbled, then winced as he tried to remove the flowers from his head. Some kind of tape was attached to the bundle, which made it impossible to dislodge the flowers without pulling out some hair. Since Jason wasn't offering to help, Geoff raised both hands to try to disengage the tape with a minimum of hair loss.

A camera flash glared in his face.

Geoff blinked to get rid of the spots in his eyes. "Very funny, David. Would you like to help?"

"No way. Too many great pictures are waiting to be taken."

Before Geoff could reply, David disappeared into the crowd.

Gradually, the laughter in the room died down. Since Geoff's seat at his table was next to the wall, only Jason and David had seen him. He wanted to keep it that way, because he didn't want to become the next source of amusement. However, since everyone's attention no longer remained focused on the mess with the cake, his chances of no one else noticing the flowers stuck to his head were shrinking. Since he was just twenty-eight, he didn't have to worry about missing a few strands from on top; his hair would grow back. Instead of waiting for help, Geoff gritted his teeth, mentally wrote off his losses, and yanked.

While he massaged the tender spot on his head, he ignored the strands of his hair stuck to the errant piece of tape and stared at the flowers.

This was the bride's bouquet or, judging from snippets of conversation around him, a fourth of Abby's bouquet.

He had no intention of keeping the bride's bouquet or any portion of it. However, the throng of husband-hungry women from the center of the room had already dispersed.

He laid the flowers on the table in front of him. Being a

Christian, he wasn't superstitious in any way, but he didn't like the idea of what keeping the bouquet implied—that he would be the next to get married. He knew, and God knew, that he would never marry.

As Geoff continued to stare blankly at the flowers, a little voice piped up behind him.

"Hi, Geoff!"

Geoff turned in the chair, then looked down. "Hi, Jenni," he said, smiling.

If David had any brains, instead of taking a picture of Geoff with the flowers in his hair, he would have been taking pictures of little Jenni.

Geoff didn't want to be biased, but he thought Jenni was the cutest and sweetest little girl he knew. Her blond hair flowed around her cherub face, and her blue eyes sparkled when she smiled. Today, wearing her little flower girl's dress, the same as the rest of the bridesmaids' dresses except in a miniature format, she looked extra special. Geoff didn't know much about ladies' clothing, but he thought that the dresses with the white tops and multicolored bottoms that were the same colors as the different flowers in Abby's bouquet—before it got all smashed up—looked just as good on six-year-old Jenni as they did on the full-grown women. Jenni had taken the responsibility of being in the bridal party very seriously.

Because he saw Jenni and her sister often, he knew that Jenni had been having a rough time over the past year after the tragic death of her parents. She was sad much of the time, even when she played with the other children. But today, she shone as the flower girl. Geoff wished there was something he could do to keep that sweet smile on her face more often.

He glanced back to the flowers on the table. Jenni had been in the throng of single women, hoping to catch the bouquet, regardless of the fact that she was only half the height of the adult women and didn't stand a chance.

Geoff picked up the flowers, rose from the chair, then hunkered down until one knee rested on the floor.

"Jenni, I think they were really meant for you."

Her face lit up like a Christmas tree as she accepted them. "Wow! You caught Abby's bouquet! That means you're going to get married soon! But if I was 'posed to get them, that means you're going to marry me!"

Geoff's smile dropped. "But—"

Before he could tell Jenni that the sequence of events wasn't necessarily related, Jenni threw her arms around him and gave him a big bear hug. "I love you, too, Geoff! I gotta tell Rissa!" She released him, turned, and skipped off into the crowd of other guests. Geoff plainly heard her animated voice announcing to anyone who would listen that she had the bouquet and she was getting married next. To him. Some of the ladies around her giggled.

"Nice one, Geoff," Jason muttered beside him.

Geoff remained in his hunkered down position. He lowered one arm to rest his hand on his knee, and the other fist he planted on his hip as he listened to Jenni showing off the flowers. "Never mind," he mumbled. "By tomorrow she'll forget all about this."

Instead of Jason's deep voice, a female pitch replied. "No, she won't."

Geoff jumped to his feet and spun around to see Clarissa, Jenni's older sister.

Like Jenni, Clarissa looked extra nice today. She was average looking—thin but not too skinny, with shoulder-length dark blond hair that flowed in gentle waves around a pleasant oval face. Clarissa and Jenni looked a lot alike, despite their age difference, except for their eyes. Jenni had big, beautiful blue eyes, yet Clarissa's eyes were a unique hazel mixture.

Lately, he'd seen her most Sundays in church, but when it wasn't winter, he saw both Clarissa and Jenni nearly every day when he was out walking his dog. He always enjoyed talking to Clarissa. Like him, she also read a lot, and they enjoyed many of the same books. She even owned a book autographed by his favorite author. In general, Clarissa was easy to talk to, and best of all, safe. Their friendship started with talking in the neighborhood when he was out with Spot and she was out with Jenni, and that was all it would ever be. No expectations, no rules, yet they could talk about anything and everything, good and bad, and then go right back to the way things were—friendly and casual.

Today, however, she was far from casual. Her pretty hazel eyes were narrowed, and her mouth had tightened into a thin line. He could almost feel the chill as she glowered at him.

Geoff cleared his throat and forced himself to smile. "Hi, Clarissa. How's it going?"

"It was going pretty well until you gave her the flowers."

"I only thought—"

"Surely you must have known that she's got a major crush on you."

"Well, I—"

"And now you're encouraging her!"

"But—" Before he could think of something worthwhile to say, Jenni's voice echoed from the crowd, telling someone else that she was going to marry him.

Clarissa waved one arm in the air in Jenni's direction, then crossed her arms again. "Look at what you've done!"

Geoff shrugged his shoulders. "She's just a little kid. She really has no idea what she's saying."

Clarissa continued to glare at him, not relaxing her stance. "That only makes it worse. Since we haven't been seeing each other as much over the winter, every time she sees you she has to recount everything you did."

Somehow, Geoff didn't think Clarissa meant to be flattering. He often saw Jenni at the living-room window as he drove past their house when he arrived home from work, since Clarissa and Jenni didn't go to the park in March. He always waved to her, and she waved back.

He rammed his hands in his pockets. "I don't know what to say. She's a great little kid."

At his words, Clarissa's posture relaxed. "I'm sorry. I guess I'm probably being overprotective. She's been so happy about being flower girl, I guess all the wedding preparation has gone to her head. For the first time in a very long time, she's been happy. When reality hits that you're not going to marry her, I hope she's not going to be too hurt."

The murmur of low voices buzzed around him. Slightly above the volume of the rest of the crowd, Jenni's excited voice once again carried to him as she continued to show off the flowers to everyone in her immediate vicinity. He didn't want to give Jenni false hopes, but he didn't want to break her heart, either.

Geoff remembered the day he'd heard the couple a few doors down had been killed in a car accident. Jenni had only been spared because she had been properly secured in her safety-approved child seat. Rather than sell the house, Clarissa moved back in to raise Jenni, and that's when he first met her.

Geoff cleared his throat and forced himself to smile. "I'll admit I don't know much about little kids, but I'm sure she doesn't expect that I'm going to jump up and marry her tomorrow. By the time the flowers are dead, so will this little thing she's got for me. Just give her some time."

"I don't know. . . ." Clarissa's voice trailed off.

"Besides, now that I know what she's thinking, I can steer her away from the topic if it ever comes up and let her down gently. Soon she'll forget all about it. Little kids have short memories."

"You just told me you didn't know much about little kids."

He shrugged his shoulders and forced himself to smile, although he knew he probably looked pretty lame. "That's just what I heard."

"I don't know about that." Clarissa turned to the crowd. "Stan and Abby are leaving now. I should take Jenni and go say good-bye."

"I've already talked to them, so I'm staying right here. I guess I'll see you and Jenni at church tomorrow."

She nodded and walked away without saying a word, which Geoff didn't think was a bad thing.

Chapter 2

Clarissa Reynolds pulled up her collar when a blast of wind caught her hair. For now, the temperature was below freezing, but by the time church got out, the day would be warmer and the snow would be melting. Still, it wasn't quite spring temperatures.

She looked down to her right. "Are you warm enough, Jenni? Did you remember to wrap your scarf up tight?"

"Yes, Rissa. I'm warm. I even gots my ears covered."

Clarissa cringed inwardly at her little sister's diction, then reminded herself that Jenni was still only in first grade. "Let's hurry. We don't want to be late."

They hustled along side by side on the three-block journey to church.

Twenty-three years ago, when she was Jenni's age, Clarissa remembered walking to church with her parents, swinging between them, all three of them laughing as they tossed her into the snow so she could make angels without making footprints to get there.

There could be no such memories for Jenni. There was no

one else to hold Jenni from the other side. It made Clarissa's reminiscences bittersweet.

Pushing those thoughts aside, Clarissa watched as Jenni started to skip. It warmed her from the inside out to see Jenni so happy. However, knowing the reason for Jenni's mood was only because they would see Geoff at church set the chill back, right down to her bones. She didn't want to think of what would happen when Jenni realized that Geoff wasn't going to marry her.

Geoff.

She couldn't help but like him. While she wouldn't have called him handsome, he was by no means ugly. His dirty blond hair was a nice, fashionable length. Some days his eyes were a dull green, other days a smoky gray, but he had the nicest, longest eyelashes she'd ever seen on a man. She didn't know why that fascinated her, but it did.

When they were together, they never lacked for conversation. Many days she didn't have the time or energy to take Jenni out, but she did anyway because she knew she would see Geoff. Since he only lived three houses away, he was easy to catch.

He'd been so nice to Jenni to give her the flowers, Clarissa had found it difficult to stay angry with him; after all, he'd meant well.

"Look, Rissa! I see Geoff's car!" Jenni started to run.

Clarissa cleared her thoughts, ran a few steps to catch up, and grabbed Jenni by the shoulder. "Don't run away from me. You hold my hand while we cross the street."

For once, Jenni didn't complain that she wasn't a baby.

Clarissa didn't know if that was good or bad.

They stomped the snow off their boots, ascended the stairs, and walked inside the foyer of the large church building. Just her luck, Geoff stood in a circle of people about their age, talking and laughing.

Before Clarissa could stop her, Jenni bolted forward, waving her arms as she ran. "Geoff! Hi, Geoff!"

He flinched at the sound of her voice, then excused himself from his group of friends. He turned around and hunkered down so he was at eye level with her when he spoke. "Hi, Jenni. It's good to see you. It's almost time for Sunday school."

"Will you walk me to my class?"

Before he could reply, Jenni grabbed his hand and pulled him away from his friends.

Together Clarissa and Geoff dropped Jenni off at her classroom, then turned in the direction of the adult classrooms.

Clarissa didn't want to be nervous about Jenni's "relationship" with Geoff, but she had to be both cautious and realistic. Jenni had never acted so infatuated with anyone of the male species before: not with a boy her own age and certainly not with a grown man. Just as Geoff had said, hopefully Jenni would soon forget about wanting to marry him. However, if Jenni didn't, she had to have a Plan B, which probably would have to involve Geoff.

The trouble was, she couldn't see getting any time alone with Geoff to talk about it. During the winter, pretty much the only time she saw him was in the foyer at church. However, she had to talk to him without her sister present.

She faced forward as she walked, hoping to appear casual

as she spoke. "I think I'm going to try out another class on Sunday mornings. Do you mind if I go in the same one as you?"

She could see him turn his head in her peripheral vision. "Not at all. You probably already know most of the people, and there's always room for one more." He stepped aside to allow her to go in before him, then took a seat beside David. Since the seat on Geoff's other side was vacant, Clarissa sat there.

Right as she opened her mouth to see if Geoff had any ideas, the leader began the session. Just her luck, the discussion went overtime, which didn't give her the time she needed to talk to Geoff since she had to run back to collect Jenni from her classroom.

She led Jenni to their usual seats near the front of the sanctuary.

"Rissa? Where's Geoff?"

Clarissa gave her sister's hand a little squeeze. "I don't know. I guess he's gone to sit with his friends. Now let's enjoy the service."

All through the service, Jenni continuously and not-so-discreetly kept glancing behind them. It was all Clarissa could do to keep herself from also looking behind to see where he was.

When the service ended, Jenni didn't give Clarissa any time to chat with the people nearby. She grabbed Clarissa's hand and nearly dragged her into the foyer. Jenni's disappointment at being unable to find Geoff was so vivid it was almost tangible.

Again, Clarissa gave her sister's hand an encouraging squeeze. "It's okay, Jenni. We'll see him again next Sunday. Now let's go home."

"But next Sunday is so long."

"The week will go by faster if you keep busy. There are cookies to bake this afternoon. We can make a nice casserole for supper, and then tomorrow is school. You'll see how fast it will be next Sunday. Now let's go home and make lunch."

Judging from Jenni's pouty-lipped frown, Clarissa could tell she wasn't convinced. However, not seeing Geoff for a week would do Jenni a world of good to help put some distance between them. The next step would be to remove the partial bouquet from Jenni's bedroom so she wouldn't think of Geoff when she couldn't see him.

Jenni's words as the cookies came out of the oven caught Clarissa completely off guard.

"Can I take some to Geoff? I bet he's home now."

"He may be home, but he's probably busy." At least she hoped he was busy.

"Please?" Jenni's eyes opened wide.

"But that means we have to get all dressed in our coats and boots again."

"That's okay. I think Geoff would really like some cookies. They're my favorite."

Clarissa opened her mouth to protest but changed her mind. While she didn't want to actively encourage Jenni, she didn't want it to look like she was trying to discourage

280

her, either. She wanted her sister's emotional attachment to Geoff to die a natural death.

"Okay, let's get dressed."

Clarissa squeezed her eyes shut as Jenni squealed with glee and ran out of the kitchen. To the sounds of the closet door banging and of boots thumping against the wall, Clarissa filled a small container with fresh, warm cookies. By the time she reached the closet, Jenni already had her boots on and was slipping into her coat.

Jenni chattered brightly while they walked to Geoff's house, three doors down.

The second their feet touched the step, Geoff's dog started barking. Even though it would have been obvious there was someone at the door, Jenni knocked loudly, then immediately turned to Clarissa, her expression very serious for a little girl. "It's a good thing Geoff lives on the same side of the street as us."

Before Clarissa could think of an appropriate response, the door opened.

Geoff stood in the doorway, still wearing the same clothes he'd worn to church, with his little dog cradled in his arms. "Uh. . .hi, Clarissa, Jenni." His gaze lowered to the container in Jenni's hand. "Uh. . .come in."

The door had barely closed behind them when Jenni held the container at arm's length in front of her toward Geoff. "I made these for you!"

He tucked the dog under one arm, then accepted the container with a smile. "Cookies! Thank you."

"If you already ate lunch, you can have one now."

He fumbled between the container and the dog until he managed to pick out one cookie. He grinned as he bit into the still-warm treat. "Would you like to sit down or something? I think I can find some juice for Jenni, and I happen to have a pot of coffee made. If you're interested."

"No, I think we'd better not. I—"

"Oh, boy!" Jenni chirped as she kicked off her boots. "Can I hold Spot?"

He squatted down, still holding the container of cookies in one hand, the dog in the other. "My hands are kind of full. You're going to have to take him."

Jenni grabbed the dog far too quickly. Spot, however, took the innocent manhandling in stride. Not only did he go without protest, he immediately started licking Jenni's face once she managed to get a decent grip on him.

Geoff grinned. "Spot obviously has missed you over the winter."

Jenni giggled.

Clarissa mumbled, "That name must have taken a lot of forethought."

Geoff's grin widened as he rose. "He really does have a spot on his back. Do you know any other dogs named Spot?"

"Well, no."

" 'Nuff said. Let's go into the living room. What do you take in your coffee?"

"Just milk or cream or whatever you have that's white, so long as it's a real liquid and not that powdered stuff."

"I agree. I'll be right back."

While Geoff poured the coffee, Clarissa took a seat and

glanced around Geoff's living room. For a man's home, she supposed it was fairly tidy, perhaps even tidier than her own living room, but he didn't have a six-year-old to pick up after. A large-screen television sat surrounded by a set of very impressive speakers. In the stand below the unit sat a VCR, a DVD player, a CD player, and some kind of video game set, along with four different-colored controllers. On the coffee table, besides a half-finished mug of coffee and a small stack of magazines, were a stack of remote controls and a digital camera.

His furniture consisted of a couch and love seat in a mixed pattern of shades of blue, and a recliner in a solid shade of the base blue of the couch, where Jenni sat playing with Spot, tugging on a colorful rope toy. The walls were an off-white color, and the carpet was a dark gray that probably shouldn't have gone with the fabric of the couch, yet it did.

The decorating was sparse. The only thing of any note on any of the living-room walls was a watercolor painting of a car, a classic Mustang if she wasn't mistaken. Both the car and the frame just happened to be the exact same shade and color as the recliner.

The place had possibilities, and she liked it.

"Sorry I took so long. Jenni, I'll put your juice right here."

Since Jenni was busy playing with Geoff's dog, Clarissa stood and spoke to Geoff as softly as she could without whispering. "I think I need more milk in my coffee. Can you show me to your kitchen?"

He stood immediately. "I'm sorry; let me take that."

Instead, she cradled the mug in both palms. "I can do it."

She motioned her head toward the opening to the kitchen as discreetly as she could. "Please show me where to go."

One of Geoff's eyebrows quirked. "This way."

Once they were in the kitchen and out of Jenni's earshot, Clarissa turned to Geoff. "I don't know what to do about this crush she's got on you. Do you think maybe we can distract her with Spot?"

He turned and glanced to the doorway leading to the living room. "Maybe. Dogs are good therapy. In fact, most pets are. Even lizards, although you can't play with a lizard like you can with a dog."

"Are you suggesting I get my sister a lizard?"

He shook his head. "Not at all. I'm just saying pets are good therapy for people of all ages. I know you work all day, so getting a puppy may not be a good idea, but maybe a kitten?"

Just what she needed. More responsibility. "I'll pass. We both know who would get stuck looking after it. Me."

"You're probably right. Sorry. I should just mind my own business."

Without thinking, Clarissa rested her palm on his forearm. "No, I'm the one who should be sorry. I had no idea she would invite herself in. You're being so nice to go along with this."

He stiffened momentarily at her touch, glanced down at her fingers on his arm, then raised his head. "No problem. I wasn't doing anything anyway."

They returned to the living room and chatted while Jenni continued to play with Spot. Clarissa had to stop Jenni from throwing a tennis ball in Geoff's house, even though he said he didn't mind. He obviously had no idea how bad a six-year-old girl's aim could be.

While Jenni and Spot played, Clarissa talked to Geoff. As the afternoon wore on, being with him reminded her of how much she missed spending time with him. Now that winter was almost over, she anticipated seeing him more, which in the summer would be nearly every day

However, seeing him more didn't fit into the trend she wanted. Jenni wouldn't lose interest in Geoff if they saw more of him instead of less.

Clarissa realized how much time had passed when the phone rang. So as not to completely monopolize Geoff's day, Clarissa convinced Jenni they had to start making supper. They thanked Geoff for his hospitality and made their way home.

Thankfully, tomorrow was back to school for Jenni. Hopefully, once she got busy, Jenni would forget about Geoff.

Chapter 3

"G eoff! Hi, Geoff!" Jenni ran toward him, waving her arms, her scarf flapping behind her.

Only two steps beyond his driveway, Geoff shuffled to a halt. Faithful to his training, Spot stopped when Geoff stopped and sat beside him.

"What are you doing here?" He glanced down the deserted sidewalk. "Where is your sister?"

"She had to get the phone. She told me to wait at the door, but I saw you. Can I come with you and Spot? Rissa will say it's okay."

Geoff frowned. He wasn't as sure as Jenni about Clarissa's reaction. He also wasn't positive that Clarissa would assume his house was the first place Jenni would go if she wasn't where she was supposed to be. Worse, her presence proved the situation wasn't fixing itself. "I'd feel better if I asked Clarissa myself. We'd better go back to your house."

"We can still take Spot for a walk, can't we?"

"That depends on Clarissa. Would you like to hold him?"

"Yes!"

He handed Jenni the leash, and they walked in silence to her house. Just as he started to go up the first stair, the door opened and Clarissa stepped outside.

"Geoff? What are you doing here?"

"I was taking Spot for a walk, and Jenni joined me. I thought maybe we should come back and ask if that's okay."

Clarissa's eyebrows knotted, and she planted her hands on her hips. "Jenni, what did we discuss about Geoff?"

Instead of learning what had been said about him in his absence, all he heard was a rather subservient "I know" from Jenni.

He looked down at Spot. Spot's tail wagged even though the dog was sitting. His back legs quivered, not from cold, but from the excitement of wanting to continue on his walk. Beside Spot, Jenni shuffled from one foot to the other as she waited for her sister's reaction.

Watching both dog and child, Geoff tried to tamp down a smile. People often teased him about the small size of his dog until they knew how demanding a Jack Russell terrier could be. However, when Spot's enthusiasm for life in general was properly controlled, his small size and willing affection was a good match for a lonely little girl.

"I don't mind if Jenni walks Spot with me. You can come, too, if you'd like."

Clarissa checked her watch. "We were going to the bakery for some fresh bread for supper."

Jenni was nearly dancing where she stood. "But Geoff is letting me walk Spot."

At the sound of his name, Spot's rear end wiggled more than ever.

"He's really reaching his level of endurance, Clarissa. I'm torturing him by making him sit there. We can detour to the bakery instead of the park. We should go now."

When Spot heard the word *go*, it was all the little dog could take. He leapt up, whined, and paced back and forth in front of Jenni.

Jenni giggled. "Please, Rissa?"

Clarissa sighed. "I suppose we could walk instead of taking the car."

Jenni clapped her hands, making only muffled thuds since she was wearing mittens. "Yippee!"

Clarissa locked the house, and they began their journey to the bakery.

The rows of wet snow piled at the sides of the sidewalk had expanded into blobs during the spring melt, narrowing the width of the sidewalk so the four of them couldn't walk side by side. Jenni walked ahead with Spot, and Geoff and Clarissa walked together behind her.

Out of the corner of his eye, Geoff could see Clarissa smiling as they sauntered along. "Spot is such a sweet little dog."

Geoff made a halfhearted laugh. "Not always. Jack Russell terriers can be very headstrong. He's also very sneaky. Especially if he figures there's food involved."

As they walked, Geoff continued to chat with Clarissa while Jenni fixed all her attention on Spot, making sure he remained at heel on her left side, just as Geoff had shown her. He felt strangely disappointed when they arrived back at Clarissa's house, because he wasn't ready to part ways.

Geoff took Spot's leash from Jenni while Clarissa inserted the key into the lock. "I guess I'll see both of you at church on Sunday."

Jenni stepped closer to him, reached up, and tugged on the corner of his jacket. "Geoff?"

"Yes, Jenni?" Geoff looked down and smiled. He couldn't help himself. Despite Jenni's misguided feelings for him, the extra time he'd spent with her made him like her now more than ever.

While being fond of a little girl was fine and acceptable, it was his growing feelings for Clarissa he struggled with. A casual friendship as had been previously established he could handle, but the more time he spent with her, the more time he wanted to spend together. He didn't know if that was an upward or downward spiral. While he enjoyed their time together, the potential for it to develop into more existed. He couldn't allow a deeper relationship, but he didn't know how to stop it.

"Will you eat supper at our house?" Without releasing his hem, Jenni turned to Clarissa. "It's okay, isn't it, Rissa? Spot can stay, too, can't he?"

Geoff raised his head to see Clarissa's face. Her cheeks suddenly turned pink, but not from the crisp spring breeze. "I suppose so. I was going to hollow out the French loaves we just bought and put stew inside. So it's nothing fancy."

Geoff's stomach grumbled at the mental picture. He hadn't thought he was hungry, but he was now.

"I obviously don't have dog food, but I don't mind giving

Spot some stew, if it's okay with you."

Geoff stood. He should have run for the hills, but instead, he told himself that he was doing this for Jenni.

He cleared his throat. "As much as Spot would enjoy the stew, I don't give him people food. He can wait for his dog food when I get home. If you don't mind that I can't stay too long afterward, I'd be delighted."

Jenni started to skip in place and clap her hands until Clarissa gave her a quelling glance, which stilled her. Clarissa opened the door, and Geoff followed Jenni into the living room while Clarissa disappeared into the kitchen. Spot followed Clarissa, hopeful beyond reason for a handout, leaving Geoff alone with Jenni.

He didn't know what to say, so he was relieved when Jenni did most of the talking. She told him about her teacher, her friends, how she was learning to print real words in first grade and even read them.

All he could do was smile and say he was proud of her accomplishments until, to his relief, Clarissa called them to come into the kitchen for supper.

Jenni led with a simple prayer of thanks, then continued to chatter freely while they ate. Clarissa responded in all the right ways, which encouraged Jenni to keep yakking, sparing Geoff from having to add to the conversation. He didn't know if Clarissa caught the reference, but during Jenni's ramblings, she mentioned that when they got married she planned to make the same kind of delicious stew that 'Rissa' made.

After supper, Clarissa sent Jenni into the living room

with Spot, telling her to select a good movie from their collection, leaving Geoff alone with Clarissa in the kitchen. When she began to tidy up the kitchen, Geoff naturally began to help.

"I'm so sorry, Geoff. I really thought she'd be over this by now. I hope she didn't embarrass you. Quite frankly, though, it's good to see her like this. I haven't seen her talk so much since Mom and Dad died."

He shrugged his shoulders as he gathered the plates from the table. "I don't mind. I'll admit she caught me off guard, inviting me like that. Supper was great, by the way. Thank you."

Clarissa turned her head from him, but not quickly enough. Her cheeks darkened, which Geoff thought quite endearing. "This is getting so out of hand. She runs to you every chance she gets. When she gave you half the batch of her favorite cookies last weekend, I nearly fainted. She's got it bad, and I don't know what to do."

While Clarissa filled the sink with water, Geoff turned his head to the doorway and listened to Jenni discussing the choice of movies with Spot, who was apparently paying attention. "I have an idea. What if I let her take some time and play with Spot every day or two? She obviously likes him, and he likes her, too. She'll soon forget all about me."

Clarissa shook her head. "You don't listen to her when you're not here. Yes, she likes Spot, but the main thing is that Spot is with you. The way you let her walk Spot and play with him makes you even better in her eyes. She told me this morning she loves you now more than ever. I almost wasn't surprised to find you on our doorstep when I came outside today."

Geoff pressed his lips together while Clarissa lowered the plates into the soapy water. Of course he was flattered, but it wasn't right. He was technically old enough to be Jenni's father, even though Jenni's father had been much older. Not knowing them well, Geoff didn't know if Jenni's mother was the father's second and much younger wife, or if both Jenni and Clarissa had the same mother, and Jenni was an "afterthought."

Geoff shook his head. The age difference between the two sisters wasn't his concern, or any of his business. What was his concern was that whatever Jenni felt for him seemed to be getting worse instead of better.

Again, he turned his head and listened to Jenni talking to Spot in the living room. Instead of loving him in the "marriage" kind of way, he suspected that because she lacked a male authority figure in her life, with neither a father nor a brother in these formative years, she considered him the next best thing. What she felt for him wasn't love at all but a desire to simply reach out for another person.

As Geoff picked up a plate and dried it, he studied Clarissa, who remained silent while she concentrated on scrubbing the pot very clean. He knew she didn't date much. Over the last year she'd told him about some of the losers she'd gone out with. Even if she hadn't told him, he would have known. Not that he paid attention to what his neighbors did, but he walked Spot every day. He knew the cars of all his neighbors, and all his neighbors' friends and relatives.

Clarissa's driveway seldom housed anything but her own car and Jenni's bike. Old Mrs. Jenkins, the widow in one of the houses between them, got more company than Clarissa.

"Isn't there anyone else you can introduce her to? Maybe a boy in school?"

Clarissa shook her head. "I've already thought of that. She has no interest in any of the boys in her class. She only wants you. She thinks she's in love with you because you're so nice to her every time you see her."

"That's not difficult. She's a darling little girl. But I don't treat her different from any other children I know."

Clarissa pulled the other towel off the oven door handle and began to dry her hands. "That's exactly why she thinks she loves you so much. For someone who claims not to know anything about small children, you're doing everything right. I saw you when you gave her the flowers."

Geoff blinked a few times. "I didn't want them. It's not like I made some big sacrifice."

"It's not that. You didn't stand up and bend down, towering above her, or hand them to her from the chair. You lowered yourself to the floor so you could see her eye to eye when you talked to her, without any part of you being above her. You also don't talk down to her or use baby words or change your voice. You talk to her as an equal. You do that kind of thing all the time. I've seen you in church, too. You're a natural with children. They all probably adore you, just like Jenni."

Something inside Geoff went stiff. He didn't want children to like him. More significant than never getting married, he was never having children. Never.

"I didn't do it on purpose."

"That only proves my point."

Geoff didn't know any other way to act toward children. It didn't take a genius child psychologist to know that if he gave children the brush-off there would be hurt feelings, and he couldn't be that way. Especially to Jenni.

This time, both of them stopped their movements and listened to Jenni, who was now trying to convince Spot to give back a sock he'd found under the couch. She was explaining to him that she would get in trouble with 'Rissa' for having it there in the first place, and she had to quickly put it in the hamper.

Geoff sighed and began to dry the pot Clarissa had scrubbed so diligently. "I wonder if I'm going about this all wrong. Maybe she's chasing me like this because I've been trying to avoid her. I'm not seeing anybody. I could pretend to be Jenni's boyfriend for a while. She's just a kid, but she isn't stupid. It shouldn't take too long before she sees that I'm not her Mr. Right. Who knows, maybe she'll even split up with me instead of the other way around. I think I could handle the day when she breaks my heart."

Clarissa stared at him blankly, glanced to the doorway where Jenni's voice was coming from, then back to him. "My first response is to say no, but I don't have a better suggestion. Maybe giving her what she wants will be the only thing that will work. I hope you're prepared for what you're getting yourself into."

Quite frankly, Geoff didn't see it as any big sacrifice. By

his own choice, he didn't have much of a social life. He wasn't sure what little kids liked to do, but he figured for starters he could take her out with him when he took Spot out for his walk every day. In just over a week the snow would be gone and the weather would be even warmer. He could take her to the park to play with other children if the ground dried fast enough. Even if he spent most of his off-work hours at the park with Jenni all summer long, it wasn't like he had anything better to do.

However, he didn't know if it would be good or bad, because that also meant seeing much more of Clarissa.

He shrugged his shoulders. "I suppose tomorrow is as good a time as any to start. I get home from work at four-thirty. When would be a good time for me to pick her up?"

"That's about the time we get home, too."

"Can I pick her up at 4:45 then? I doubt the restaurant will be crowded so early on a weeknight."

"You're going to take Jenni out for dinner?"

Geoff felt his blush. "Most people go out to dinner for a first date, so I thought that was a good start. I'll probably take her for a burger, and then she'll want to go to the play center with the other kids. It might be a good idea for you to come, too. You can help me make more plans while she's busy."

Clarissa smiled and nodded. "I can tell her it's a date, and that as her sister, it's my job to chaperone."

Geoff hung up the towel on the oven door. "That sounds like a good plan. Now, if you don't mind, I should take Spot home and feed him. I'll see you both tomorrow."

Chapter 4

Clarissa sucked her bottom lip between her teeth to keep herself from laughing. Since this was Jenni's first official "date," Jenni made it more than clear that she would be sitting in the front seat with Geoff, and Clarissa was to sit in the back. Fortunately, Jenni didn't think it at all strange for her big sister to accompany her.

From the back seat, Clarissa watched Geoff interact with Jenni. She couldn't help but be impressed.

While Geoff positioned Jenni's booster car seat and made sure she was properly buckled in, he asked about her day at school. As they traveled, Jenni eagerly recounted how well she could print the letter *J*, not only for her own name, but so she could print Geoff's name. Clarissa bit her bottom lip at how Geoff gently informed Jenni that he spelled his name the other way, with a *G*, and then offered to show her how to print it.

She could see why Jenni liked Geoff so much. He had a way with children one didn't often see with people who weren't parents themselves. He was patient and kind and sensitive to young children, making her think that when the time came, Geoff would make an excellent father. Likewise, he would also make some lucky woman a wonderful husband. Not only was he a strong Christian, he was fun to talk to, interesting, and considerate. She'd been very impressed when he had helped with the dishes without being asked. He could just as easily have gone into the living room with Jenni.

Geoff nodded in understanding as Jenni explained the intricacies of how to sort and fit all her school supplies into her cubby at the end of her last class. Everything that was important to Jenni for today also appeared equally important to Geoff.

Clarissa wondered if he would be equally attentive and caring to an adult. Something told her he would.

Once they arrived at the fast-food restaurant, Geoff insisted on paying for everyone's burger and fries. They found a table near the play center, bowed their heads, and, ignoring the din around them, waited while Jenni said a short prayer of thanks for their food.

"This is such fun, Geoff! Look what I got!" Jenni held up the toy that came with the kid's meal.

He nodded, listening to Jenni as she chattered away about the other toys that came in the set and then elaborated on the movie that featured the characters. Before long, just as she had every other time Clarissa had taken her to the restaurant, Jenni politely asked permission to go to the play center.

Geoff smiled as Jenni ran to the enclosed area. Together, Clarissa and Geoff watched Jenni through the large glass window that soundproofed the play center from the restaurant area, not looking at each other as they spoke.

She could hear the grin in Geoff's voice. "It looks like Jenni is enjoying our date, although I've never had a date bolt on me like that."

"You're doing great. She's going to talk about this for a long time."

"While she's occupied, we should talk about other places I can take her. She's probably too small to go bowling."

"You'd be surprised. They have glo-bowling for the kids. The music is so loud you can't hear anyone talking, it's quite dark, and they have black lights that make stuff glow in the dark. They have rubber bumpers on the sides of the lanes, so instead of gutter balls, the bowling balls bounce off and every ball makes it down to the end."

"That sounds like cheating."

"Maybe, but the kids love it, and Jenni is no exception. It's fun, and that's all that matters when you're six years old."

"Then if you don't think it will be too much for her, I'll take her bowling later this week. Unless you have other plans."

Suddenly, Clarissa didn't feel like smiling anymore. Now more than ever, Clarissa could understand why Jenni had attached herself to Geoff. Clarissa was an adult, not an impressionable young girl, and she could feel herself also falling for his charm. He wasn't doing this begrudgingly; he seemed intent on everyone enjoying himself or herself. His attention to Jenni was bringing back the perky personality she'd had before the death of their parents, something Clarissa hadn't been able to do, no matter how hard she tried.

"No," she muttered, pointedly keeping all her attention on Jenni while she spoke. "I don't have other plans. I just don't want her to get too tired by going out too often."

"I'll take all my cues from you. How about if you give me some secret, prearranged signal so I'll know when it's time to go home? If you suggest it's time to go, Jenni might resent you, but if I say it, I have a feeling everything will be fine. After all, at least for now, I can do no wrong."

He wasn't doing too badly in doing no wrong for Clarissa, either. Going along with Jenni's boyfriend fantasy was surely a sacrifice, yet Geoff was doing it gladly and willingly so he wouldn't hurt Jenni's feelings. At the same time, he was also spending some quality time with her.

Clarissa turned to face him, knowing Jenni was safe and really didn't have to be watched intently every second in the enclosed kid-zone environment. "Are you sure you really want to do this? You know it could go on for a long time."

He shrugged his shoulders. "I don't mind. Really. Besides, I'm curious about glo-bowling. This gives me an excuse to try it. You know. Like when you want to see a movie made for kids, and you're too embarrassed to go as an adult, so you have to wait until it comes out as a rental. Actually, there's one that starts this weekend, a computer-animated flick I'd love to see. Now I won't look like a wimp, because I'll have a little kid with me."

Clarissa immediately knew which movie he meant. "Every time she sees the commercial, she makes me come watch it with her."

He leaned closer, grinning as he spoke. "You wanna come,

too? Just promise me you won't cry if it's a sappy ending."

Clarissa's heart stopped beating, then started up in double time. Geoff's eyes sparkled beneath his gorgeous long lashes, almost daring her to challenge him.

She couldn't. All she could do was stare back. More than ever, she could see how Geoff had become the man of Jenni's dreams. If she wasn't careful, Geoff could easily become the man of her own dreams.

"I won't cry," she mumbled. "I promise."

"Great. What else do you think I can do to take Jenni out on dates until she tires of me? I've got Spot entered in a flyball tournament in July. The weekly practices end past her bedtime, but I could take her a few times and leave early. That might be sufficiently boring for a small child to sit through and might hasten her decision to find a man who's more likely to join her in the sandbox on a summer day."

"I don't allow Jenni to play in sandboxes. You never know what's in there. What's a flyball tournament?"

"It's kind of like a relay race for dogs. A team of four dogs runs one dog at a time over a set of hurdles, grabs a tennis ball, and takes the ball back to the starting point; then the next dog goes. The teams race against each other."

"But Spot is so small. How could he possibly win a race?"

Geoff grinned, once again sending Clarissa's heart into a flutter. "Teams consist of three big dogs and one small dog. The hurdles are set four inches below the shoulder height of the smallest dog, so the large dogs literally fly over the low hurdles. The smaller the last dog, the more advantageous to the other dogs. For a small dog, Spot's pretty fast, especially when there's a tennis ball involved. I think he really understands the game, and he really does try to win. They also have an agility competition. That's when the dogs run through hoops and tunnels and climb things. I haven't decided if I'm going to enter him this year because we haven't practiced as much as we should have. The deadline is in a couple of days; I guess I'd better make up my mind."

"That sounds interesting. I think Jenni would like to go."

His voice lowered, but this time he wasn't smiling. "And what about you? Would you like to go?"

She opened her mouth, but no sound came out. Most of the men she knew considered team sports to be hockey, football, and baseball, and most of the time, their only activity with those sports was to move from the couch to the kitchen when they were hungry. She'd never known anyone who participated in a team activity with his dog. Jenni would probably want to go to such a thing to watch the dogs. Clarissa wanted to go so she could watch Geoff.

Finally, her vocal chords decided to function. "Yes. I think I'd like that."

Before Clarissa could collect her thoughts to think of something else to say, Jenni returned, huffing and puffing, to have a long sip of her drink while she stood beside their table.

Geoff shuffled until he was sitting sideways in the seat, then leaned forward until his elbows rested on his knees. "Are you having fun, Jenni?"

She nodded rapidly. "Mmmm hmmm!" she muttered without her lips leaving the straw. In a flash, the drink was back on the table. "This is the bestest date ever!" Before either of them could respond, Jenni was back inside the play area.

Geoff made a lopsided grin as he repositioned himself to sit properly once again. "Considering her big sister came, and Jenni doesn't mind that I've spent more time with you than I have with her, it's obvious she doesn't date much."

Clarissa nodded. "Guess not."

Once again, they both turned their heads to watch Jenni playing with the other children.

Naturally, this was Jenni's first "date," if one could call it a date, but the truth was that Clarissa didn't date much, either, at least not much in the last year since she'd taken the responsibility to raise her little sister.

She'd been going steady with Kyle for nearly two years, and he'd even hinted at marriage before her parents' accident. She'd always thought he liked Jenni the few times he'd seen her. But when suddenly Clarissa became responsible for Jenni's care, everything changed. Kyle didn't want to be Jenni's quasi-father, as he so bluntly described the position. What had hurt the most was when he accused Clarissa of being unfair to him, to suddenly bring a child into their relationship. He wanted children, but he only wanted his own. When Kyle told Clarissa to make up her mind, whether it was him or Jenni, the choice had not been difficult. From that day on, she hadn't seen Kyle again. When she gave up her apartment, he hadn't even joined the rest of their friends to help her move back into her parents' house to raise her sister.

She discovered the hard way that Kyle was not unique. Most of the men who already knew her suddenly shied away, knowing that if a serious relationship developed, Jenni was part of the package.

More shocking was the reaction of men whom she didn't already know when her parents died. Because she was so much older than Jenni, most people assumed Jenni was her daughter, not her sister. When they discovered Clarissa was neither widowed nor divorced, yet came with a child, many wrongly assumed that she was easy on a date. Between the men who didn't want to become an instant father and those who had something else in mind when they went out, Clarissa didn't date much, either.

She tried not to let her pride be bruised, knowing the only reason she was with a man now was because he was allegedly dating her little sister.

The next time Jenni appeared for a drink, Geoff and Clarissa stopped her from going back to the play area. They spent a little time at the table talking and decided it was time to go home—after all, it was a school night.

Like a gentleman, Geoff parked his car in the driveway and saw them both safely inside.

Before he left, Jenni turned to him and looked up, her eyes open wide. "Thank you for taking us, Geoff. That was lots of fun."

He squatted down to talk eye to eye with her. "I had fun, too."

"Are we going out tomorrow?"

"I'm sorry, Jenni, no. Tomorrow is Bible study night, and the next day is when I go to practice with Spot. How would you like to go glo-bowling on Friday?"

"Yes!" she squealed, throwing her arms around Geoff. "I love glo-bowling! We went for Matthew's birthday party. It's so fun!"

Very slowly, Geoff returned Jenni's hug. As he gave her a gentle squeeze, his eyes closed, and for a split second, his whole face tightened, as if Jenni had somehow hurt him.

The second Jenni released him, he stood. "Then I guess I'll see you Friday." He turned toward Clarissa. "How's five-thirty? I hope you don't have anything else to do. If not, we can reschedule."

She shook her head. "That's fine." She reached down and rested one hand on Jenni's shoulder. "We had better let Geoff go home, Jenni. You've got to take a bath tonight and get to bed early. Tomorrow is school."

Jenni nodded solemnly. "Bye, Geoff."

Geoff nodded, turned, and let himself out.

Clarissa stared for a few seconds at the closed door. Even though they were together for Jenni's sake, she had wanted him to stay and have coffee. She wanted to talk some more about things that had nothing to do with Jenni. She was already starting to fear that when Jenni's crush on him ended, they would go back to only seeing each other in the park, and she didn't want that to happen.

Like Jenni, Clarissa also found herself looking forward to Friday.

Chapter 5

Geoff stared at the calendar on the wall of his kitchen. Never in his life had he lived with such a schedule. Of course, he went to Bible study meetings every Wednesday and flyball and agility practice with Spot on Thursdays, but somehow, almost every other day of the month had something penciled in, and the same with the previous month.

Every date had something to do with Jenni and Clarissa. They went to movies together; they went glo-bowling once a month. As a unit, they were on a first-name basis with many of the staff at the hamburger restaurant. On Sundays they naturally attended church together, and after the service, they stayed together for lunch and supper, too. He spent so much time at their house, they'd bought a bag of dog food.

With the arrival of summer, they were able to do more outdoor activities, and Jenni wanted to do them all. In the time since Stan and Abby's wedding, when Geoff first started "dating" Jenni, both he and Clarissa had noticed a big difference in the little girl. There were times Clarissa still heard Jenni crying at night, but those times were happening less often. When they were together, Jenni's laughter happened more spontaneously, and she was starting to reach out to the other children, participating instead of waiting to be asked to join in.

After Jenni was in bed, Geoff often stayed with Clarissa. They prayed together, they talked, and they watched television together. They shared their joys and their sorrows, or at least, most of them. There were still things he hadn't told Clarissa, things he didn't ever intend to tell her.

He didn't want to ruin what was there, but being with them so much forced him to think about things he didn't want to deal with.

Family life.

Just to put some noise in the house, Geoff turned on the television and flipped to a popular blow-'em-up space series, pointedly ignoring anything remotely related to a family setting. It didn't quell the sensation of restlessness.

Leaving the television on, he picked up his Bible and flipped through, trying to find verses telling him to be happy with what he had and not to want what God didn't want him to have.

He seldom dated because he couldn't risk opening any doors he couldn't close. He only went out with a woman as a friend, when they both knew nothing would develop from it. He'd never regretted when the time came to say good-bye.

But Clarissa was different. He didn't want to see his time with Clarissa end, but it had to. They both knew that when Jenni's puppy-love crush on him faded, their lives would go back to normal—for Clarissa it would be again just her and Jenni, and for Geoff it would be just him and Spot. It wasn't ideal, but it was the way it had to be.

He continued to flip through the pages in his Bible. He wanted to pray for God's will, but he didn't know what God's will was in this situation. He knew God didn't want him to have a family of his own—he'd been told that in more ways and more times than he could count. One day Clarissa would meet the man who would be the perfect husband for her, and he could never be that man.

Even though it wasn't realistic, he wanted to keep seeing Clarissa, regardless of when Jenni experienced a change of heart toward him. He knew he was being selfish and that was wrong, but he couldn't help himself. He thought about Clarissa at the oddest times during the day, including while he was at work. She even found her way into his dreams. He didn't find it annoying—he enjoyed thinking about her. Her warm smile. Her generous spirit. Her patience. Her kindness. He didn't know why he had thought she was only average looking before, because now that he'd been with her almost daily, he realized she was absolutely beautiful. She had the most gorgeous hazel eyes he'd ever seen.

He'd even thought about what it would be like to kiss her.

Geoff wondered if this was what it was like to be falling in love. Even though he knew it was wrong, he didn't want to stop seeing her. It made him want to pray that Jenni would be "in love" with him forever to give him an excuse to keep seeing Clarissa. Of course, he knew that was neither realistic nor fair.

He tried to let the verses he read comfort him, but they didn't completely dull the ache. Instead, Geoff called Spot for a walk, hoping the night air would clear his head.

He was sinking into a hole, and every time he saw them again, he sucked himself down deeper.

Geoff walked into the Sunday school classroom and sat in his usual place beside David.

David turned to him as soon as he finished his conversation. "I saw an ad in the paper for that dog thing you've got Spot entered in. I meant to ask, did you ever decide if you were going to do the obstacle course thing?"

"It's called agility trials. And yes, I did enter him."

David shrugged his shoulders. "Do you think you stand a chance of winning? He's kind of small."

"We're entering because it's fun. It's not about winning or losing. Are you going to be there to take pictures for the paper?"

"Wouldn't miss it. I got some great pictures last year. Do you remember that big black dog that went in the tunnel and wouldn't come out?"

Before Geoff answered, Clarissa walked in, halting his thought processes. She smiled and made a beeline for the empty seat beside him. Geoff tried not to let it show that he was happy to see her. When David saw her approaching, he turned and continued the conversation he was involved in before Geoff sat down.

Clarissa slid into the seat, tucked her purse under her chair, and turned to him. "Long time, no see," she said, grinning as she spoke.

Geoff lifted his wrist and checked his watch. "Yeah. It's been a whole eleven hours. Did Jenni sleep okay?"

"Yes. I checked on her after you left, and she didn't move."

He was about to ask if she kept her promise to get ready for church with no problem since they let her stay up late, but the leader directed everyone's attention to the front, and the lesson began.

After the class ended, when they went to pick up Jenni from her classroom, they found Jenni pacing in the back. When she looked up at them, her eyes were glassy.

Clarissa knelt·down in front of her and rested one hand on Jenni's arm. "What's wrong? Did someone hurt you?"

Jenni shook her head so fast her blond curls flipped back and forth. "No. Mrs. Morgan says she's gotta have a operation. So she can't be our teacher anymore until school starts again. She said we gotta have another teacher, but no one is good like Mrs. Morgan."

Geoff frowned. Two of the prayer requests this morning had centered around Julia Morgan. First was for a quick recovery after her unexpected surgery, which would be Monday. Second was that a suitable teacher could be found for the primary-level class on short notice.

Clarissa smiled and stroked Jenni's hair. "I'm sure someone nice will come and teach while Mrs. Morgan gets better. Would you like it if I was your teacher until Mrs. Morgan can come back?"

Jenni's eyes widened. "Really?"

Clarissa nodded. "I've never taught Sunday school before, but I might like to try."

Jenni glanced at Geoff, then turned back to her sister. "Mrs. Morgan sometimes gets a helper. Can Geoff be your helper? Or maybe since you didn't do Sunday school before, Geoff can be the teacher, and you can be the helper."

Geoff tried not to choke. "But, Jenni, I've never taught Sunday school, either."

"But Rissa says you know the Bible real good."

Geoff felt his cheeks heat up. It both flattered him and made him nervous that the two of them talked about him at such length. "I like to read my Bible, but that doesn't mean I know enough to be a good teacher."

Geoff wouldn't have thought it possible, but Jenni's big blue eyes widened even more. Her lower lip quivered. "Please?"

He knew he was a goner. "I'll ask the Sunday school superintendent, but I'm not making any promises."

Before he could move, Jenni lunged forward and threw her arms around his legs. "Thank you, Geoff!" she mumbled against his thigh. "You're the best!"

Beside him, Clarissa made a strangled cough.

Geoff pried Jenni's arms off him and stepped back. "Let's go in for the service now. I think I have some praying to do."

Chapter 6

Clarissa kissed Jenni on the forehead as she tucked her sister into bed. By the time she tiptoed out of the room, she was sure Jenni was already asleep. It had been a long day.

Clarissa sighed as she sank into the couch. It might have been a long day, but it had been a short week. Or if not a short one, definitely a busy one. Monday they'd again gone out for burgers with Geoff. Tuesday he took them to the mall, where they walked and walked and didn't buy a single thing. Wednesday she got a sitter for Jenni and went with Geoff to his home group for Bible study. After the class they sat with the Sunday school superintendent and talked about taking over the primary class on a temporary basis. Thursday Jenni played with Spot in the living room while Clarissa and Geoff brainstormed in the kitchen about the lesson they would do on Sunday. Clarissa couldn't believe how disappointed she was when Geoff and Spot had to run off to their flyball and agility practice.

Friday they'd rented a movie, and the four of them huddled

together on the couch to watch it, although Spot got kicked off when he started stealing Jenni's popcorn.

Then today, Saturday, Geoff had taken them to an environmental awareness event. They'd built bird feeders and then gone into wooded areas of the park to hang them. Clarissa didn't know who was more tired, herself or Jenni, but it was a good tired. She knew she would be stiff tomorrow, but she didn't care. Being with Geoff had made it all worthwhile. She'd be seeing him again tomorrow when he picked them up earlier than usual so they'd be ready to teach their first Sunday school class together.

She smiled through her exhaustion, mentally kicking herself for not noticing Geoff before Jenni fell in "love" with him.

They both knew whatever was happening was temporary, that they were only together until Jenni fell out of "love" with him. But Geoff being the man he was, Clarissa thought it very possible that would never happen. Just like Jenni, she felt herself falling in love with him, but in a different and very adult way.

It was a given that she found him attractive, but more important than that, they shared anything and everything. The only thing they hadn't talked much about was his family. She'd told him so much about her parents, including why there was such a large age difference between herself and Jenni. Yet she knew almost nothing of Geoff's parents or his family—she only knew that his family lived across town, and he had one older brother who was married. She assumed there was some kind of problem in the family. One day, she hoped he would confide in her, but that hadn't happened yet.

Clarissa yawned and stared at the remote control for the television, lying just out of reach in her current position. She lifted her arm, knowing the remote was too far away, then let her arm drop.

She smiled at herself. If she was too tired to reach the remote, she should just go to bed. Besides, the sooner she fell asleep, the sooner it would be morning.

And the sooner she would see Geoff.

⟡

"Rissa! Rissa! Where are you?"

"I'm in the bathroom," Clarissa mumbled around her toothbrush, her head over the sink. "What do you want?"

"You gotta come!" Jenni yelled from down the hall.

With her toothbrush still in her mouth, Clarissa rushed out of the bathroom. She took exactly one step and skidded to a halt.

Instead of little Jenni, a much taller person stood in the hallway. "Hi, Rissa," he said.

Clarissa yanked the toothbrush out of her mouth, then swallowed the sudsy water, trying to ignore the momentary queasy feeling. Hastily she swiped her arm over her mouth. "You're early. I didn't hear you come in." She looked down at the toothbrush in her hand, then quickly swished her arm behind her back.

Geoff made no effort to hide his grin. "Jenni opened the door before I had a chance to knock. She asked me to put the craft stuff in the car, but I didn't know where it was."

"It's on the kitchen table. She knew that."

Clarissa narrowed her eyes and glared at Jenni, who didn't

seem to notice her displeasure. Clarissa knew she probably shouldn't have been annoyed with Jenni. Jenni still wasn't old enough to be embarrassed when caught doing personal things, but Clarissa was. Now, not only had Geoff seen her with toothpaste dripping down her face, but her hair wasn't combed, and she hadn't yet applied her makeup. The only positive was that she was properly dressed, even if she didn't have her shoes on.

When Geoff turned around and disappeared into the kitchen to get the box, she couldn't see if he was laughing at her indignation.

She finished getting ready as quickly as she could while Geoff sat in the kitchen with Jenni. Before too long, they were at the church setting up their classroom.

Clarissa stacked the supplies they brought into neat piles while Jenni helped Geoff get the felts, scissors, and glue from the bins in the closet, since Jenni knew where everything was.

Geoff's voice echoed from within the closet. "Look at this. I never had colored glue when I was a kid. The stuff in here is amazing."

Clarissa checked her watch. "Never mind the supplies. We only have a few minutes until people start dropping their kids off. I'm too new at this to be playing with craft supplies while I'm supposed to be watching kids."

The shuffling in the closet stopped, which caused her to look up. Geoff stood in the opening to the closet, grinning. "What's the matter? You nervous?"

"Maybe just a little. Are you?"

"A little. But between the two of us, we'll do fine."

Jenni's voice piped up from the back of the storage closet. "What about me? Can't I be the helper today?"

Geoff turned around. "Of course you're the helper today. Are you nervous?"

Jenni shook her head, her effort to appear grown-up almost laughable. "No. I been the helper before."

Clarissa cleared her throat. "*I've been* the helper before," she echoed.

Jenni stepped all the way out of the closet, her eyes wide. "You were? I don't 'member when you been the helper."

Geoff bit his lower lip and didn't say a word.

"No, Jenni, I was just trying to help you say it right. Now let's get busy so we can be ready."

The first student arrived at the classroom as the last box of felt pens made it to the teacher's desk.

Not only did the class and craft time go better than anticipated, Geoff was not at all what Clarissa expected, although in retrospect, she should have known. They had previously agreed that Geoff would teach the lesson and Clarissa would lead the craft time. Geoff was a computer programmer, but he would have made a wonderful teacher. He was entertaining, yet serious enough on the key points to drive the lesson home. He could see when their attention spans waned, and he then changed his presentation accordingly.

The craft time went quickly, as she knew it would. They finished just as the first parent arrived.

As usual, Geoff, Clarissa, and Jenni sat together for the

main service, and also as usual, they went to the same fast-food restaurant for lunch. The same as every other time, Jenni gobbled down her lunch and ran to the play center before either Geoff or Clarissa had halfway finished theirs.

"After all this time, I still must not be a very interesting date," Geoff said as the glass door closed behind Jenni. "She keeps running off on me."

"Then I must not be a very good big sister, because she does the same thing to me when I bring her here."

He grinned. "I guess we're even then."

"Now that she's gone, what did you think of our Sunday school lesson? I think we did pretty well, don't you?"

Geoff nodded. "We made a pretty good team. Do you want to take turns between teaching the lesson and the craft? Although I have to warn you, I don't think I'd do any better at cutting and gluing than any of the kids."

Clarissa could almost picture Geoff struggling to cut shapes with the awkward child's safety scissors and glue the pieces together using the colored glue he was so enamored with. "Maybe we should stick to the way we did it today. My father always used to say, 'If it ain't broke, don't fix it.' I think that's good advice."

Geoff's expression turned serious. "I'm sorry to say that I didn't really talk much to your father. Your parents sound like they were good Christian people."

"Yes, they were. I still miss them; I probably always will. Do you see your parents often?"

He started absently swirling one fry in the blob of ketchup on the corner of the wrapper. "I see them about once a month or so, sometimes less. I know that sounds bad, but we don't always see eye to eye on things, so I don't go as often as I should."

She wanted to ask him more, but the silence that hung after his words told her he didn't want to elaborate. Moreover, sitting in the middle of the loud and crowded fast-food restaurant wasn't the ideal place to discuss personal issues. However, Clarissa had learned the hard way that often opportunities had to be forced or they were lost forever.

She reached over the table and wrapped her fingers around Geoff's wrist. He stopped moving but didn't pull away.

"Sometimes it helps to talk. I'm a pretty good listener."

"There's nothing to talk about. I keep praying God will open their hearts to see my point, and they're probably doing the same thing about me."

"Is there a middle ground? Can't you meet halfway?"

"Not in this case."

Again, he let his words hang without explaining or letting her know what kind of dispute had no room for middle ground. Clarissa wanted to ask more questions, but Jenni's reappearance closed the window of opportunity.

They ended up back at Geoff's house, where they played video games all afternoon, then nearly destroyed Geoff's kitchen trying to make a gourmet dinner to celebrate the success of their first Sunday school lesson.

By the time Clarissa and Jenni left, it was dark. This time, Geoff walked them home, which Clarissa thought very romantic.

After she unlocked the door and sent Jenni inside to get ready for bed, Clarissa stood on the doorstep beneath the starry sky to say goodnight to Geoff.

It would have been a perfect ending to a perfect day if he kissed her good night beneath the starry sky.

She even thought about asking if he'd like to kiss her, but before she could get a word out, he mumbled a quick "Good night" and left.

Clarissa crossed her arms and watched him walk the short distance between their homes until he disappeared inside his own front door.

If only. . .

Chapter 7

Geoff sucked in a deep breath as he stood behind the line with the rest of Spot's team, the Flying Fuzz-buttons. He stiffened and looked into the bleachers, where Clarissa and Jenni sat, their attention locked on Spot and the other three dogs on the team.

The weather was warm, although not hot. The sky was overcast, but it didn't feel like it was going to rain. A perfect spring day for an outdoor event.

He almost turned away when Clarissa turned her head slightly and looked straight at him. She smiled, made an exaggerated wink, and gave him a big thumbs-up.

Something funny happened in the pit of Geoff's stomach, only he knew he wasn't hungry.

He hadn't been sure that Spot's team was ready for the big competition, but with Clarissa behind him, he felt like he could do anything, which was ridiculous. She'd never even been to a practice, although he'd taken Jenni a few times. Jenni had been totally enamored with all the dogs, and she'd even jumped the hurdles herself the first time she'd gone.

Fortunately, no one present had asked why he'd brought a little girl with him, because he didn't have an answer.

He didn't know when it happened, but in the time since he'd started "dating" Jenni, his whole life had shifted on its axis. He didn't know if it would ever be right again.

He didn't want a relationship, and he didn't want a family, yet not only was he spending most of his time with a woman and a girl young enough to be his daughter, but he missed them whenever they weren't together.

It was wrong. Very wrong. God wasn't supposed to let this happen, but it was happening, and there was nothing he could do about it.

Geoff's mental meanderings were interrupted by the applause as the scores of the teams before them were shown. The heat between the Flying Fuzzbuttons and the Racing Rovers was next.

Both teams took their positions, and at the signal, the lead dogs were off. Geoff positioned Spot, then released him as soon as Buddy returned and crossed the line.

Spot ran for all he was worth. For a dog with such short legs, he cleared all four hurdles in excellent time, activated the flyball box, caught the ball, and made the return trip even faster than the outgoing run. The split second Spot crossed the line, Shesha bounded forward.

Spot jumped into Geoff's arms, and Geoff praised him for a good run. As the team's height dog, Spot had done well, but the speed needed to win had to be made by the other, bigger dogs. So he wouldn't distract the other team members, Geoff whispered to Spot to tell him how good he'd done, and in so doing, he looked up to Clarissa and Jenni.

Jenni was watching the other dogs racing, but Clarissa was watching him. When she saw him looking back, she smiled and waved. Hesitantly, Geoff waved back, then turned as Bonkers, their fourth dog, crossed the line a full second before the other team's last dog, scoring them at 23.41 seconds. Almost in unison, both teams of four dog handlers turned to see their scores for the heat. The fastest team was not always the winner, the final score being dependent on errors and how many hurdles the dogs knocked down. So far today, none of the dogs had been red-flagged for starting too soon.

"We did it!" A cheer raised for the Flying Fuzzbuttons winning the heat. Geoff could hear Jenni cheering loudest of all.

The Flying Fuzzbuttons placed third in the competition, earning them a ribbon. All handlers praised their dogs fully, since this was the best they'd ever done.

The group broke up for lunch, during which time the flyball equipment would be taken down and the agility equipment set up for the afternoon's events.

Clarissa had packed a picnic lunch. Like most participants, they found a location as private as possible with so many people and dogs sharing the park. They ate quickly, and Geoff returned to the competitors' area with Spot.

The ten-inch division was the first to start. Since Spot was a relative newcomer to Agility, his level, Starters, was first, and unfortunately, his group, the Regulars, began the competition, which didn't give him much time to get used to the setting. Geoff did the preliminary walk through the course, said a short prayer for speed and strength, and took his place.

At the signal they began their run. First Geoff directed Spot over two hurdles and through a chute. He directed Spot to make a slight left and pointed him to the dog walk, giving him the signal to slow down so his feet touched the yellow contact zone, to avoid having points deducted for a fault. When his paws were back on the grass, they turned, and Spot ran through the "L" tunnel, which ended up back under the dog walk.

As Geoff ran beside Spot, directing him over another hurdle, Geoff turned for a split second to see David wave at him, giving Geoff a bad feeling he was going to be in Monday's newspaper. Spot was the smallest dog to be entered in the agility trial competition this year, making him somewhat of a point of interest.

Geoff gritted his teeth and tensed, ready to run again, while he waited for the judge's count at the pause table. At the word "Go," Geoff directed Spot through the weave poles and then into the collapsed chute tunnel. He ran forward and called to Spot as he appeared through the opening, then waved him to the hardest obstacle, the teeter-totter. Unfortunately, Spot's feet didn't touch the contact zone before he jumped off, but Geoff pushed the thought from his mind as he directed Spot over another couple of hurdles, then over the A-frame. In a last burst of energy, they ran at top speed, and Spot flew through the tire jump. By the time Spot made it to the final platform, Geoff was panting as hard as the dog. At the signal that they were done, Spot leapt into Geoff's arms, and Geoff gave him a big hug. Their score was good, but not good enough to win a prize.

Since there were many dogs after them, Geoff headed for the bleachers to sit with Clarissa and Jenni to watch the rest of the competition.

As he approached them, Clarissa and Jenni jumped to their feet. Jenni immediately dropped to the ground to hug Spot, but to Geoff's surprise, Clarissa stepped forward and hugged him.

With her arms over his shoulders and around the back of his neck, they were so close their noses were almost touching. "You both were wonderful! I know you'll get a good score! Congratulations!"

"We don't do it for the score, we do it beca—"

The sudden pressure of Clarissa's lips on his cut off Geoff's words. At first he stiffened, but it only took a split second for the shock to turn to pleasure as he rested his hands on Clarissa's shoulders and kissed her right back.

Her lips were soft and warm and wonderful against his. She started to pull back before he was ready to stop, so he raised his hands and cupped her chin, angled his head a little to the right, and then kissed her again, this time with every bit of his heart and soul involved. He was kissing the woman he loved.

"Ewww!!! You're kissing on the lips! That's yucky!"

Jenni's voice was as effective as dumping a pail of cold water on his head. They separated in a split second.

Clarissa wouldn't look at him, but he looked at her. Her

cheeks flamed, and her lips looked as soft as they had just felt.

His gut clenched. What they had done was wrong. Not only had he kissed Clarissa in front of Jenni, he'd kissed her in front of everyone at the park.

Clarissa cleared her throat, but her voice still sounded choked. "Jenni, I think we should go get something to drink. Let's go to the concession stand."

Without giving Jenni a chance to respond, Clarissa rested her hands on Jenni's shoulders, turned her around, and walked away.

Geoff sank to the wooden seat and opened the cooler to get a drink for Spot without thinking about what he was doing.

He'd kissed Clarissa. And he wanted to kiss her again. In private. Where they wouldn't be interrupted.

While Spot slopped at the water, Geoff slumped and buried his face in his hands. He'd known that whatever was happening between himself and Clarissa had been spiraling out of control, but today proved it. He'd fallen in love. That wasn't supposed to happen; yet it had.

Geoff shook his head, then let his arms drop so his elbows rested on his knees. For lack of something better to do, he stared at Spot, who had nothing better in the world to think of than sniffing the corner of the bleacher stand.

Geoff had to do something to extricate himself from this disaster, but he didn't know how. The only thing he did know was that it was going to hurt.

Jenni's voice indicated their imminent return. Geoff stood and watched their approach, drinks in hand.

Clarissa's smile made him feel like he was being poleaxed. His stomach churned, and his heart pounded. He wanted to kiss her again, and he didn't care that Jenni was watching.

But he couldn't. Things had gone too far.

Tonight when he drove them home, he would have to tell them he couldn't see them anymore.

But until then, he didn't want to spoil the day for them, or for himself, either. Like Cinderella, he would wait until the end of the day. At midnight, the dream would be over.

Clarissa reached forward with one of the drinks. "It's grape soda. I remembered you saying you haven't had this since you were a kid, and I couldn't resist."

Their hands brushed as he accepted the drink. Geoff's chest tightened, which he knew was stupid, but he couldn't control it.

"Thanks," he muttered.

Clarissa beamed ear to ear, apparently unaffected. Geoff felt like an idiot.

"I think we should celebrate how good Spot did, but since Spot can't go into a restaurant, I'll order pizza for dinner."

"That sounds nice," he mumbled.

He reminded himself that midnight was many hours way. Until then, he would enjoy the evening, because after tonight, it was over.

Tomorrow, life would be back to normal, and he'd never felt so depressed.

Chapter 8

Clarissa closed her eyes while Jenni prayed over their pizza. She almost had to bite her lip not to interrupt Jenni and shout out praises to God.

Today had been the best day of her life.

After they all chorused a big "Amen" together, they dug in. Clarissa remained silent while Jenni chattered about the dogs she'd seen. It gave her time to think.

Even though she'd been thinking about what it would be like to be kissed by Geoff, she could barely believe what she'd done.

But now that it had happened, she didn't regret it. Not only had he kissed her back, he'd kissed her a second time.

She didn't know why it had taken so long—maybe it was because the last year had been difficult—but she felt like suddenly her eyes had been opened.

Ever since Kyle had left her, she'd been incredibly lonely yet too busy to make the effort to get back into the dating scene. The few times she'd tried to meet someone with whom she might be able to share her life, she'd been terribly disappointed. She'd even told Geoff about a few of her misadventures with men, and he'd gently reminded her that God was in control, and when the right man came along, she'd know it.

Geoff had been half right. God had placed that right man under her nose, but she hadn't known it. At least not until today.

For the last year, Geoff had been the one person she could talk to when she needed someone. He'd always been there when she needed a friend. She knew his schedule. Unless he was sick, he always took Spot out as soon as he got home from work. They'd spent countless hours talking while Jenni and the other children played with Spot.

Even during moments when there was nothing to say, they simply enjoyed each other's company. She'd go home feeling like all was right with the world after spending time with him. She'd never met a man like Geoff, and she knew she never would again. Today, she finally realized that Geoff was the man God had set aside for her to marry and love until her dying day.

Clarissa lowered her head so neither Geoff nor Jenni could see the smile she couldn't wipe off her face. At first he'd been surprised when she kissed him, and she couldn't blame him for that. Geoff was never one to demonstrate strong emotions, especially in public. For him to kiss her in the way he had, openly, in front of all those people, could only indicate that he felt the same way.

If she wasn't sure before, she was positive now. Not only had she fallen in love, she was pretty sure he loved her back.

Spot barking at the back door interrupted her thoughts.

"I'll do it!" Jenni chirped as she dropped her half-eaten piece of pizza onto the plate and ran from the room.

Clarissa found herself staring across the table at Geoff, no doubt with stars in her eyes.

She cleared her throat. "I had no idea you could do that kind of stuff with dogs. It's like a team sport, except it's the dogs that do all the action. But that's not true, either. All the owners run through the course with their dogs."

He nodded, smiling hesitantly. "We have to be in good shape to keep up that pace, that's for sure." His smile widened, making Clarissa's heart pound. "You wouldn't believe what it takes to get some of those dogs to properly trigger the flyball box. If they just take the ball out with their teeth, it's considered cheating."

Before Clarissa could think of anything to say that didn't include dogs, Jenni returned. Having heard talk of flyball, Jenni bombarded Geoff with more questions until they were finished eating and the pizza boxes were cleared.

Once in the living room, they watched a movie Jenni had borrowed from a friend. As usual, Geoff positioned himself in the middle of the couch, Clarissa sat on one side of him, Jenni on the other, and Spot climbed onto Jenni's lap.

Clarissa dearly wished that Geoff would put his arm around her, but he didn't. She tried to convince herself that the reason was because he was supposed to be dating Jenni. However, Jenni had seen them kissing, and Jenni's biggest concern was not that Geoff was kissing the "wrong" woman. It was that they were kissing on the mouth.

By the time the movie was over, Jenni was yawning, which gave Clarissa the opportunity she needed. Before Geoff stood, she tapped him on the arm. "How would you like to carry Jenny to bed? I think we should, you know. . .talk."

Because Geoff was, after all, a man, she expected him to make some kind of comment that it wasn't talking they would do, but more kissing, which would have been fine with Clarissa. Instead, his face paled, and he jumped off the couch. The quick movement startled Jenni, and Jenni's movement startled Spot. Spot sprang out of her arms, Jenni shuffled to the floor, and Spot ran around in small circles, barking at her feet.

"Actually, I think I should leave."

"Leave?" Clarissa sputtered. "But—"

Jenni ran to Geoff and wrapped her arms around his legs. "You can't go yet! I promise I'll be good when it's time to get up for church tomorrow!"

He bent down and gently disengaged Jenni. "I really have to go."

Clarissa, who was the only person left sitting, looked up at Geoff. "What time are you going to pick us up for Sunday school? Same as usual?"

"Maybe it would be best if we met there."

A queasy sensation rolled through the pit of her stomach. She didn't think he meant just for one day. It sounded like the separation was meant to be permanent. Clarissa rose, stepped forward, and rested one hand on Geoff's arm. "What's wrong?"

He stepped back, and she withdrew her touch. "This isn't

working out. I think we're seeing too much of each other."

Her stomach turned to lead. "I don't understand. What have I done wrong?" The thought that he was bolting because she'd kissed him confused her. He seemed to enjoy it as much as she had.

"You've done nothing wrong. It's me. I can't do this." He bent down toward Jenni. "I'll take Spot, please."

Jenni started to sniffle as she passed Spot into Geoff's hands.

Clarissa was too much in shock to cry, but she knew that if they didn't deal with whatever was wrong now, the second the door closed behind him, she would never know. She had to go for broke and be completely honest.

When Kyle left her, she'd demanded to know why, and she was glad she had pushed the issue. He'd left her because Jenni had been added to their relationship. However, she hadn't been that upset. While she certainly liked Kyle, she had still been waiting for love to happen, and it hadn't—even after two years of steady dating. Kyle was no significant loss.

If Geoff left her, she would never recover.

Clarissa forced herself to speak through the tightness in her throat. "Please tell me why you're going. . ." Her eyes burned, but she blinked the tears back. Her voice constricted to barely above a squeak. "Because I love you."

All Geoff's movements froze. His voice cracked when he spoke. "You can't. Love isn't an option for me." He blinked a few times, then shuffled backward. With his hesitation, Spot bolted from his arms.

Clarissa regained her senses in time to scoop Spot up.

She backed up a step, holding the dog close to her heart. Geoff couldn't leave without explaining if she held his dog hostage. "Why not? I think you're a very lovable person. You've been a good friend since Mom and Dad died." Jenni chose that moment to wrap her arms around Clarissa's legs. She didn't have to look down. The sniffles told her Jenni was already crying enough for both of them.

"Being friends was fine. But we can't be just friends anymore, so it's over."

"But isn't that the way it's supposed to work? Friendship first, then falling in love?" The ditty she learned as a child playing jump rope sang in her head. *First comes love, then comes marriage, then comes Clarissa with the baby carriage.* Only in this case, she didn't want the baby carriage. But she definitely wanted the love and marriage part.

"Not for me. Give me back my dog."

Pangs of desperation stabbed through her. Common sense deserted her. She made her fingers into the shape of a gun and pressed the tip of her index finger to Spot's head. "Tell me why, or the dog gets it."

"That's not funny, Clarissa. Quit fooling around."

She shuffled back as much as she could with Jenni still attached to her legs. "I'm not trying to be funny. I'm not giving him back until you tell me."

She could see by the tightening of his cheeks and the narrowing of his eyes that he was gritting his teeth.

Clarissa cleared her throat. "I have to know what I did. This afternoon, I thought things were going. . .well."

He dragged one hand down his face, then ran his fingers

through his hair. "That shouldn't have happened. If you're looking for anything more than friendship, and I know now you are, then you're going to have to find that elsewhere. I can't be anymore than a casual friend with you."

"How can you say that? What's between us has gone on for over a year."

"Suddenly things have changed. I know you want more." He rammed one hand in his pocket and waved the other in the air. "Love. Marriage. Babies. That's not for me."

"I don't understand. When you kissed me. . ." She let her voice trail off until the room was silent, except for Jenni's sniffling.

Clarissa lightly touched Jenni's shoulder with her free hand. "Geoff and I have to talk alone now. Go get your pajamas on, brush your teeth, and I'll be up to say prayers in a few minutes."

Fortunately, Jenni disappeared without argument.

Geoff crossed his arms over his chest. "Why do you want to drag this out? Isn't it enough for you to hear that I'm not interested in a relationship?"

"No, it's not. I don't believe you. Everything about you says that's not true. You've stuck with me and helped me with Jenni. You're dependable and trustworthy. You're wonderful with children. You're a good Christian man."

"Yeah. With a definite message from God. God doesn't want me to have kids, and that means I'm not getting married."

Images of Geoff and Jenni together cascaded through her mind. She'd heard many excuses from many different men about not wanting to be involved with children, or not being "ready." Everything Geoff did with Jenni denied his words, which only made her angry. "How dare you! I thought you, of all people, could be honest with me."

He stepped closer. His eyes narrowed, and his whole face became tight. "You want honesty? How's this then? I'm hemophiliac. My grandfather was hemophiliac, and he passed it on to my mother, who passed it on to both my brother and me. I've been in the hospital so many times I've lost count. It's no fun for me, and it's no fun for my parents to worry. A male carrier can't pass it on to a son, but I would definitely pass it on to a daughter. My brother and his wife decided to take a chance with a family. They had a daughter, and she died. My parents keep pushing me to get married and have kids, even after everything that's happened. It may be more treatable now than when I was a kid, but there's still no cure."

He stepped closer and grabbed Spot from her limp arms. "You don't know what it's like to grow up with everyone treating you like some freak made of glass. I don't think God would fault me for not wanting to put another innocent child through what happened to me. I'm not willing to take the chance that I wouldn't have a girl, so I went out and made sure I would never be able to pass it on. Just like Spot on his last trip to the vet."

He backed up until he was close enough to twist slightly and grab the doorknob with one hand. "Every woman who gets married deserves to have kids, but no one is having kids with me, and that means you, too."

In a split second, he turned fully and opened the door wide.

"Geoff! Wait! This doesn't change anything! I'm not interested in having children. I have Jenni, and she's enough for me."

"You say that now, but in a couple of years your biological clock will be ticking and you'll change your mind. Go fall in love with someone else, because having kids is no longer an option for me."

Before she could say another word, the door slammed shut behind him.

Everything remained silent while his words slowly sank in. She continued to stare at the back of the closed door until Jenni appeared in her pajamas, clutching her big brown teddy bear. "Where's Geoff? Isn't he going to kiss me good night? Just not on the mouth."

Clarissa squatted and pulled Jenni and the bear in for a big hug. "I'm sorry, Sweetie, he had to go. Geoff, uh, isn't feeling very good."

"Is he sick?"

Clarissa didn't know enough about hemophilia to give her sister an answer. "In a way, but not really. Tell you what. How would you like to stay up and look it up on the Internet with me?"

Jenni nodded so fast her hair bounced. "Yes! I don't want Geoff to be sick."

"Some things are beyond our control. But that doesn't mean there's nothing we can do. Let's say a prayer, and we'll see what we can find."

Chapter 9

Geoff sat at the kitchen table and stared blankly at the wall. If he were a drinking man, and if he had any alcohol in the house, this would have been the time to tie one on. But the Bible spoke clearly against drunkenness, proving God really did know best—he couldn't take the chance of hurting himself if things got out of control.

He crossed his arms on the table and let his head sink between them.

Against all his better judgment, he'd fallen in love with both Clarissa and Jenni, and it hurt.

Again, he asked God why he was so afflicted, but he didn't receive an answer. More than anything he'd ever wanted in his life, he wanted Clarissa. But he couldn't have her, because he couldn't give her what she deserved.

He ventured into the living room, where he mindlessly flipped channels until he gave up and turned the television off. Finally, he did what he should have done in the first place, what he usually did when life tormented him, and that was to read God's Word. In the silence of his empty house, he picked up the devotional book he'd been following for that year and read the page for the day. The verse it referred to, 1 Peter 4:19, somehow perfectly fit his day: "So then, those who suffer according to God's will should commit themselves to their faithful Creator and continue to do good."

He closed his Bible and squeezed his eyes shut. He indeed was suffering, because he did want children and he did want to marry Clarissa. However, in his actions today, he hadn't been faithful to his Creator. He'd abandoned Jenni, and she still needed him. Despite his own struggles, he had to continue to do the good God was asking him to do, and that was to help Jenni until she didn't need him anymore.

With that thought, Geoff went to bed. Tomorrow he was teaching Sunday school. He would never have seen himself as a Sunday school teacher, yet not only did he enjoy teaching, but the children responded to him. Therefore, he would continue, despite his pain. God's will was more important than his own.

Geoff flexed his sore fingers, then continued on his mission to pick up every piece of scrap yarn and snip of paper. He almost felt like writing a letter to the manufacturer, but none of the children had difficulty managing the safety scissors, only him.

With perfect timing, he picked up the last scrap as Clarissa directed the last child out with her parents. However, before he could dash out, Jenni dropped the box of felts into the bin and rushed to him.

"We looked up what you gots on the computer. We also is getting a book from the lieberry."

"That's library," Clarissa whispered behind Jenni, then looked up at him. "We did a little research last night, and we also reserved a book online. We want to learn all we can."

His heart pounded. "Why are you doing this? Don't you understand what I told you?"

"I understand. But you don't seem to understand what I told you. I have Jenni, and she's all I need. Besides you, of course. We both love you too much to let this go."

He backed up until the corner of one of the tables dug into the back of his legs. "I told you yesterday. Let it go, Clarissa."

"No. I won't. Jenni won't, either. You're the one who has to let it go. We can handle this together."

"Drop it, Clarissa. This isn't the time to argue. We're in God's house."

"Jenni and I aren't arguing. It's you who's doing all the arguing."

Geoff knew differently, but to say so would only make the discussion continue. He stared first at Clarissa's expectant face and then Jenni's. He knew anything Jenni thought or did was out of pure innocence, but Clarissa should have known better. "I'm not arguing. That's just the way it is," he muttered, then grabbed his Bible and dashed out of the room.

He hurried to the sanctuary, for the first time not stopping to chat with any of his friends. He sat in his usual seat near the front, starting to think how strange, even depressing it felt to be sitting alone once again, when Clarissa and Jenni shuffled in, one on either side of him.

He lowered his voice to a harsh whisper. "What are you two doing here?"

Clarissa smiled so sweetly his stomach did a flip. "This is God's house. We're here to worship with friends. One friend actually."

He gritted his teeth. She knew he wouldn't cause a scene by moving. Besides, he had a feeling that if he got up and chose another seat, they would only follow him again. If there was anything he'd learned about Clarissa in the last year and a half, it was that she was tenacious.

"You win, for now. But you're not going to change my mind."

He noticed he was getting somewhere when she didn't respond or smile. Fortunately, the lights dimmed and the worship leader came on to begin the service, giving Geoff something else to concentrate on, which was worshiping God, the reason he was there in the first place.

Unfortunately, he kept getting distracted, not from Jenni misbehaving, but because she sat perfectly still and participated in the worship. She even listened to the pastor's sermon between trying to read the bulletin notes and playing quietly with a toy in her lap.

Part of him was so proud of her he thought he would burst, but before he could get too carried away, the more sensible and realistic part of him was reminded that he was cutting off all ties with Jenni.

As the service closed, he took advantage of being in God's house to pray extra hard for an answer. He didn't want to lose either Clarissa or Jenni, but to allow them to keep their hopes up was being very unfair, especially to Clarissa. When it came time for her to get married, she deserved someone with whom she could have a real marriage, which included a real family.

The pastor's "Amen" and closing benediction signaled the congregation to stand, but before Geoff could move, Jenni scrambled onto his lap. Before he realized what she was doing, she threw her arms around his neck and gave him a big hug. "I still love you, Geoff. Don't you love me anymore?"

His eyes burned, and his throat constricted. "Of course I still love you, Jenni," he finally managed to choke out, hopefully not sounding like an emotional basket case. But more than loving Jenni as a sweet little girl, he loved Clarissa as a woman. Against all logic, the annoying way she wouldn't leave him alone made him love her even more.

At his words, Jenni slipped her hands around the back of his neck, ready to hug him again, when suddenly, she froze. Very slowly, she ran her fingers along the chain of the Medic Alert tag he always wore around his neck. Without speaking, she pulled it out. "What's this?" she asked as she ran her fingers on the punched-in lettering.

His fingers shook as he slowly turned it over for her to see the universal logo. "It's a tag that says what's wrong with me, in case I'm in an accident and can't talk."

Before he could remove the medallion from Jenni's small fingers and tuck it back under his shirt, Clarissa snatched it from them both. "It says you're B positive."

Geoff grabbed the medallion out of Clarissa's hand and dropped it back into his shirt. He set Jenni back into the chair and stood.

Their concern for him only reminded him once again of what he couldn't have. "So now you know my blood type. I hope you found that interesting. Now if you'll excuse me, I'm going home for lunch. Alone."

He heard Clarissa's sharp gasp as he turned around and walked out.

He didn't want it to end this way, but to keep going and to keep her hopes up would only make it hurt worse, although Geoff didn't know if that was possible.

Chapter 10

Clarissa watched Jenni squeeze her eyes shut and grit her teeth to shut out the hurt.

She'd never been so proud of her little sister as she was right now.

The nurse smiled as she wrapped a label around the vial containing Jenni's blood sample and tucked it into the holder beside Clarissa's vial. "We should have the results later today. We'll give you a call."

The second the door closed, Jenni squirmed off Clarissa's lap. "Do you think this will make Geoff feel better? Do you think he'll want to see us again?"

Clarissa gave her sister a hug. "I don't know. Do you remember when Melissa's mom stepped on their puppy's tail and it growled and hid from everyone? That's kind of how Geoff feels right now."

Jenni nodded thoughtfully, making Clarissa hope that Jenni wouldn't minimize Geoff's pain by thinking of him as an injured puppy, but it was the best analogy she could think of.

She'd never seen such pain in his face as yesterday when he walked out of the church. Her heart ached for him, but this was the best she could think of that they could do for him.

The whole drive home, they talked more about Geoff and what they could possibly do to make him feel better. Of course, there were no answers. All she could do was try to convince Jenni that if Geoff still closed the door to their love and friendship, it wasn't her fault.

She continued to think more about him after she tucked Jenni into bed. She could understand Geoff's conviction about not wanting to get married because he refused to pass on a genetic disorder. She even found his sacrifice noble.

If only she could find a way to convince him that she meant what she said. Not every woman wanted to be a mother, and she was one of those women. She loved her sister more than life itself and held no resentment or bitterness that she had to be as a parent to Jenni. But that situation aside, she very seriously had no desire to have children of her own.

Clarissa closed her eyes and prayed. Even though Geoff thought he wasn't a candidate for marriage, Clarissa still thought that God had dropped him into her lap for that very reason. She knew Geoff loved her the same way she loved him. He only needed to open his heart and admit it. Together, they could work around his medical condition.

Instead of turning on the television and mindlessly flipping channels, Clarissa went to bed to pray. Hopefully, she would have some answers soon.

Clarissa had just touched the door handle on her car after

dropping Jenni off at the sitter for the Wednesday night Bible study meeting when her cell phone rang. As quickly as she could, she fumbled with the zipper and mumbled a quick hello.

"Hi, Clarissa. It's Geoff. I need a favor."

Clarissa's heart pounded. Ever since the weekend, Geoff had tried to avoid her, but she'd been diligent in not letting him push her away. Monday when she and Jenni arrived back from the clinic, they had knocked on his door, bringing Chinese food for dinner. She could see that part of him still wanted to be with her, but part of him wanted to push her away. Fortunately, the part of him that she knew loved her won, and he invited them in.

Tuesday she and Jenni had waited behind the bush in the front yard and then pounced on Geoff when he took Spot for their daily walk. Again, she could tell he was having a hard time pushing her away. So they made his decision for him. Jenni lured Spot inside with a treat and a tennis ball, knowing Geoff would have to follow, and he did.

Since Clarissa planned on seeing him at the Bible study meeting, they had left him alone today, for a few hours, anyway.

That he was phoning her could only mean that he was finally starting to weaken, and that he could finally see how God had put them together.

She tried to sound serious and dignified, when what she really wanted to do was dance. "Sure, anything you want, just ask."

"I need you to go get Spot for me. I was in a car accident

on the way home from work today. I'm fine, but they want to keep me in the hospital for twenty-four hours as a precaution. Spot probably needs to be let out real bad, but this is the first chance I had to use the phone."

Clarissa's heart nearly stopped beating. Like most people, she'd assumed that a hemophiliac's greatest danger was of bleeding to death, even from a minor cut. However, she'd learned that instead the greatest danger was what couldn't be seen. The greatest risk was of internal bleeding, because that was something that often wasn't noticed until too late. He also was at greater risk of complications from a concussion because of the failure of his blood to clot like everyone else's.

"Don't worry; I'll take him to my place overnight. How are you, really?"

"I'm fine. It's not like this has never happened to me before. I guess I'll see you tomorrow when I pick up Spot. Thanks, Clarissa. Bye."

Clarissa tucked the phone in her purse and ran to Geoff's house.

Her hands shook as she unlocked his front door. He'd given her the key to his house, but he refused to give her the key to his heart.

As soon as she saw to Spot's needs, Clarissa drove to the hospital as fast as she could without getting a ticket. She found Geoff with the back of the bed raised to a seating position, reading. When she stepped into the room, he flinched and fumbled the book.

Clarissa walked to his side, pulled up a chair, and sat. "Jenni and I both got our blood typed a couple of days ago.

I'm O positive, so I can donate if you need. Jenni's B positive like you, so she can donate when she's older."

He inhaled sharply and set the book aside. "I don't know what to say. After the accident they gave me a number of drugs that make my blood clot. Things have changed a lot over the years. I'd only need a donation if I had surgery or if I had been bleeding already. But I'm touched that you both would go to all that trouble just for me."

"I'd do anything for you. I love you, Geoff. I know you think you're doing what's best for me, but you're wrong. How can I convince you that I don't want any more children besides Jenni? No one seems to understand. I love Jenni, but she's really all I will ever need or want."

Taking her chances, she wrapped her fingers around Geoff's hand. Her voice dropped to barely above a hoarse croak. "I need you, Geoff, but you won't take me. Why? I know you love me, too."

Beneath her fingers, Geoff's pulse raced. His voice cracked when he finally spoke. "I can't impose all my problems on you. The stress and worry every time something like this happens would get to you eventually. You're better off without me."

She gave his hand a gentle squeeze. "No. We're better off together. It feels good to know I can donate to you in case of an emergency. I'll do that whether you marry me or not. But I do want us to get married. Try and put aside your preconceived notions and think about what it could be like. Please."

He squeezed his eyes shut. "Dear God. . .," he mumbled,

and she could tell that he wasn't using their Lord's name in vain. He was praying from the depths of his soul for an answer.

Clarissa squeezed her eyes shut and did the same.

For a few minutes, the only noise was that of the usual traffic in the hall.

Geoff cleared his throat and spoke very softly "Are you really sure of this? I don't do typical 'guy' things like team sports, but I have to always keep exercising. That's why I do agility with Spot. We go for a long walk every day, regardless of the weather. I'm very diligent with my diet. Still, there are going to be some scary moments in the future. I consider marriage a lifetime commitment. I have no intention of just trying it to see if it works. "

She squeezed his hand. Beneath her fingers, she could feel him trembling. Clarissa gave him a shaky smile. "I still think you're a keeper."

He slid his hands out from hers, reached over, and embraced her as best he could from his position on the hospital bed. "I love you so much, Clarissa. If you'll have a pathetic specimen like me, I'll be honored if you'll marry me."

A nurse's voice echoed over the PA system that visiting hours were over. Clarissa stood and leaned over the bed toward him.

She brushed a short kiss across his lips and backed up just as a nurse stepped in and reminded her that it was time to leave.

Clarissa waved and blew him a kiss on her way out the door. "Jenni's with a sitter; I have to run. See you tomorrow when you get home."

Epilogue

So if you don't mind, Jenni, with your permission, I would like to marry your sister. I know we originally thought I was going to marry you, but it didn't work out that way." Geoff held his breath, waiting for either tears or an argument.

Jenni looked up at him, her eyes wide. "That's okay. I been talking to Bradley, and he says you're too old for me. But Bradley says you'd make a good big brother."

Geoff let go a relieved sigh. "Bradley sounds like a smart person. Who is Bradley?"

Jenni grinned ear to ear. "Bradley is in my class at school. He's very smart. I think one day I'm going to marry Bradley! I was too 'fraid to tell you because I didn't want to make you sad. But you're going to marry Rissa, so that's okay."

Geoff tried to hold back a groan as Jenni skipped off.

Clarissa's fingers intertwined with his. "She wouldn't have been like this six months ago. God really did put you with us to protect Jenni's heart."

Geoff nodded. "I guess. But now who is going to protect

the world from Jenni?"

Before Clarissa could answer, Jenni reappeared. "Do I gets to be flower girl again?"

Geoff hunkered down to be at eye level with her. "Yes, I guess you do."

She clapped her hands. "Yippee! Then Spot can carry the rings like Cody did for Stan and Abby! And this time, I'll catch the bouquet all by myself!"

Geoff and Clarissa looked at each other. "Uh-oh. . ."

GAIL SATTLER

Gail Sattler lives on the West Coast with her husband, three sons, two dogs, five lizards, and countless fish, many of which have names. Gail loves to write tales of romance that can be complete only with God in their center. She's had many books out with Barbour Publishing and its **Heartsong Presents** line. Gail was voted as the Favorite **Heartsong Presents** Author for three years in a row and is now in the **Heartsong Presents** Author Hall of Fame. Visit Gail's web site at http://www.gailsattler.com.

A Letter to Our Readers

Dear Readers:

In order that we might better contribute to your reading enjoyment, we would appreciate your taking a few minutes to respond to the following questions. When completed, please return to the following: Fiction Editor, Barbour Publishing, Inc., P.O. Box 719, Uhrichsville, OH 44683.

1. Did you enjoy reading *The Bouquet?*
   - ❑ Very much—I would like to see more books like this.
   - ❑ Moderately—I would have enjoyed it more if _____

   _____

   _____

2. What influenced your decision to purchase this book?
   (Check those that apply.)
   - ❑ Cover ❑ Back cover copy ❑ Title ❑ Price
   - ❑ Friends ❑ Publicity ❑ Other

3. Which story was your favorite?
   - ❑ *Flowers by Felicity* ❑ *Rose in Bloom*
   - ❑ *Petals of Promise* ❑ *Flowers for a Friend*

4. Please check your age range:
   - ❑ Under 18 ❑ 18–24 ❑ 25–34
   - ❑ 35–45 ❑ 46–55 ❑ Over 55

5. How many hours per week do you read? _____

Name _____

Occupation _____

Address _____

City _____ State _____ Zip _____

E-mail _____